Readers love the Marshals
series by MARY CALMES

All Kinds of Tied Down

"This book is classic Mary Calmes, from the characters that are easily lovable down to the quick and witty banter."
—Joyfully Jay

"…a lot of laughs, some serious hotness, wrapped around action/adventure and an incredible story."
—Rainbow Book Reviews

Fit to Be Tied

"Mary Calmes takes us on a fast-paced, action-packed ride that will have you holding onto to the edge of your seat. You will be so wrapped up in the drama you will forget to breathe."
—MM Good Book Reviews

"All in all, this book was better than the first and possibly one of the best layered stories written by Queen Calmes."
—Boys in Our Books

Tied Up in Knots

"This story grabs you by the throat and doesn't let go. *Tied Up in Knots* is an absolute gem in this series, polished to a brilliant, glittering shine…"
—Gay Book Reviews

"Mary Calmes is absolutely smashing it with this series, and she has hit another home run with *Tied Up in Knots*."
—The Novel Approach

More praise for
MARY CALMES

Late in the Day

"*Late In The Day* is at its heart a beautiful love story."
—Divine Magazine

"Mary Calmes has a way of making you care about her side characters… She makes you want to know more about these people… It's one of those Mary Magic things."
—Just Love: Queer Book Reviews

You Never Know

"*You Never Know* is pure Mary Calmes. Main characters to fall in love with, secondary characters who fill out the story, dialogue that is real… and an HEA for everybody."
—Happy Ever After - *USA Today*

"If you know me at all, you know that MC is my crack. But when she throws in the second-chance-at-love trope? I'm all… *heart eyes*"
—Gay Book Reviews

A Day Makes

"*A Day Makes* is just fabulous. It is exciting, romantic, sexy, and totally captivating."
—Joyfully Jay

"Once again, Mary Calmes has written a book that I couldn't put down."
—Under the Covers Book Reviews

By Mary Calmes

Published by Dreamspinner Press
www.dreamspinnerpress.com

TWISTED ANDTIED

Mary Calmes

REAMSPINNER
PRESS

Published by

DREAMSPINNER PRESS

5032 Capital Circle SW, Suite 2, PMB# 279, Tallahassee, FL 32305-7886 USA
www.dreamspinnerpress.com

This is a work of fiction. Names, characters, places, and incidents either are the product of author imagination or are used fictitiously, and any resemblance to actual persons, living or dead, business establishments, events, or locales is entirely coincidental.

Trade Paperback ISBN: 978-1-64080-171-4
Digital ISBN: 978-1-64080-172-1
Library of Congress Control Number: 2017916039
Trade Paperback published March 2018
v. 1.0

Printed in the United States of America

(∞)

This paper meets the requirements of
ANSI/NISO Z39.48-1992 (Permanence of Paper).

Again, and always, my constant thanks to Lynn West,
without whom I would be in BIG trouble.
To Lisa Horan, who holds my hand.
To Jessie Potts, who was there in a crunch with the title.
And to Rhys Ford and Jaime Samms,
who checked in every day to make sure I wasn't dead.
And lastly, but never leastly, to my wonderful, amazing readers,
who have taken Miro and Ian to heart. XXOO

CHAPTER 1

SURREAL.

My day had gone from being moderately normal by deputy US marshal standards to insane in a matter of seconds, all because the one person I counted on to always make rational choices had done the exact opposite.

He wasn't supposed to jump off buildings.

In the movies people always talked about seeing their whole lives flash before their eyes when they thought they were going to die. I always sort of figured that for bullshit, but the moment I saw my boss, the chief deputy marshal of the Northern District of Illinois, Sam Kage, leap after a suspect into nothing, there it was, whoosh, me in a freaky-fast montage that brought me to the moment where I was sure I had no choice but to follow the man into the sky. Who knew that shit actually happened?

It all started that morning when SOG, the Special Operations Group—the marshals' version of Special Forces—led the way into an enormous warehouse on 48th Place. They were followed quickly by TOD, Tactical Operations Division—our badass SWAT-style guys covered in body armor and Kevlar, toting serious firepower—with the marshals behind them, then uniformed Chicago Police Department bringing up the rear. Just with that many guys, the opportunity for a clusterfuck was already a possibility.

The point of this operation was to apprehend or stop Kevin and Caradoc Gannon, neo-Nazi pieces of crap who had gotten their hands on a small quantity of VX gas, and so SOG was deployed to execute the men responsible for threatening the civilian populace of Chicago. With TOD there was a good chance of survivors, and nine times out of ten, everyone came out in one piece. The SOG guys would make the decision right there on-site whether to put people down. It didn't happen often. Unlike how it was in the movies, capturing a fugitive normally went fairly smoothly. The marshals rolled up somewhere, and some of us went around back while the rest of us went in hard through the front. Sometimes we even knocked.

My partner and now husband, Ian Doyle, went in with the first wave alongside SOG—how, I had no idea—because we'd rock-paper-scissored for who would take point in our group and who would hang back and keep an eye on our boss. Ian and I were stuck watching him because we were last on the scene. That was the agreement among the investigators on Kage's team: whoever rolled up behind the big man had to babysit. Not that we would ever say that to his face, none of us being suicidal or insane, but it was simply understood.

So Ian was inside the warehouse with the rest of the guys and the tactical experts, and I was keeping an eye on my boss. When Kage saw a guy drop out of a second-story window onto the top of a delivery truck and then down onto the pavement, he shouted and gave chase, and I followed.

This was *not* supposed to happen.

There were good and bad things about being Kage's backup. The positive part was if I was the one charging after him, then I was in the best position to protect him. I would be the one to guard him, and make sure he went home to his family that night, and stayed at the top of the food chain in charge of an entire team of deputy US marshals.

The flipside was exactly the same. Being his backup meant if I fucked up, not only was I screwing up the life he shared with his family, but also luck of the draw said the next man in his job would be worthless by comparison. Kage carried all of us on his shoulders, above the shit of red tape and politics, and he also provided shelter and protection, so losing him was *not* an option. For that reason, I liked him safe in his office. But Kage was on-site because it was his circus. He was the top stop of information for the marshals service in Chicago, as his boss, Tom Kenwood, had to travel back and forth a lot to Washington as well as all over the great state of Illinois. So when something big went down and the press got wind of it—as they always did—then Kage had to be there to do his voice-of-God thing and give short answers to reassure the public without confirming or denying squat.

At the moment, however, the man in question was flying down the sidewalk in front of me, his long legs eating up the concrete in pursuit of an escaped felon.

I had no idea Kage could run like that. He was fiftysomething, definitely not the thirty-three I was, so I was honestly surprised that not only could he run, but run pretty fast. Plus he was six four, with massive shoulders and a lot of hard, heavy muscle, really big, so his speed was even more shocking. He not only kept pace with the much younger fleeing fugitive but was gaining on him as well.

A parked car didn't stop our suspect; he did an impressive parkour leap over it, completing a maneuver that had him using his hands to go down on all fours for a second before he vaulted the ancient Oldsmobile. Kage didn't stop either, doing the classic *Dukes of Hazzard* slide over the hood that all the men in my life had perfected.

Ridiculous.

"Why is going around the car so difficult?" I roared after him. "Jones!"

Because apprehending the fugitives was a coordinated strike, I had a stupid earpiece in from when the breach happened, and we were all connected. But after things got squared away afterward, everyone else dropped off except the guys I worked with on a day-to-day basis. Normally I was the only person in my head, but because I was chasing Kage and they were all thinking they were being helpful, I had my entire team of deputy US marshals not only checking on me but shouting directions at the same time.

"Can you see him?" Wes Ching yelled.

"Pull your gun, Jones, just to be on the safe side!" Jack Dorsey suggested loudly. "But don't shoot him, for fuck's sake."

He was being a dick. "I'm gonna shoot you when I get back!" I growled. We never ran with our guns out. That was a rookie move.

"You gotta stay right with him!" Chris Becker barked into my ear.

Like I didn't know that?

"If he slows down, don't leave him!" Mike Ryan insisted with a snarl.

Because I couldn't stop or mess with my momentum in any way, there was no time to reach up and pull out the tiny earpiece to silence them. "Will you guys quit with the screaming already? Fuck!"

"Yeah, don't leave his side, Jones!" Ethan Sharpe demanded, ignoring me.

"I know," I roared to everyone in general. "For fuck's sake!"

"Make sure you yell for people to get out of his way!" Jer Kowalski instructed.

"Really?" I snapped. "'Yell for people to move' is your advice?"

"Somebody's pissy," he commented snidely. "I suggest more running, less talking, Jones."

"Keep up with him!" Ching cautioned.

I needed all these orders because *clearly* I'd only been a goddamn marshal for one day.

"Are you close enough to shoot anyone who tries to touch him?" This from Chandler White, who normally didn't try to boss me around but was clearly making an exception this time because, again, I was apparently some kind of newb who couldn't tell his ass from a hole in the ground.

"You have him in your line of sight, right?" Eli Kohn wanted to know.

"Fuck, yes!" I shouted.

"You gotta get close, but not too close," Sharpe felt the need to tell me.

I growled.

"Try and get in front of him. That would be better," Kowalski suggested.

"I swear to fuckin' God, you all—"

"You know he can't do that," Eli objected. "Since Kage is the first one in pursuit, Miro can't—"

"Kill the chatter," Ching broke in angrily. "You're all lucky Kage doesn't have an earpiece in, or we'd all be dead."

It was true, but since Kage was in the command center during the initial breach and was only allowed to come out when we got the all-clear, he never put in an earpiece like the rest of us.

I saw the guy turn into an apartment building and Kage follow right behind. "No, no, no," I grumbled under my breath.

"God fucking dammit, Jones, you better not let any—"

"Will you guys all lay off!" Ian warned gruffly, and his rough whiskey voice was a welcome relief. "You know Miro's got this covered. He's not stupid; he knows what he's doing. Give the man a little fuckin' credit!"

It was good to have someone on my side who didn't doubt my mental or physical ability and who would champion me to the others. But that wasn't surprising; I could always count on Ian. The moment of silence that followed his outburst was soothing.

"But you can see him, right?"

"Ian!" I howled, utterly betrayed.

"I'm just asking!" he yelled back defensively.

"You can all go straight to hell!" I bellowed before I tore through the front door of the apartment building after Kage, going up the stairs right on his heels, one level after the next, Ian in my ear the whole time along with everyone else.

"You're very sensitive, M," Eli commented.

"Kiss my ass," I said, careening around a corner as I followed Kage up and up.

Funny how much Eli and I had changed in the past five months. From November to March, Thanksgiving to St. Patrick's Day, our friendship progressed, and he'd evolved from Kohn to Eli, a permanent shift in my head.

"And Ian, you can—"

"Are you still on the street?" Eli pressed.

"Where the hell is Ian?"

"He's offline. The SOG team made the secondary interior breach," Dorsey informed us. And while I wasn't crazy about that, he was one of many, not leading the rest of the men.

"Miro, where the fuck are you, because GPS is showing you now at—"

"Shut the fuck up," Dorsey griped at Eli, who'd spoken. "Miro, did you turn in somewhere? Because it looks like we lost you on the last corner."

"The fuck do you mean, you lost—Miro, where the hell are you?" Becker yelled.

But I'd run flat-out after Kage for at least eight blocks, and we were on the fifth floor now. I was done being able to form words.

I heard Kage hit the door that led to the roof—it had a panic bar, and that sound, like a giant rubber stamp, was hard to miss—and charged out into the open after him. From where I was, maybe ten feet behind him, the sound of leather-soled shoes scraping over the rough concrete sounded like nails on a chalkboard, and the noise added to my quickly ratcheting fear the closer they got to running out of roof.

I thought Kage was going to stop.

There was no way he wasn't going to stop.

As many times as he had said to me, "Marshals don't jump off buildings, Jones," I would have bet my life on the fact that when the other guy took a running leap toward the next building over, Kage would come to a stop. He didn't. He *followed*, and I was so astonished that I found myself sliding awkwardly, my feet slipping on the gravel, arms windmilling for balance, out of control for a moment as I finally came to a bracing halt at the edge of the building I too would have had to hurdle as I'd just watched Kage do.

And then came that second, my life in a blur up to that moment when I realized the one person I knew I could always count on... was gone.

No one but Ian could ever understand what Kage meant to me. It was cliché, yes, but I'd never had a father; there was never an older man who took me under his wing, never one who was both mentor and guardian, not just because he had to but because he wanted to. I would never be the same from this second on.

What was worse was that I knew him even better after just one awkward, ridiculous, scary dinner in February. One weird Valentine's Day, and everything was different. It wasn't like we were buddies or that I understood at all how his mind worked, but I did know how much he loved his husband and what lengths he would go to keep him safe. It wasn't every man who took a bullet for someone he loved. Ian and I knew a secret others didn't, because he hadn't even told the rest of the team he'd been shot. Instead he simply showed up for work the following Monday, having taken the two days of vacation already on the books, like nothing remotely interesting had happened. Since he liked to look bulletproof, Ian and I saw no reason to muck around with that perception.

I knew the loyalty I saw him give his men, give me and everyone else who worked for him, extended to his friends as well. He worried about his family, his friends, his team, and honestly, just seeing him grounded me. But now....

My heart clenched, my stomach sank, and my breath caught as I closed my eyes for a second and tried to reconcile what I believed in—his invincibility—with what I'd just seen—his death—before I stepped up to the wall and peered over the side.

There, braced on a thin lip of what could only be called an ornamental flight of whimsy on the architect's part—no more than molding on the building—was Kage, dangling by a one-handed death grip over a fifty-foot plunge, holding on to the guy he'd been chasing with the other.

I nearly dropped dead.

"Take him," Kage growled while heaving the guy up to me.

I couldn't have done it. Ian couldn't have done it. It required muscles neither of us possessed and the ability to deadlift at least two hundred pounds. And he was doing it from basically the shoulder alone.

I was strong, but not like that, and I couldn't imagine the concentration needed to keep the guy from falling in the first place.

I grabbed the fugitive, realized I was looking at none other than Kevin Gannon—which was why, of course, Kage took off after him in the first place—hauled him up over the edge, and then cuffed him. "Don't move," I warned. Normally I put a knee on a suspect's back when I had them on the ground, but this guy wasn't fighting or squirming. He just lay there, limp.

"No," he said between gasps, "not moving."

Bending back over, I saw Kage had both hands on the top edge of the roof. I leaned forward to offer him a hand.

"Secure your prisoner, Jones," he ordered gruffly before he pressed himself onto the ledge, turned to sit and swing his legs around, and then stood.

I stepped back, watching as he gave himself a quick dusting, straightened his navy suit, adjusted the tie, and then faced me.

I couldn't stop staring.

He scowled.

I had no clue what to say.

"Don't tell anybody," he instructed before turning for the door of the roof.

Don't tell anybody? Was he fucking kidding? I could barely breathe!

Holy motherfucking hell.

I had to concentrate on not hyperventilating.

Once I could move air through my lungs again—because Jesus Christ, I thought *Ian* was good at stopping my heart—I finally turned to look at my prisoner.

"That man is insane," Gannon said.

I nodded in earnest.

"But, yanno," he said on a sharp exhale, "kind of awesome."

He got a wan smile from me that time.

Kage waited for us at the bottom of the last flight of stairs and then opened the door to seven uniformed CPD officers. Because his face was now recognizable, along with those of the mayor, the police superintendent, and the state's attorney, they straightened, holstered their drawn weapons, and waited for his order.

He only glowered and told them to move so we could get through. When we got closer to the warehouse, I saw Ching and Becker waiting for us along with Dorsey and Ryan, plus Sharpe and White. I didn't see Ian anywhere, which didn't concern me since the area of operation was swarming with law enforcement. Kowalski and Eli weren't there, instead back at the office on desk duty, running warrants and playing liaison to those of us in the field. Technically it was Ian's and my day to do it, but Eli had his cousin Ira coming in from San Francisco, and he didn't want to be stuck in the field when he was supposed to be picking the guy up at O'Hare. I understood. With our job, it could go off the rails at any time. It was best to simply not engage than to try to get away.

"—secured, and all the VX gas canisters have been recovered."

My mind had been drifting, so I was lucky the glut of information was not directed at me.

"But SOG was called to an emergency in Hyde Park, so they're gone."

"We need to run warrants on all these men," Kage began, indicating the people lying on the ground, facedown with their hands zip-tied behind their backs. "Run everyone through NCIC and then—"

"Is that really necessary?" asked Darren Mills, the new supervisory deputy who took over Kage's spot after he was promoted.

First, holy God, he interrupted Kage.

Second, not only did he question our boss, *his* boss, but what he asked was stupid.

I glanced at Ching, who shot a look over to Becker, who winced. It was not the first time Mills, who had been chosen by a committee without the benefit of endorsement from Kage or Kage's boss, Tom Kenwood, had opened his mouth and inserted his foot. He had also missed a filing for Asset Forfeiture, so we missed the monthly auction where we got the cars we drove, or sometimes didn't want to drive but got stuck with anyway—a horrific carnation-pink Cabriolet came instantly to mind—and he still didn't know who did what in our building.

Over the years, I'd come to realize there were two kinds of transfers, which was probably true of all workplace environments. There were people who came in quietly, got the lay of the land, and worked really hard to make sure everyone saw they could be counted on to do the job. Then there were others like Mills, who swaggered in, put on airs, and pretended to run the place and direct the team. In his defense, the investigator team normally did report to the supervisory deputy, as we all did to Kage when he was in that position, but when he moved up, Kage changed the reporting system so the lead investigator, currently Becker, remained in direct contact with him—basically circumventing Mills. In response Mills had spoken to Kenwood, US marshal in charge of the Northern District of Illinois, one of the ninety-four men appointed by the president and confirmed by the Senate, to complain that Kage hadn't relinquished all his duties.

That was the gist of it, anyway, and I only knew that much because Dorsey and Ryan had been in the office processing a fugitive when Mills barged into Kage's office without an invitation.

"Really?" I'd deadpanned over wings, eating one after another, licking my fingers and listening while we sat at Crisp on Broadway. Ian was shoved up beside me, laughing as he watched me but also listening. "Mills just rolled into his office without checking with Elyes?"

Kage had needed an assistant for as long as I'd known him, and he finally got one in the form of small, slender, hyperefficient Elyes Salerno, easily one of the most beautiful women I'd ever met in my life. She had a pixie cut, dark tan skin with bronze undertones, and huge chestnut-brown eyes with the thickest black lashes I'd ever seen. She had fantastic fashion sense, and as many compliments as I gave her, she gave me the same back, telling me often that if only her husband had my shoe collection, she'd have no complaints. The fact that she could be midsentence with me, check her email, and answer a question for Kage if he popped his head out of his office all at the same time told me she was absolutely on top of all facets of her boss's life, from remembering when he was supposed to be somewhere to intuitively knowing what report he needed. Elyes only left the office when Kage did. So the fact that Mills disregarded her and walked past her into the office was, I was sure, his first mistake.

"Yep," Dorsey reported, sighing when the server put the next basket of wings down on the table. It was always good to go to Crisp with Dorsey and Ryan because they ate the same wings as me and Ian: the Seoul Sassy and the Crisp BBQ. The others liked to mix it up, but I never saw the appeal of straying from the tried and true. "Mills yells at Kage and says he's got Kenwood on the line, and he's about to slam the door when Kage leans out, apologizes to Elyes, and then closes the door behind him."

I couldn't control my smile. "Ohmygod, I can't believe Mills is still breathing!"

"Right?" Dorsey chuckled.

"So what happened?" Ian asked, smiling as he wiped the side of my mouth. "Jesus, I can't take you anywhere."

I waggled my eyebrows at him as Ryan snapped his fingers between us. "Listen, this is about to get good."

"It is," Dorsey promised, smiling evilly. "'Cause alluva sudden Mills straightens up like you see people do in the movies when they're freezing or turning to stone or something."

Kage's office was a wall of windows, so the show had to have been a good one, from where Ryan and Dorsey sat in the bullpen.

"Yeah," Ryan agreed, grinning with his deep dimples and the glinting blue eyes that explained how he had so many women hanging off him when we went out. He was one of those guys you didn't realize was handsome until he smiled. "Mills goes rigid, and his face turns this bright red, and then Kage does that thing where he turns and looks at you like you're the stupidest fuckin' thing on the planet."

"I've seen that one," Ian and I said in sync.

Dorsey scoffed. "We all have. It's the one Phillip—"

"Call me Phil, there, buddy," I chimed in, and Dorsey, Ryan, and I all made gun motions at each other instead of pointing.

"I think I missed something," Ian commented, squinting.

Ryan gave a dismissive wave. "You missed nothing. Tull was the nozzle who sent us all over the fuckin' place when you were deployed and Kage was on vacation."

"Oh, when you were in San Francisco." Ian made the connection, wiping my mouth again and running his thumb over my bottom lip in the process.

The heat in his eyes made me shift a bit in my seat, my chinos suddenly tighter. He had a very decadent effect on me. "Yeah," I croaked.

"Tull was a fuckin' douchebag," Dorsey assured Ian, "and Kage made sure he understood that his time with the marshals service had come to an end, and when he was doing it in front of all of us, he gave him that same look, like, you are such a fuckin' fucktard, how are you even in my goddamn office right now?"

Ryan was laughing and nodding because, just like the rest of us, he was familiar with the Kage glare of disapproval.

"He wanted to go back to JSD, but those guys work too hard to have to deal with assholes like him," Dorsey went on, mustering up even more disdain for Tull.

"Agreed," I said as Ian curled a piece of hair around my ear. I had been letting it grow out for a while and was still waiting for Kage to say something. "Judicial security doesn't need a guy like Tull any more than we did."

"So what happened with Mills?" Ian asked, wiping his hands before draping an arm around the back of my chair.

Dorsey chuckled. "He stands there for a second, looking back at Kage, and then he whips around and almost runs out of the office without closing the door."

"Oh shit," I breathed. "Then what?"

"Then Kage walks over to the door, gives me and Mike a head tip, and then slowly closes the door," Dorsey wrapped up. "I mean, I don't know what Kenwood said in there, but I'm betting things didn't go down how Mills thought they would."

Ryan cackled. "What a dick."

So now even after that debacle—when Mills knew his decision to try to go over Kage's head so epically failed—*still* he asked him, in front of all of us, if checking warrants was necessary when every marshal on the planet knew that was procedure. Kage said it because he was programmed to say it, not that he didn't think it was our first step. He was like a parent reminding a child to put something away, habit and nothing more.

"Yes," Kage said with a huff, the annoyance rolling off him. "We must."

Mills coughed nervously.

"Where's Doyle," Kage snapped.

"Oh, uhm, he left with the SOG team," Mills answered, clearly flustered, fidgeting, shifting nervously from one foot to the other.

"On whose authority?"

"Mine," he said, darting his eyes to Kage's face.

"Do you have his earpiece?"

He cleared his throat. "I do."

Kage tipped his head at me. "That's his partner. Give it to him."

"Oh, yes," he acknowledged, passing me the earpiece Ian should have turned back in the second he finished the operation. "SOG lost a man on the breach. He'll be okay but had to be taken to the hospital, so Lieutenant Saford asked for Doyle, and I gave the okay."

I glanced at Kage, whose clenched jaw told me he was not happy with that.

"Between Doyle volunteering for their ops, Saford requesting him, and you approving it—I think maybe I should look into reassigning him."

I realized, horrified, that he was looking at me. "Sir?"

Seriously, why the hell was *I* in trouble? Guilt by marriage?

"Jones?"

I had no idea what I was supposed to say.

"May I make an observation?" Mills asked.

Kage didn't answer, but he gave him his attention.

"You know as well as I do the command of SOG here is vacant, and a former Green Beret, who's also a marshal, would be a great fit for that office."

Kage crossed his arms, giving Mills, who looked as though he was actually shrinking before my eyes, a look that would have peeled paint. "Really? He'd be a good fit, you think?"

I could tell when it hit Mills that maybe he'd overstepped. Like his boss hadn't come to that same conclusion a long time ago, eons before.

"But of course you know that already, sir."

Kage made a noise like an irritated grunt and then turned to me. "Run warrants and prints on everyone. You and the others are here until it's done."

Why he said it again, I had no clue, but I didn't dare groan—he'd gut me—so instead I nodded and turned away, tugging my prisoner with me, walking with Becker and Ching.

"So Captain America bailed again, huh?" Ching taunted as soon as we were out of Kage's earshot.

I flipped him off.

"So touchy." Becker snickered before pointing at the end of the twenty-four-man line.

"Jesus," I muttered, looking at all of them, wanting to find out where Ian was—and more importantly, *how* he was—but instead I was stuck running fingerprints and checking warrants for what looked like hours yet.

Earlier that morning before work, when I'd been making breakfast and he was reading his email, he'd suddenly asked me what "upcycled" meant.

"What?" I asked, turning away from the eggs in a basket.

"You don't know what that is either?"

"I have a guess, but gimme some context."

"Well, Josue says he's getting an Etsy shop, and he's going to upcycle vintage jewelry," he answered, looking up at me, squinting. "The fuck does that mean?"

Josue Morant, who used to be Josue Hess, was a witness I had brought back from Las Vegas last November. He had become, like Cabot Kincaid and Drake Palmer before him, more than a witness. He was like a ward to Ian and me. The fact that he was emailing Ian meant he was trying to circumvent me for some reason, and I could hazard a guess as to why.

"Etsy is an online site where artists and folks like that sell stuff they make," I explained.

"Okay," he said as if I hadn't helped in the least.

"And I'm guessing 'upcycling' means repurposing."

"Whatever," he said dismissively, done, I could tell, discussing things he didn't give a crap about. "I just reminded him that he can't use his real name, can't use any name remotely attached to his former life, and can't post a picture of himself, or one he created, so we'll see what he does from here."

"Poor kid. He was supposed to testify in February."

"Yep." Ian yawned and stretched. "That's what happens when rich criminals get good lawyers. Trials get pushed back."

"I think that—"

"Hungry," he whined petulantly, "need food. How long does it take to drop eggs into a hole in a piece of bread and fry them? I would've had this done hours ago."

I scoffed, turned back to the eggs looking good at the center of the sourdough bread, and put the red peppers I'd sautéed earlier on top.

"And not that I'm complaining, because you cooking for me is very domestic and all, but we usually just have coffee, so what gives?"

"I just—I'm worried that something will come up and you won't get a chance to eat," I answered, and a second later was surprised to find him there at my back, mouth on the side of my neck, biting gently. "Knock it off. You're gonna turn me into a giant goose bump, and I'm trying to make the presentation on the eggs perfect, which is why it's taking so long."

He didn't listen, instead nuzzling my hair and then kissing my ear, his warm breath making me shiver as he wrapped his arms around my waist and pulled me against his hard body, my ass pressed to his groin.

"Jesus, Ian," I groaned, going boneless in his arms, my head back on his shoulder, as always loving the feel of him, his strength and heat, the power in a simple hold.

"Let's move this off the burner so I can get what I really need," he rumbled, one hand on my belt buckle, tugging my dress shirt out of my pants with the other.

"You need to eat," I managed hoarsely, the way my voice cracked not hot in the least. It wasn't my fault, though; Ian could make me forget my name with not much work on his part. He had a drugging effect on me that was utterly sinful. "I want to feed you."

"Well, I wanna—"

"Eat," I asserted, grinning.

"Eat something," he assured me before he turned me around, moving the pan off the burner at the same time, then laid a kiss on me that left no doubt in my mind about what he wanted. If his stomach hadn't picked that moment to growl so loud it startled us both, I knew we would have been late for work.

I chuckled as he stepped back.

"Shut up."

"Maybe you should eat, huh, baby?"

He grunted.

"What do you think?"

"Maybe," he allowed, coming clean. "And don't smile at me."

I couldn't help it. Just looking at him made me stupidly happy.

Minutes later, as he was inhaling his food, I got a begrudging smile coupled with flashing eyes that made my knees wobble as I clutched at the counter. There was no doubt about it. Ian Doyle had me wrapped around his finger.

"Jones!"

Brought back sharply to the present from my wandering thoughts, I saw Kage gesturing to me, and I looked back at Becker.

"I got him," he said, taking hold of my prisoner's arm. "Go."

I bolted over to Kage, and he put a hand on my bicep—which he never did, not a big touchy-feely guy, my boss—while still listening to others standing in a semicircle around him but clearly about to give me directions.

He turned his attention on me, and I saw the concern there in his eyes. "You remember the marshal from Alabama who came in last week, the one working out of the Middle District in Montgomery?"

"Yeah, uhm." I had to think a second. "Juanita Hicks. She was looking to talk to the couple from Madison who were put into WITSEC here."

He nodded. "Well, it turns out that wasn't Hicks. She was killed two weeks ago, and that woman is Bellamy Pine, Dennis Pine's wife."

"Oh shit," I sighed, suddenly glad I'd put her off because of protocol. It was simple dumb luck: because I had put the adorable young couple into witness protection in Chicago, I had to be the one to go with her to see them. Since I hadn't had time until this week, she'd had to wait, much, I recalled now, to her annoyance.

They were a nice couple, a ballet teacher named Jolie Ballard and her website-designer husband, Brett, who did not deserve to have Dennis Pine in their home at three in the morning along with three other men toting two witnesses. How they managed to witness Pine killing three people—the two he planned, plus one of his own who'd grown a conscience—and get out of the house with their two dogs was a miracle. They did it with misdirection and, apparently, as Jolie told me, a well-timed leap—or *grand jeté*, as she called it—over a smallish sinkhole in their backyard. Jolie could do it, years and years of intensive ballet training, even carrying her Pomeranian, but Pine went down, and that was that. Brett told me the county was supposed to fix the sinkhole, and he'd never been more thankful for red tape in his life.

As it turned out, Pine's trial was in two weeks, and if Jolie and Brett took the stand, Pine would get the needle. His wife, Bellamy, was trying not to let that happen.

"Jones?"

"Yeah, I-I was supposed to call her today."

He nodded. "Well, you need to keep that meeting. We'll monitor you because Hicks had a partner, Christopher Warren, and he's missing as well. They discovered Hicks's body this morning behind an RV park in Mobile, but no sign of Warren."

"So they want to take Bellamy alive."

"That's the plan, yes."

"Okay."

"Did Doyle go with you to meet Bellamy? Will she think it's odd that you come alone?"

"No, sir, Ian went with Sharpe and White on the fugitive pickup out in Skokie last week, the guy who busted out of that prison in California—I forget which," I told him honestly. "But that's when I met with her, when most everyone else was out."

"Okay, then," he said, meeting the eyes of everyone else there, some in suits, some in tactical gear. "We need you to call her and meet her, and we'll do the rest."

"Yessir," I replied, reaching for the phone in my back pocket.

He put a hand on my arm to stop me and then glanced around the circle, making sure everyone understood he was talking to them. "All eyes on my man, you understand?"

And everyone listened to him, like always.

I WAS at the food trucks a block away from the office because I'd called Bellamy, who was still posing as Hicks, and told her to meet me there so we could talk before I took her to see Jolie and Brett. She rolled up twenty minutes later and stopped the car beside the curb but didn't park it or get out. I gave her a head tip so she'd know I'd seen her and continued to pretend to talk on the phone, when really I was just speaking out loud to my team, the earpiece picking up everything.

"Is she there?" Becker asked.

"Yep, right here."

"Do me a favor and do not get in the car," Ching told me.

"Like I've never been kidnapped before," I scoffed and made a show of hanging up, for all it mattered with him and Becker on the open channel.

"He's got a point there," Becker agreed.

"Shuddup," I groused.

"Enough with the chatter," Dorsey grumbled.

Approaching the car, I leaned over as she lowered the window, not getting too close, instead sinking to my haunches on the curb.

"We going for a ride?" she asked.

I shook my head.

"And why not?"

"They're coming here instead. That way we can just meet in the office," I told her, realizing she looked the part of a marshal. The black suit, white shirt, badge clipped to her belt, gun holster, all of it seemed like she'd been putting it on for years. Instead I knew she'd memorized how the real Hicks dressed. It made me sick to see the badge clipped to her belt, but I swallowed it down.

She must have seen something there on my face: revulsion, hatred, loathing. Even though I was playing it cool, it might have seeped through. "What's with you?" she asked, quiet, concerned, brows furrowed.

"Nothing, why?" I shrugged, standing, thinking the movement would stop her from staring at me. "Hey, you hungry? I haven't had lunch yet."

"Wait."

I stopped moving, brows lifted, hoping I was the epitome of nonchalance.

"When I talked to you before, you said this wouldn't be a problem."

"It's not," I said, shrugging. "And it's even less of an issue now, since instead of us taking an hour out of our day to drive out to where they are, they agreed to come to us."

She stared at me.

"Food?" I prodded.

She took a breath and shook her head. "I'm sorry, but that's not going to work."

"What's not?" I played dumb, standing there on the sidewalk.

"I need to see them at their home," she pressed.

"But you know that's not how we do things," I reminded her, assuring her of the protocol and trying not to sound like a wiseass, maybe missing it a little bit. I was getting angrier by the second. How dare she pretend to be Hicks. It was disgusting.

"You're going to have to do better, Jones."

"And why is that?" I asked right as I heard a noise behind me. I didn't get the chance to turn, the muzzle of the gun stilling me as it was shoved into my right side while a hand curled over my left shoulder, holding tight.

"Hold still, Marshal," a man commanded, taking the device from my ear and crushing it under the toe of his boot.

"What's going on?" I asked, feigning surprise.

She narrowed her eyes as she stared at me. "Give me an address."

Letting go of all pretense, I glared at her. "You know I can't do that."

"I will kill you, Marshal," she threatened. "I'm working against a deadline here."

"And if you actually were a marshal, you'd know we never give up our witnesses," I promised. "It's the whole what-we-do thing."

"Fuck." Up until that second, I would have bet my life on the fact that I had the situation well in hand, but then another set of hands closed on me, and two men propelled me toward the car.

Bellamy got out and held open the back door of the Audi sedan so they could stuff me in, and I knew it was my one chance to get free. My team was coming—they weren't far, I knew that—so I jerked back even with the gun pressed to my ribs because I was never being kidnapped again. Once was more than enough.

When Craig Hartley—the serial killer known as Prince Charming—had taken me two years prior, I was chained up and tortured. The whole ordeal culminated in Hartley, a former doctor, removing one of my ribs. And while I knew, logically, the same was not about to happen—I'd be shot and killed, not beaten and cut open—I still couldn't stop my immediate terror. My brain shut down, and because there was no flight, all that was left was fight.

Twisting free, I rounded on the guy with the gun. But instead of shooting, he pistol-whipped me. I understood. A dead man could not lead them to Jolie and Brett; I was safe until I gave up their location. So even though it felt like my right eye exploded before I was suddenly blinded, I swung and caught the guy with an uppercut that flung him back against the passenger-side door.

I was caught in the jaw hard and then the stomach harder, but as I went down, I still managed to kick the guy's feet out from under him. Of course he came down on top of me, which wasn't great, but then I heard Dorsey—he had a bellow that was unforgettable—and I relaxed.

"Jones!"

Ching was there, and Becker, and they shoved the guy off me so I could breathe. Dorsey lifted me to my feet. He was kind of big.

"Jesus Christ," Ryan breathed, doubling over, hands on his knees. "I thought you were shot when you went down."

"So did I," Ching huffed, hand on my shoulder, squeezing. "I haven't run that fast in a long fuckin' time.'

"You took years off my life, Jones," Becker grumbled like it was my fault.

It was nice they were all worried. I was sort of touched. "You guys start running when the earpiece went dead?"

"Hell yes," Dorsey told me as he led the zip-tied Bellamy from beside the car to the sidewalk and helped her to her knees, then laid her facedown on the sidewalk.

"Where's Warren?" Ryan demanded as he squatted beside her. "We want him."

"He's in the same ditch she is," Bellamy snarled, "but you'll never find either of those stupid fucks if you don't let—"

"Take her phone," I told him quickly. "She told me when I met with her before that this was her first trip to Chicago. At least we'll have the route to check."

"Jones!" she shrieked.

"Got it," Ryan informed me before he got on his phone and ordered the download on hers. Hopefully it would be quick.

"I'll tell you where they are," offered the guy who hit me with his gun. "You guys make me a deal, I'll talk. I haven't done shit but drive."

He was an accessory, but there were levels, for sure.

"I swear to God, I wasn't even with them when they killed the marshals."

It hurt to hear they were both gone, even though I hadn't known either of them. But they were my tribe, and I'd miss them.

"Hey."

I turned my head to see Becker, who took my face in his hands and lifted my chin, checking me over, gentler than I'd ever known him to be.

"You need stitches, Jones. Let's get you to the hospital. They're gonna have to take a picture of your head an' see if you've got a concussion."

"I didn't even—"

"I'm sorry; did you have something to say?"

Sometimes Becker made me feel really stupid. "Nope."

"I didn't think so. Let's go."

"Yessir," I groaned as Bellamy screamed in rage behind me.

I was surprised when he took hold of my arm.

"I can walk, you know."

"I know," he told me as he continued to lead me to the car.

"What's with you?" I asked.

"You could've left us today," he said gruffly. "I don't think I'm ready to lose anybody on this team just yet."

It was hearing about Hicks and Warren. Everything had become real in an instant.

CHAPTER 2

MY EYEBROW only needed five stitches, which, compared to some of the other lacerations I'd suffered over the years, was nothing. The doctor on call checked me out—I got jumped in line because I got hurt, technically, in the line of duty, and because Ching looked pissed and no one wanted to tell him no.

Because I was a federal marshal and had to carry a gun 24-7, I always had to be checked out so a doctor could vouch for my brain not being scrambled. No one wanted someone to get shot accidentally because a marshal had a concussion and mistook them for a bear or something. I certainly never wanted to be the guy on the wrong end of a shooting incident.

As I sat there in the ER, blood on my shirt and sweater, waiting as Becker talked to Kage and Ching paced as he talked to Dorsey, the curtain that separated me from the next bed was yanked open and Eli appeared, another man right behind him, like it was a magic show.

"Hey," I greeted, smiling, finding it odd he was there.

"I was driving by from the airport and told you were still here. Since we're supposed to be eating tonight, and I figured Doyle stranded you at the pickup site when he left with the SOG guys, it made sense to come grab you."

I nodded. "That seems reasonable," I teased. "I find your logic sound."

He rolled his eyes theatrically but moved quickly, his nonchalance belied by how fast he got to me.

Stepping between my parted legs, he checked my eye and face, upon which, Dorsey had informed me, the bruises had started to darken. Eli winced at the damage and my clothes. "I'm thinking we have to go by your place so you can clean up and put on something without blood splatter on it."

I grunted before holding out my hand to greet the man who must be his cousin but looked only fleetingly like Eli. Where Eli was tall and built like a swimmer with wide shoulders, a broad chest, narrow waist, and long legs, Ira was leaner with long muscles, not ones defined in a gym like Eli's.

"Oh yeah," Eli said. "This is my cousin, Ira. Ira, this is Miro Jones."

The smaller, nerdier, bespectacled cousin of a guy I trusted with my life moved forward to take my outstretched hand.

"Pleasure to meet you, Ira."

"And you," he said with a half grimace, half smile.

I patted our gripped hands with my other, then let go, gesturing at my face. "Oh, this is nothing. Par for the course."

He nodded. "I have a friend, Tracy. This kind of thing happens to him too."

"Is he in law enforcement?"

"No, but his brother is."

"Turns out you know the brother indirectly," Eli explained. "Me and Ira were putting it together in the car that you know Alex Brandt, and he's Ira's friend's brother."

How did I know that name?

Eli, who read me pretty well after the years between us, noticed me struggling. "You worked with my buddy Kane Morgan in San Fran the last time you were there and—"

"Oh, Brandt's the DEA agent," I realized. "Shit, how is he?"

"Good," Ira said, grinning. "He's annoying and kind of a douche, but yeah, all in one piece."

"Oh, I'm glad." Even though I'd never met Brandt myself, Inspector Morgan struck me as the kind of man who didn't take his friendships lightly. I was pleased to hear he wasn't missing anybody. "And damn, that's a small world," I said to Eli.

"It is. I mean, I know Kane, but I had no idea Ira knew the Brandts."

I looked back at Ira. "So you like San Fran?"

"I do," he said, then indicated Eli with a tip of his head. "This one liked it too until Natalie."

Eli inhaled sharply, which made me ready to hear all about whoever Natalie was.

"Hey," Becker said, snapping his fingers to get our attention.

Eli and I turned to look at him.

"State police in Huntsville, Alabama, already found a shallow grave off I-65 North."

"So they recovered both bodies?"

He nodded.

"That's good."

Becker half shrugged, and I understood. Yes, it was good they'd been found because this way their families got closure—but bad for the obvious reason—they were dead.

I twisted back around, taking a breath before smiling at Ira, giving him an eyebrow waggle, needing the diversion of a good story. "Okay, so, dish about Natalie."

"No," Eli barked, putting it on. "Shut up, Ira. Don't you say a fuckin' word."

Ira chuckled.

"I'm not kidding." He pointed at him. "Just—you don't need to tell him about—"

I grabbed Eli's arm and drew him closer, upsetting his balance just enough that we bumped and he had to put his hand on my shoulder to steady himself. "Tell me all about Natalie," I instructed Ira.

Ira was enjoying seeing us jostle around, the delight easy to read on his face.

"Don't," Eli warned.

"Do," I pressed, holding Eli's arm tighter when he tried to lunge at Ira.

"He followed Natalie out here from San Fran, and a week later, she dumped him."

I moved my hand to Eli's shoulder, squeezing tight. "Aww, buddy, is that before you started dressing well?"

"Fuck you," he groused as he eased back into my hold, not struggling, content to stand there beside me.

It was funny. We were fooling around, and in the midst of waiting in the ER, I was comfortable, and I realized that was because I was with Eli and the rest of the guys.

I realized at Thanksgiving last year that I'd stopped looking for companionship outside of my circle, outside of the guys I worked with and counted on. My last friendship with a nice attorney who moved in next door to me and Ian turned out to be nothing but a ruse, and in the aftermath of that betrayal, I found myself hesitant to open up to anyone new. I was never a real trusting guy to begin with—foster care did that to you, made you wary of strangers—but now where I used to smile and make conversation with everyone, I was far more reserved, downright quiet. I listened a lot, which was good, and as a result, the guys, especially Eli, had become the ones I looked to for companionship.

"So," I said, looking at Eli. "You followed a woman out here and, what, fell in love with the city?"

He shrugged. "She left to go back, couldn't take the winter, and I stayed here."

"And then your mom moved here too?"

"Well, yeah," he replied with a smirk. "She can't live without her baby."

"Which sucks for the rest of us," Ira chimed in, "because his mother can cook."

I smiled at him. "And yours can't?"

He winced. "Just don't—if you ever meet her, don't tell her I said that."

"Said what?"

Ira pointed at me, grinning at Eli. "Oh, I like him."

Eli was going to say something shitty back, I was sure, but a commotion in the hall interrupted us, and we all watched uniformed hospital security rush by, and then a nurse and a doctor followed. Before I could even open my mouth to ask, a person—I couldn't tell if it was a kid or a woman—bolted past, and then Ching, who was still behind me, drew the curtain wide, opening it around my bed so we could see what was going on.

The heavy coat was thrown off, and a teenaged girl emerged from underneath, clad in booty shorts and a tank top that were too skimpy for March in Chicago, where the weather went up and down so fast that it could be sixty on one day and thirty the next. The shoes she had on, platform strappy heels, also made no sense. When she went down, the heel twisting under her, I hopped off the table to go help, and when I moved forward, she looked up.

"Jesus," I gasped because it hit me. "Wen?"

She heaved out a sob, got her feet under her just as security reached her, and charged forward, closing on me in seconds and hurling herself into my arms.

I clutched her tight, tucking her head to my chest but still careful not to crush her since it was like holding a baby bird. I had no idea what the hell was going on. The last time I saw her, she was not this skinny, was not wearing mascara that was running down her face in black rivulets, and certainly was not dressed to walk the streets. I was horrified and filling with slow, seething rage as every protective instinct inside of me went off. The urge to shelter her thrummed under my skin.

Security guards moved forward, and I took a step back, bumping my bed. They might have advanced a second time, but Eli was there, hand out to still them.

"We need you to hand over that patient," one of the guards ordered, addressing me. "She assaulted her guardian and hit a nurse who was trying to help her and—"

"You need to step back," Becker informed them, opening his coat so they could see the badge hanging from the chain around his neck. "We're federal marshals, so you need to explain what the hell is going on here."

"There, there," Wen cried, pointing at a man bolting for the exit.

"Stop," Ching bellowed, drawing his gun as people screamed around him and dropped to the ground. "Or I'll be forced to fire."

The man did a slow pan, and the arrogant smile slowly crumbled as he took in Eli, who had pulled his gun as well, and Ching, both advancing on him. From his reaction I bet he had been ready to face security guards, not federal marshals. "I haven't done anything wrong," he assured them.

"We'll see," Ching informed him, holstering his gun, pulling the zip ties from the pocket in his cargo pants as Eli covered him.

The guy wasn't looking at Eli anymore, though; it was Becker, his gun trained on him, who was suddenly making him shake.

"Benjamin James," Becker said as Ching shoved the guy to his knees and secured his hands tightly behind him. "Picking up where Rego left off? You pimping out underage girls?"

The shaking turned into a tremor, but I didn't care. It was Wen sobbing in my arms, holding on so tight, who had all my attention. Lifting her head, I looked down into her face.

"What happened, sweetheart? Where's your sister?"

"Han," she gasped, "she got hurt real bad. The man... he hurt when he—when—Miro!"

Howling cries then, and she dissolved in my arms as I lifted her and put her on the bed I'd been on. She weighed nothing, a mere slip of her former self, and I wrapped her in a blanket that Ira, now off the floor where Eli had pushed him, handed me. Swallowing down my desire to go kick the shit out of James, I made myself stay there and be strong for Wen, letting her lean forward and bump her head on my chest.

"We gotta go see Han, okay?" she pleaded.

"Sure thing, honey."

"And you won't let them get us again, right?"

"No, you know I won't."

She nodded. "I knew you wouldn't. I told Mrs. Cullen to let me call you, but she wouldn't. I told her we weren't going to school, but she said for Chinese girls to miss studying wasn't a big thing because I was just going to be a maid anyway."

My stomach roiled, and the anger swept through me, but I kept my voice calm, solid, matter-of-fact for the trembling girl. "You're going to be a doctor like your father was."

She lifted her head and gazed at me with wounded, terrified eyes. "Can I still be a doctor after what those men did?"

Fuck. "Absolutely," I assured her, confident in my answer, letting her hear the certainty in my voice as I tucked her head back against my chest.

Glancing over at Eli, I saw him swallow hard, watched his jaw clench, and knew, like me, he was holding on by a thread not to tear James limb from limb.

"Oh, don't you guys worry," Ching said, darkly certain, a cold grin on his face that was by far the scariest expression I'd ever seen on him. "Prison's gonna be a blast for this one, I'll make sure." I remembered that just like some of Dorsey's family, some of Ching's were serving time as well. "No one likes guys who hurt little girls."

I had always heard that but didn't know it was a real thing until I started putting people in jail for a living. It was, without a doubt, a true statement. Scary prisoners locked up for life had daughters too.

"Take me to Han," I told the fourteen-year-old girl in my arms. "Let's go see your little sister."

It was one of the longest walks of my life.

MOST PEOPLE, if asked, probably thought the number of people who went into WITSEC every year was in the thousands, but it was actually far less. From when witness protection became a program in the 1970s to today, the number hovered somewhere between ten and eleven thousand, depending on what report you accessed or who you asked. Of that number, most were married or there was a significant other, some had families, and some were underage.

Because kids who had seen a crime committed—normally the death of one or both of their parents—could not be turned over to relatives unless they too entered WITSEC, most of them went into foster care. In Chicago there were, at the moment, a hundred and twelve underage kids placed with the Department of Child and Family Services, and while that agency was in charge of them, the caveat was that, along with their case manager/social worker, a liaison from the marshals' office supervised them. So while DCFS struggled with the same things as every government agency—the deplorable lack of funding, the chronically understaffed clusterfuck, and widespread unreliable reporting—for the kids in WITSEC, it was supposed to be better because they had someone from the marshals' office advocating for them. Sadly they dropped the ball on Wen and Han Li, whose parents, Dr. Herman Li and his wife, Jia, had been killed in a home invasion in Jacksonville, Florida.

It was a mistake. Gil "Piston" Baker, head of a local meth ring who had ties to a biker gang that was big in Florida, thought he was killing a rival when he was, in fact, killing a gifted cardiologist. In the dark, hopped up on meth, having mixed up the numbers of the address, he shot first, murdering the doctor and then his wife, who charged down the stairs after Dr. Li. The girls saw it all from the second floor and ran to their room, locked the door, and then climbed out the window and up onto the roof, cell phones in hand, before Baker even figured out what he'd done. Jacksonville PD caught him before he pulled out of the driveway.

Baker would have remained strong and not rolled over on the motorcycle club, but facing the needle for murdering the Lis, he turned on everyone he'd ever called friend. It was a long, arduous process, dismantling a gang that had ties to a cartel with fingers in prostitution, drugs, and guns. And because everything had to be disclosed, Baker's gang knew all about Han and Wen, so they were placed into protective custody until the entire trial concluded—which was still years away—or Baker died. Since Baker was in fine health and had basically put out a bounty on each girl, WITSEC was their only option. Five months ago, they had been brought to Chicago. Ian and I did their intake paperwork and took them upstairs to Custodial WITSEC, run by Sebreta Cullen and overseen by new Supervisory Deputy Darren Mills.

Normally there was red tape. Normally there was a process and things took time—if and when an individual or a department was investigated, that would move at a glacial speed. The difference in this instance was the office faced a PR nightmare of biblical proportions that could effectively cripple the Northern District. It would blow the reputation of the marshals' office to kingdom come. But more important than all of that was we were talking about underage children. Kage was so furious he wasn't even yelling, which was a very, *very* bad sign. Heads were going to roll.

The problem was new because Mills put Cullen in her position after Maureen Prescott retired, and he was not required to run his pick by Kage. Because of that, and because Kage had his hands full with everything else, he hadn't checked in on Custodial WITSEC.

I went with Kage to confront Cullen because I was the guy who'd called him. He charged into that office at four in the afternoon like the wrath of God.

He rattled off directions to his team, the accountants—because there were fiscal concerns if people weren't watching the kids—then the social workers from the DCFS who would know what they were looking for, and of course, Prescott, who'd worked for Kage for years before retiring and still came when called. Kage brought some of the guys up from Judicial Security too, four total, and positioned them around the room so that when he told everyone to get up and walk to the conference room—he was clearing the area before he spoke to Cullen—no one hesitated. They just got up from their desks and moved.

I followed him into Cullen's office, where he didn't knock. He shut down her assistant with a sharp word that sent her scuttling after the others, strode to Cullen's desk, took the phone out of her hand, and hung it up.

Cullen was a short blonde woman with a medium-length bob with bangs. She shot up out of her chair. "How dare you—"

"No." He punched a button on the phone so it was on speaker. "Marshal Kenwood."

"Kage," the US Marshal for the Northern District answered.

"I'm here with Sebreta Cullen, sir."

"And is Prescott there?"

"I am, sir," she answered, moving around to stand beside Cullen.

"And who's taking over in the interim?"

"Deputy US Marshal Miro Jones, sir," Kage replied smoothly, leaving me stunned and staring, gulping like a fish on dry land. "He's the one with the commendation from the State Department and the Spanish consulate for the recovery of a cultural attaché's children."

"Oh yes, excellent," he agreed quickly. "Sounds like you have it well in hand. Have the DOJ get the investigation done to find out if it's criminal or merely gross negligence. Make sure she's escorted from the building after Public Affairs meets with her and reminds her of the agreements she signed when she was hired."

"Yessir."

"Do you have a team at her home now?"

"I do, sir."

"Excellent. I'll expect a report in two hours."

"Yessir."

When he hung up, I looked back at Cullen and noticed she was shaking. She had to step aside as Prescott plugged into her computer a flash drive I knew from experience gave her immediate access to the desktop.

"What the hell is going on?" Cullen shrieked, and I noticed her peaches-and-cream complexion was steadily pinking with anger.

"Well, that's what we're going to find out," Kage explained, scowling.

"I don't understand. My record is impeccable with—"

"White middle-class kids," Prescott interrupted, her fingers flying over the keyboard. "But with black kids, Asian, mixed, gay, bi, transgender—your record is for crap, Ms. Cullen."

"I don't—that's not true," she shouted, banging her hand on the desk. "I'm a Christian and—"

"You hypocritical piece of crap," I snarled. "How could you—"

"I won't stand for—"

"You will stand for it!" Kage roared, and holy crap, was he loud. I forgot sometimes, considering how good he was about keeping his tone modulated, that when he wanted to, he could bounce his voice off the walls. But it made sense. He was massive with muscle, his arms, shoulders, and chest built like a tank, so when he wanted to yell, Jesus Christ, he *could*. "No Christian I know treats a child—any child—with the willful disrespect, disinterest, and disdain you've shown."

"I—"

He turned and pointed at two women and a man, all in suits, who stood just inside the office door. "These people are here to advise you of your rights, place you on administrative leave for the duration of the inquiry, and take your statement about the welfare of the children who are supposed to be cared for by the department you manage."

"You cannot expect me to take care of the bad children like I do the good ones," she told him, her voice rising a second time. "Many of those kids have serious mental issues, or they're juvenile delinquents or—"

"They're *children*," Kage said, his voice so hollow and cold I could feel the chill. "It's your job to protect them. You failed."

"I can't be expected to help the black boys, because they hate me, and those horrible kids who don't know if they're boys or girls, or the dirty little faggots—"

Prescott gasped, which snapped Cullen from her tirade, prompting her to cover her mouth with her hand.

Instantly I thought of Josue and Cabot and Drake, all young men, not children, but still in need of direction, guidance, and protection. A few years younger and they would have been treated to Sebreta Cullen's icy indifference and possibly may have gotten as lost as Han and Wen. I was nauseated thinking about what could have happened to my boys—or even me—in a different time and place. I was gay and in the foster care system, but I never faced anything like Cullen. She looked into the hopeful, needy eyes of children turning to her for salvation and shelter, care and concern, and threw them away like garbage. The surge of disgust was visceral, and I had to breathe through my nose not to vomit.

Kage turned his head to the suits in the room, focusing on one woman who was clearly in charge. She got on her phone as another man strode forward, folder open while he wrote frantically.

"Done," the woman on the phone said to Kage, looking up for only a moment before returning to her conversation. I saw her badge before she started closing the blinds in the office, *Department of Justice* easy to read above her name: Rhonda Taylor. She was tall—at least six two—a stunning woman with long blonde hair who looked more like a model than a DOJ lawyer.

Kage turned back to Cullen. "Sebreta S. Cullen, you are hereby dismissed from your position as director of Custodial WITSEC here at the Northern District of Illinois."

"But I didn't mean—"

"And off the record," he said icily, "you're a vile human being, and I will personally make certain that criminal charges will be filed against you."

"You won't find—"

"Oh, we will," Prescott assured her, her voice and hands shaking. "We most certainly will."

"Come with us, please," Taylor directed, now off the phone, lips pursed, eyes blazing, utterly rippling with barely controlled anger.

Cullen moved around her desk and stood before Kage. "This is a witch hunt because you're gay and you've hated me from the start."

The muscles in his jaw corded, and really, I knew he'd never hit a woman, but if he did, no one in that room would have said a word. "Madam, before today I had no earthly idea who you were or that you were not doing your job, and that's my failure. I trust others to oversee different departments in this building and have recently been reminded that, unless I pick the supervisor myself, I can have no real confidence in the reporting. Had you done your job, you would never have seen me. As things stand, you're terminated with charges pending a formal inquiry. You will remain on house arrest until we complete our investigation."

"You can't do—"

"He can, he has," Taylor informed Cullen, her voice brittle. "And had he not, I would have, so come with us, Ms. Cullen. We need to go over the expectations of you during this transition time, and the limits of your travel to and from your home."

"I'm not a criminal!"

"You certainly are," Kage intoned, turning his back on the room, clearly done speaking to the horrible excuse for a human being, purposely breathing in slowly, I suspected, so he didn't explode.

After Cullen was removed, we stood quietly for a few minutes as a team in coveralls came in and started dismantling the office in front of my eyes, taking photographs and paintings from the walls, packing up framed awards and certificates, boxing up tchotchkes and candles, the pens on her desk, and pictures of her family. It was so cold and impersonal to watch.

"Oh, Sam," Prescott said, taking a halting breath.

He turned to look at her.

Elbow braced on the desk, her face was in her hand as she stared at the screen, trembling, her eyes filling fast. "You need to have Jones meet with a lot of these kids right now—yesterday—or we're going to have more—oh God."

"Tell me," Kage demanded.

She took a shaky breath, hand over her mouth for a moment, moving her fingers as though tiny shocks were moving through them before she straightened and put her palm down on the desk with what seemed like considerable effort, getting herself under control before she addressed him. "You've got a boy in the morgue right now."

"How old?"

"Sixteen."

He nodded. "I'm sorry, but I need you to come back for at least three months. I need you to tell me who's good, if any, in this department, and supervise here on-site while Jones conducts the field interviews. It's a two-person job until we can get all the current, as well as the incoming, kids accounted for and situated."

"Yes," she agreed.

"And he needs an assistant."

"For an interim position?"

It appeared their eyes locked, like they were sharing a brain for a second, and I felt like I was witnessing that silent communion I'd read about but never seen in real life. A moment later, they both turned to me.

"Sir?" I asked Kage.

"Get him an assistant," he told Prescott before he turned for the door.

"Mills?" she asked.

"Mills," he echoed as he walked out.

I watched him leave, his retreating back holding my attention.

"Jones."

All my focus returned to Prescott.

"That man has all the faith in the world in you. You get that, right?"

I tried not to grimace because... was she serious? Me? All he had? All Sam Kage had? Anyone in their right mind would leap at the chance to be the one he called upon for anything because if he had any kind of trust in you at all, it was worth the world. But I wasn't his go-to guy; I couldn't be. There were others so much more qualified than me. "I think I'm all he's got at the moment."

She shook her head. "I worked for him a long time, and he's never unprepared." Quick breath. "You need to give yourself some credit here. If he didn't think you could do the job, he'd never put you in charge."

I let that sink in. What I knew of him and what a dumbass he always treated me like were at odds with her words. Could it possibly be that Kage did not think I was a complete doofus? And I knew he didn't because otherwise I wouldn't be on his team, but would it have killed him to tell me that? To say, even in passing, "You know, Jones, you don't totally suck." I could only imagine what being his child must be like. Strong and silent was all well and good if you knew you were loved, or in my case, respected.

"On the other hand, you have to realize that this is not a glory job."

"What do you mean?"

"I mean that this is not the job for an adrenaline junkie. This is a small office in the corner of the monolith, and when you're outside with your badge, no one really looks at it. They're much more interested in the lanyard around your neck. You still carry a gun, but in all my years on the job, I only drew mine twice."

"That's good. I'd prefer never to have to pull my weapon," I answered woodenly, saying what I thought I should at the moment instead of screaming.

She spoke like I was done in the field doing what I knew best and backing up Ian. It sounded so normal coming from her, like this was of course my new path and not at all the life-and-death decision it actually was. I couldn't imagine not being a member of Sam Kage's team, not being Ian's backup, not doing what I had been for the past five years. The idea of something new, of change, was terrifying, but instead of arguing, I shoved down the fear because, at the very same time, there were aspects of the job I was doing now that I was better at and a huge piece of what she was talking about. Maybe the nurturing side of me, the part that wanted to help and not punish, was something Sam Kage could actually see.

"Jones?"

"I'm listening," I advised her because I was just processing at the same time.

She nodded. "Once you take this job, Jones, your power isn't about heroic feats anymore. There won't be any news articles or photos ops, instead simply quiet moments where kids thank you before they go off to college."

I crossed my arms as I looked at her. "There's nobility in that."

She scrutinized me. "But you don't care about that."

She said it like she knew already, and I shrugged.

"You're not a glory hound, are you, Jones?"

"No, ma'am," I replied, now taking the time to study her face, liking her dimples, her kind smile, her deep brown eyes, dark sepia skin with the gold undertones, and the intricate braids swept up carelessly into a bun that looked heavier than her hair fork could actually hold in place.

"I've read your file."

"Mine?" I was surprised.

"Yes."

"Why?"

She stared at me until I got it. "He had you check me out."

"He did."

"But that makes no sense."

"Like I told you, he's always prepared."

"But he just told Cullen he had no idea who—oh," I said, jolting with the realization of what I knew, for certain, about my boss, that being caught off guard was not an option for him. "If Mills hadn't filled the position, he wanted to be ready."

"Yes."

"So I was on the back burner this whole time?"

She nodded.

"That's kinda scary, right?"

"It's something, yes."

I took a breath. "Well, give it to me. What did you tell him?"

"I said that you seem to have a natural drive to create a family."

"Explain it to the whole class, willya?"

She raised her thick eyebrows. "Cabot Jenner and Drake Ford?" I opened my mouth to correct her because those weren't their last names anymore. "Yes, yes," she hushed me. "I know, you put them into protective custody and changed their lives."

"I guided them a bit."

"And Josue Hess?"

"He's only been with me for a little while."

"Yes," she said, nodding. "*With* you. I heard that."

"I just want to make sure that you're not mixing up regular—"

"Where are Wen and Han Li now?"

"They're at the hospital in protective custody, waiting for their… stepaunt, I guess is what you'd call her, to collect them."

"Why weren't they placed with this aunt to begin with?"

"They're not really related to her."

"Explain."

"I got permission to contact their mother's stepsister, who lives in San Antonio. She's going to graduate school there, and she's agreed to take the girls."

"And how are you keeping them safe?"

"Well, the sister, Rowan is her name, she's related to Mrs. Li through her father's second marriage. Rowan was his second wife's kid when Mr. Wu, Mrs. Li's dad, married her."

"So Mr. Wu, Mrs. Li's dad, was Rowan's stepfather."

"Yes."

She smiled kindly, tipping her head for me to go on.

"So Mrs. Li and this Rowan are stepsisters and—"

"I got that, but how does that keep the girls safe? I mean, if you found out, don't you think other people will be able to?"

"It's a stretch. I only know because the girls told me. Mrs. Li and Rowan were friendly, but they had a big gap in their ages. They only met after Mrs. Li's father, Gene, passed away."

She nodded. "I like the sound of this, of them having family, but you still haven't convinced me of the long-term viability of your plan."

"They'll have exactly what they would have had if their parents had lived. They live on their own with federal marshals checking in on them, plus I put them on SRT status until they're both eighteen and—"

"SRT status?" Her eyes were wide. "How did you get that put in place for two non-high-profile witnesses?"

Special Response Team status was for emergency lockdown situations in case an entire family had to be moved at a moment's notice. It was normally reserved for organized crime families, cartel heads, or people who had turned state's evidence. It was not usually put in place for witnesses testifying against single individuals.

"I told them that because the girls were abused, it makes them especially likely to reach out to old friends of theirs, old friends of their parents, people they used to know, which in turn makes them vulnerable to discovery."

"But you don't actually think they would do that, do you?"

"I have no idea. They didn't do it when they were in hell these past few months, but that doesn't mean it won't happen."

She scrutinized me. "But you let the office there in... where?"

"San Antonio."

"You let them think it could."

"It just puts them on everyone's radar so they can't slip through the cracks again."

"That's very smart. Did you include that in their transfer paperwork?"

"I did."

She nodded. "That's quick thinking, Jones, to have it in as part of their official plan."

"You know as well as I do that whatever stipulations are included in a witness plan initially are a pain in the ass to get changed."

"Very true."

"So this way I figured there would be no question that their aunt would be accompanying them if the new living arrangement was ever discovered."

"And the aunt was fine with this? Being uprooted if there ever came a need?"

"She said she was all-in for the girls," I reported, leaving out the fact that Rowan Wu was livid when I told her how Wen and Han had been living. Why hadn't she been contacted after her stepsister was killed? Wasn't it usual to ask family before anyone else?

I had no answers for her other than to say no one had any idea about her or her connection to the girls until I was told.

"Well, that seems like a good thing, then, if I want to take them," Rowan had said over the phone. "And I do want to take them. I may not be mother material, but I can be a kickass aunt."

I had no doubt. Her absolute willingness to jump in spoke volumes. She had already lined up a therapist for the girls.

"It sounds as though you're confident about this new arrangement," Maureen said.

"I am, and the girls can contact me as well. They have my cell number."

"When are they leaving?"

"They'll be taken to San Antonio by judicial transport tonight."

"So the girls only told *you* about this."

"Wen did, yeah."

"Because she knew you."

"Well, she doesn't know me that well, of course. She just remembered me from when I did her intake paperwork. I haven't seen her since then."

"Which was one time."

I nodded.

"You must make quite an impression."

Me?

It was a weird thing to say, because I doubted that was the case. "Actually, it's Ian who makes the impression. I sort of fade into the background when he's around."

"And yet, not for little girls who are looking for a savior."

"Savior's laying it on a little thick, don't you think?"

"What do you think Wen Li would say? She saw you at the hospital today by some freakish stroke of luck, and her whole life changed in an instant. Do you think she sees you as her savior or not?"

"She's just a little girl."

"Exactly. A little girl looking for a miracle."

I shook my head. She was jumbling things up in my head. I knew who I was, and some kind of hero wasn't it. There was a difference between doing your job and going above and beyond. I did more for Josue and Cabot and Drake because it had been that way from the start. But Wen and Han Li had not been on my radar because they weren't supposed to be. It hadn't been my job to....

"Ah," Maureen said, flashing me a quick grin, pointing at my face. "You got it. It was supposed to be Sebreta Cullen's job to stand between the world and those girls. She didn't do it, she didn't perform her job, and as a result, atrocities occurred. It is heroic in certain instances to simply do what you're supposed to, and Custodial WITSEC is one of those jobs. If you drop the ball here, it's a child's life."

We fell quiet, just looking at each other.

"You know this is all just crap, right? I mean, I'm not the long-term solution here. You heard Kage: I'm the interim guy. He'll find the person he wants directing this department. I'm just filling in until he finds a new you."

"I think you're the new me."

"That's just silly. We don't even look alike," I quipped to try to soothe myself after the bomb detonated in my chest. How could she simply say something like that and think she wasn't turning my whole life upside down? Because if I was the new her, then where did that leave my partnership with Ian? Where did that leave me as a member of the team that had become a vital part of my life? The unit was my family. Leaving was not an option.

She gave me a bright grin. "The question truly is what you can live with and what you can live without."

"What do you mean?"

"Do you have to be a hero every day? Do you crave the excitement of being in the field?"

I would miss being with the others, but the fugitive pickups, the chases—just everything I'd done that morning with Kage—none of that was really me. Ian was the guy who liked kicking down doors; I liked the mop-up part of it, protecting the innocents, extricating them from filth. That was the part that gave me satisfaction, the knowledge that I'd set someone on a new road. "I like helping people," I told her.

She nodded. "Will you miss your partner?"

"Well, actually, I'm married to my partner."

"Yes, I know," she said, surprising me. "But what I mean is will you miss working with him during the day?"

Absently I touched the stitches in my eyebrow, and it hit me that I hadn't really worked with Ian in weeks. It seemed like he was loaned out to SOG or on ops with them almost daily now. It was why I wanted to make sure he ate in the morning, because he'd walk in the door after me at the end of the day like a ravenous wolf. I didn't get to look after him over the course of a day anymore because I didn't see him.

"Custodial WITSEC is the liaison between social services and underage witnesses."

"Yeah, I know."

"Also reports of child abuse, including endangerment, physical as well as environmental neglect, issues of adoption, and things like college placement all fall under our purview."

"Well, I had to put Cabot, Drake, and Josue all in college."

She smiled. "Yes, I know you did."

"So at least that part I can do."

"I understand that you yourself were once a ward of the state."

I glared at her. "Exactly how long were you studying up on me?"

"Sam has had this idea for a while—as I told you—of you in Custodial. You must have done something that impressed him."

Again came that feeling of surprise because that was not at all the impression I got from him on a day-to-day basis. "He always acts like all I do is piss him off."

"It's probably more that he worries about you getting hurt."

"Hurt?"

"Mmmm-hmmm," she mused.

"Not physically."

"No."

I cleared my throat. "I don't think that's it."

"You were in the system," she commented. "Were you homeless at eighteen when you graduated from high school?"

"Yes."

"So you had nowhere to go except college."

I nodded.

"Well, that might be a lot to make you relive over and over, don't you think?"

I shrugged. "It doesn't bother me. It was a long time ago."

"Over and done is not the same thing as seeing other children carry their belongings from one house to another just as you did."

I felt the tightness in my chest as I remembered that, remembered having to leave people's houses and feeling like I was nothing, my clothes and knickknacks in garbage bags, making that whole experience that much worse. I was worthless—so was everything that was mine, which was why now, today, all my possessions were quality.

I spent too much on shoes, socks, everything, anything. I knew that, and I knew why. It was why people became hoarders: because once you lost it all, had not one thing to point to and call your own, it was a brand seared into your soul. The second that changed, once you could have whatever, buy whatever, there had to be more and more until the hole inside was all filled up.

I got lucky there. When I turned eighteen and went to college, I met the four women who were still my dearest friends. Through them, because we all lived together and they shared everything with me from food and money to paintings on the walls and rugs on the floor, from their TVs and game systems to getting me a phone for Christmas… as a direct result of being shown that friendship was the real prize, not stuff, I learned the ebb and flow of possessions. I didn't become a hoarder, though my shoe collection was vast, but kids I didn't know also needed to learn those lessons. Trust took longer, trust I had just recently mastered with Ian coming into my life, but maybe I was supposed to pass on something. Pay it forward, as it were.

"You're thinking really hard," Prescott apprised me.

"Yeah, I do that sometimes."

She chuckled.

"Not often, mind you."

She sighed deeply. "Well, tomorrow's your first day here. I suggest you go talk to your partner and find out what he thinks about all of this. At this point this is an interim assignment, and it's up to you what you want it to be. I know Sam Kage, and he would never simply do something without asking you; that's not how he works. You just need to figure out what it is you want."

I did. She was right. If Ian wasn't my work partner anymore, and if he actually wanted to be transferred to SOG, then did I still want to be a marshal? Was the real thrill of the job being with him? And if I wasn't his partner, did Ian still want to be one? But maybe I was misreading the guy I loved. Maybe he was just helping out because he missed being in Special Forces, and that desire would fade over time.

"I think you need to figure out your life, Miro Jones."

She wasn't wrong.

CHAPTER 3

SINCE MY day was over at six, I went back down to our office, got an apple from the ridiculously large basket in the break room that was currently filled with, among other things, papaya and mango, and stopped at White's desk after I grabbed my mouse off Becker's. Why someone had to move it every frickin' day was beyond me.

"Hey," I greeted him, sinking down into the chair to his right, propping my elbow beside his inbox. "Any luck?"

White grunted. "No, and I checked through all the human resources files today."

"You realize if Kage ever catches you or Sharpe in there, you're dead."

He shrugged. "I figure I'll blame Kowalski."

"How you figure?" I asked, then took a bite of the Fuji apple. "Didn't he just leave on that fishing trip with his family?"

"Yeah, he left right after the op this morning. Ching called him about Hicks, though, and he felt like crap when he found out you got hurt."

"Well, that's all heartwarming and shit, but that doesn't change what has to be done."

He scoffed.

"What? If he would just tell us what the hell Jer stands for, we wouldn't have to go looking through all the records," I said indignantly.

"You realize you sound ridiculous," Sharpe commented from his desk.

"Kowalski's the one who's bein' a dick."

A month ago I mentioned to White that only Eli knew his partner's real name and that he wasn't telling, and wasn't that annoying? What followed was White and Sharpe pushing and digging to see if Kowalski or Eli would break. Neither had, not surprising in the least, so now whenever both of them were out of the office—like Kowalski now taking his annual vacation with his brother and their extended family, and Eli chauffeuring his cousin around—White and Sharpe and I were left snooping. It wasn't like we were giving up nights or work hours to the quest, but when we had any downtime… we tried to dig up Kowalski's full name from somewhere. Sharpe had even looked up old yearbooks and pretended to be from the homecoming committee and called his mother, but she was smarter than he was and told him if he did it again, she'd tell her son. Nobody wanted that, so we closed the door on that angle.

"All his paperwork actually says 'Jer' on it," Sharpe pointed out. "Are we sure Jer isn't just it?"

"It's not," White assured him, gesturing at me. "On Miro's paperwork it just says 'Miro,' and we know that's not right."

"This is an excellent point you're making," I commended Sharpe. When he actually looked at me after I spoke, he jolted like I'd startled him. "What?"

"You look like shit."

"I got beat up and hit with a gun," I reminded him. "Can I get a fuckin' break?"

"Yeah, but aren't you going with us to drink with Kohn and his cousin?"

"Yeah, why?"

Sharpe gestured at me.

"What?"

"You've got blood all over you."

"Which is why I gotta go home and change."

"No, no, no," White grumbled. "You go all the way home, and we're stuck waiting on you for hours to eat. Just—" He looked at his partner. "Don't you have extra shirts in your locker?"

"Lockers" were what they had at the gym; these were more like tiny hall closets with locks on them. You could hang a couple suits, store a couple pairs of shoes in the cubby at the top, and that was about it.

"I don't have anything that's gonna fit him," Sharpe groused. "I'm taller than he is."

"Yeah, but he's got a lot more muscle."

There was a pause.

"Pardon me?"

I started laughing.

"Fuck you, Chandler, more muscle my ass!"

I realized with a heave of breath that I missed Ian and wished he were here.

"Where the fuck is Doyle?" Sharpe complained, looking at me. "Is he home? 'Cause if he is, he could bring you something."

That reminded me that Ian had driven today because after work he had to go see his father out in Marynook. Ian had been sketchy on the details, but I suspected Colin Doyle wanted to talk about Ian's stepbrother's upcoming sentencing on drug charges. Ian also alluded to the fact that his father found some old photo albums that belonged to Ian's mother and wanted to return them. So since he planned on doing that, I was going with Eli and Ira to have drinks, and then Ian was supposed to rendezvous with us for dinner. I wasn't surprised there were no messages or missed calls from him, and none of the guys had seen him since he left with SOG earlier.

"He was going to see his dad; I'm not sure where he is."

"Well call him, for fuck's sake, and find out."

"You're really fuckin' bossy, you know that?"

He flipped me off as I tried Ian. Finally on the fifth ring, he picked up.

"Hey," he said, no endearment, no warmth, so I knew he was still with the SOG guys. Even though we were married now, he wasn't letting those guys know anything about his personal life until he was ready.

"Hey," I sighed. "Did you get over to see your dad yet?"

"No, I had to reschedule. The op took way longer than I thought it would. We just got done, so we're over at Cortland's gettin' a beer and some food."

"You and the guys?"

"Yeah."

I cleared my throat. "So I guess you're not meeting us for drinks and then dinner?"

He was quiet.

"Ian?"

"Shit, was that tonight?"

"It is."

"Fuck."

"No, it's fine, don't worry 'bout it," I soothed. "I'll call Aruna and have her keep the dog, and I'll meet you at home later."

Again he was silent, and I couldn't tell if it was because he wasn't listening to me—drinking with a lot of guys was distracting and loud—or if he was thinking. I could hear a lot of noise in the background, so I was guessing it was hard to hear.

"What?"

Nope. He was distracted. "I'll talk to you later," I told him.

Nothing.

"Ian?"

"Yeah?"

"Bye," I said and hung up. Of course I was disappointed he wasn't going to meet me, but I understood too. Ian wasn't going out on missions with his unit anymore. He was an ex–Green Beret now, so the camaraderie of men in life-and-death situations, that was still something he craved, whether he wanted to cop to it or not. So while I wanted to see him, I got it.

Sharpe and White were both looking at me.

"What?"

"Not a thing," Sharpe assured me, standing up. "C'mon, let's see if I have a shirt that'll fit over all the muscles that my partner's been noticing."

It took a second, and then, "Oh, fuck you," White grumbled, punching the keys, grabbing the half-eaten apple I passed him and taking an angry bite.

Sharpe cackled as we walked away.

WHEN SHARPE, White, and I made it to Howells and Hood over on Michigan Avenue, I discovered Eli had invited several guys from his gym to hang out, as well as the rest of the team. Eli had already had more than a few drinks; I could tell from the way he wrapped his arm around my neck and gave me a sloppy kiss on the cheek.

Whenever one of us had family in town, the rest of us always showed up to meet or hang with them because it told members of our team that the people who were important in their lives were also important in ours. Ian not being there was kind of shitty, but since all the rest of us were—except Kowalski, who had a legitimate reason—I hoped he wouldn't notice.

I thought we were getting dinner, but apparently Ira never got a chance to play pool at home, so when the others bailed to get food— none of us ever ate at the same place we drank, I had no idea why—I stuck with him and Eli, figuring any sports bar we hit would have at least a burger.

We cabbed it over to Milwaukee to find the pool hall Eli wanted to try crowded, even though it was a Wednesday night. Inside it was hot, and blaring classic rock made it impossible to speak to the person standing beside you without your mouth at their ear. It worked out great: we had enough guys to play teams, and the more drinks Ira had, the louder he got, which was funny since he came off all buttoned-up and buttoned-down, but with a few more beers in him, he was ready to start a fight.

"Such a nice Jewish boy," Eli laughed, pinching his cousin's cheek.

When I was bent over, ready to shoot, someone pulled my phone from the back pocket of my pants. Turning, I found Eli grinning at me, answering a question from a guy leaning into him. As soon as I was done shooting, having sunk the three ball in the side pocket, I straightened, and Eli bumped into me, put an arm around my neck, and snapped a selfie of us with my phone. He was texting someone, but I was winning, so I didn't care. It wasn't as easy to do as usual because the purple silk shirt I had on was tighter than I normally wore. I did actually have a wider chest, broader shoulders, and bigger biceps than Sharpe.

Once everyone got hungry, I talked them all into Superdawg because it was close. We could walk, and with so much alcohol in our systems, we needed carbs.

"Where's the ketchup?" Ira asked after we were done ordering. Eli gasped.

"What?" Ira asked, annoyed, scowling at his cousin.

"Absofuckinglutely not," I chided. "No ketchup on the dog, man. Have your lost your mind? This is fuckin' Chicago, yeah?"

He looked at me like I was nuts.

"Get extra fries and tamales too," Eli told me when I was ordering, head on my shoulder, smiling at the girl behind the counter.

She was distracted by Eli, gazing at him instead of listening to me, but finally I got my food ordered and moved sideways so the next guy could go.

"Careful," one of Eli's friends said, taking hold of my side so I didn't step off the curb.

"Sorry," I said quickly, grinning wide.

"No, it's fine," he said, letting go but not stepping back. "Really."

"I don't—not sure I got your name at the bar."

"And no one could hear shit at the pool hall," he said, smiling at me, holding my gaze.

"Right?" I agreed, offering him my hand. "Miro Jones."

He greeted me, taking my hand. "Daley O'Meara."

I squinted at him.

"What?" he asked, teasing. "I smell?"

"No, you...." He smelled great, actually, some kind of woodsy cologne. "I just.... You on the job?"

His lazy smile got bigger and brighter. "I am. I'm following in my old man's footsteps."

"He a cop?"

"He's the commander out at the Eighth," he explained, and only then did I realize he was still holding my hand.

"I'm gonna need that," I said, tipping my head at our clasped hands.

"Yeah," he agreed, letting me go but still not taking a step back. "How'd you get hurt?"

"Oh, you know, a little undercover work."

"I don't, actually. I wasn't recruited straight outta the academy to do that like you apparently were."

"Oh no, I—"

"Which district are you at? I'm over at the Fourth."

"I'm not a cop anymore. I'm a marshal like Eli."

"Ah, you and those other guys that bailed, you're his friends from work."

"Yeah."

He was quiet a moment, just looking at me, so I figured it was my turn to talk. "So the Fourth, huh?" I grimaced. "You guys got a new commander yet since they canned Vaughn?"

"Oh man," he groaned, raking his fingers through his thick hair. "That was such a clusterfuck. I don't even know how I'm supposed to deal with that shit."

Earlier in the month, Leland Vaughn, commander of the Fourth District—which, interestingly enough, was where my first partner worked before he transferred to Boston—was implicated on murder charges, racketeering, drugs.... You name it, he was guilty of it, as he'd been in deep with the Irish mob.

"He was a piece of shit," I said, shrugging. "I mean, he deserves what he gets."

"Well, you guys gotta watch him, right? We were told he turned state's evidence and went into protective custody. That's the marshals' office, isn't it?"

"Yeah, but that's not us here in Chicago, I can promise you that." As far as I knew, Leland Vaughn was either in Alaska or New Mexico and nowhere near the Windy City. He was an extremely high-profile target. "There's no way to protect Vaughn in this city. The police and the mob are both after him."

"It's been bad. We got the O'Brien crew and the Murphy crew dropping each other like flies." He sighed. "I hate that it's just more bad press too."

"It'll run its course," I offered frankly. "I mean, they always do."

He nodded, tipping his head, appreciating something about me. "What?"

"May I just say that this purple shirt is really something."

"Oh yeah? You like that?" I snorted.

"It's... very purple," he teased, the grin making his eyes glitter. "I just haven't seen this—what is this, silk?—in a while."

I laughed, not about to give Sharpe credit for the atrocity of a shirt. "Are you kidding? This is my clubbing gear, man."

He nodded. "I'm concerned about the clubs that you might frequent."

I patted his arm, and he followed me to grab our food. He sat across from me while we ate, and I realized Eli still had my phone.

"Hey!"

Eli looked up at me from the other end of the table.

"I don't have any calls from Kage, do I? Or a Prescott?" Those were the only two I was worried about at the moment.

"Uh, no." He snickered. "Nothing from anyone you work for."

"Okay," I said, returning to the mouthwatering goodness in front of me. I had no idea how hungry I was until I started eating.

"Why does he have your phone?" Daley asked, and I could hear the judgment in his tone.

I looked up at him. "He's a little drunkish and he's fuckin' around, but he knows better than to leave with it because, technically, we're never off duty."

"Makes sense."

"But since my partner is gone at the moment, and so is his, we're covering each other's asses," I explained before I took another bite. "We're fine," I finished with my mouth full.

He laughed at me and wiped mustard off the corner of my mouth.

Eli wanted to end the night dancing at a new place called Troubadour over in River North. He'd been trying for a while to get me and the rest of the guys to go there. I could not imagine the others dancing—though Becker assured me that back in his Marine Corps days, he was a total club kid—except me and Sharpe, so I figured since I usually said no, I'd go tonight, especially since I had nowhere to be and it was just a bit after midnight. We all loaded into cabs, and I had Daley wedged in on my left and Eli more or less in my lap with Ira dancing in the front seat next to the driver, who found the sight of a drunk bespectacled accountant quite amusing.

The club was loud, the music visceral, but interestingly enough, the drinks were not watered down. At all. It made no sense until I realized the stunningly beautiful six-foot-tall Nubian goddess of a bartender knew Eli. Whatever he passed me nearly burned the back of my throat.

"The fuck was in that?" I asked after I gulped it down.

"Moonshine!" He cackled in my ear. "Bourbon, scotch, whiskey, rum, and mescal."

"Oh for fuck's sake," I groused as Daley snickered on the other side of me, sipping a whiskey cola.

"Even the smell of that glass is enough to make me drunk," Eli teased, arm draped around my shoulders.

"I need my liver, you know," I muttered, taking the old-fashioned he passed me. After a long sip of the drink, I tasted the heavy hand of bourbon in that as well.

Eli laughed into my neck before following a beautiful woman out onto the dance floor, with Ira trailing him. I drained the glass and then felt hands on my hips before Daley took my empty, left it on the table, and piloted me into the crowd.

Dancing in a group was fun. I hadn't been for ages since it was not something Ian enjoyed, and truly, I didn't miss it that much; it was never my forte. But I used to go with my girls when we were in college, and with them, like now, lots of people moving together, acting stupid, nothing serious, buzzing from a few too many drinks, it was a good time.

The music never stopped, never slowed, so we were all sweaty and laughing, and when we finally stopped to hydrate, our table had been taken over, so we headed toward the lounge area. I detoured to the bathroom before my bladder burst, ran some water through my hair after washing my hands, gave my face a quick splash as well, and was finished and on my way back out, walking down the hallway, when I was shoved against the wall.

It was instinctive to fight. Some of it, the heart-pounding, head-clearing spike of adrenaline was from dealing with Craig Hartley, my psyche as permanently scarred as my body. The rest of it, the way I rounded instantly, fists raised, braced for battle, was all training, first as a cop and then as a marshal. The only reason I didn't pull my gun was because I was wearing an ankle holster, but all I needed was enough room to crouch and draw. When I hit whoever knocked me into the wall, that would give me the space I needed.

Daley's laughter caught me by surprise, and then my brain registered "maybe friend and not foe." I didn't relax, though, so all things considered, Daley was lucky I hadn't hit him.

"I guess I should know better than to jump a federal marshal."

"Hey," I rasped, taking a breath, calming, forcing a smile, not comfortable in my own skin yet, needing another few seconds. "You—"

He stepped into my space, took my face in his hands, and would have kissed me, but I took hold of his wrists and pushed him back harder than I should have. I didn't hurt him, but as the motion came directly on the heels of him ambushing me seconds earlier— it was more abrupt than it should have been. Feeling bad about overreacting, I did two things at once: I made certain he couldn't complete his motion and kiss me but rendered him immobile at the same time. And even though he was a big, strong guy, I did have a lot of muscle on him.

Everything happened in quick succession, so it was not surprising when his eyes went wide. It took that extra moment for my brain to make the jump from keeping him off me to what was actually going on. He'd tried to kiss me, and now he was looking at me like I'd kicked his puppy. I had to clear things up, so I held tighter when he tried to pull away.

"Wait, no, it's not like that," I soothed, quickly knowing exactly where his mind had gone when it appeared I was rebuffing his advances. "I *am* gay."

"Then what?" he asked angrily. He knew what he looked like— handsome man, great body, with tight, compact muscle—and there had to be reason I was telling him no.

"I'm married, so I can't kiss attractive men anymore." I saw the alarm wash away from his handsome features, and understanding flooded them instead. "Sorry," I whispered.

All his irritation and confusion was gone in an instant, and for that, I was thankful. I'd been there myself many times in the past, hitting on the wrong guy. "For what?"

I shrugged. "I dunno, sending the wrong signals, maybe."

He shook his head, reaching up to push my hair out of my face. "You didn't. I just got excited meeting someone so pretty and funny."

I snorted. "Awww. Man, that's a nice thing to say."

His eyes darted to the thick gold band on my left hand. "I saw the ring, but lots of guys wear them. I can't tell you how many of them I've met in clubs, only to be told that it's just a piece of jewelry."

I arched a brow for his benefit, and he squinted in response. "What?"

"You think maybe you've been picking up guys who actually are married?"

"No," he said defensively.

"Oh, okay," I said patronizingly, playfully, feeling better, normal, back on solid ground with him.

"Shut up," he grumbled.

I grimaced. "If you're not getting many calls back, I think you gotta figure that some of the guys wearing rings are in fact very taken, and that you, my friend, were a booty call."

"You really are a smartass."

"Maybe stay clear of guys with bling from now on."

"But they're all so hot," he confessed, his voice husky.

I snorted, which made him smile in response.

"So how long have you been married?" he asked, hands on his hips, still standing in my personal space.

"Four months," I answered quickly.

He nodded. "Your guy away?"

"No, actually, he used to get deployed a lot, but not now."

"So he just stayed home, and you came out?"

"No, he went out with some guys he was working with today."

"Instead of coming with you?"

"Yeah, but—"

"That is not smart," he told me.

"It's perfectly fine," I said like it was a given. "I'm made loyal, and I can handle myself, right?"

"Sure," he agreed, putting his hand on the wall beside my head. "But it's stupid to let you out alone."

"I don't—"

"It is."

Ian.

We both turned to see Ian walking down the hall toward us, and I heard Daley's breath catch beside me.

Until that moment, Daley had not seen pretty. Not that "pretty" was the word I would use to describe Ian. "Breathtaking" was the one that applied.

What I had going for me in the looks department was thick, defined muscles; good hair; and according to my husband, big, dark, beautiful brown eyes. But the man coming toward us had been blessed genetically. From the sleek, sculpted muscles that moved fluidly in a fusion of power and grace that combined seamlessly to put the rolling rise and fall in his stride, to his sharp, chiseled features: strong square jawline, lush mouth with a smirk of recklessness, and killer blue eyes—he embodied breathtaking.

He'd gone home to change—he'd put on the olive-green henley that molded to his sculpted shoulders and biceps, sleeves shoved up to show off veined forearms, and the faded jeans clung like a second skin to his long, powerful legs. Watching his advance overwhelmed me for a moment, but I managed to smile as he reached us.

"Hey," I said, my voice a dry croak of desire.

He stared at me for a moment before turning to Daley and offering his hand. "Ian Doyle."

"Daley O'Meara," he greeted, clearly amused. "Doyle, huh? Apparently your husband's fond of Irishmen."

"One Irishman, certainly," he said, his voice rough with a sliver of danger.

From Daley's smirk and half shrug, he seemed not at all intimidated, more amused, and that was interesting because most men were, if not fearful, definitely wary of Ian.

He turned back to me. "I'll get your number from Eli. I'd love to have you along for a gym workout or the next time we all go out."

"Sure," I agreed fast and hugged him when he leaned in.

It was quick, and then he gave Ian a nod before taking his leave. When I turned to Ian, he was glaring at me.

"What?"

"Are you kidding?"

I was at a loss, and then it hit me. "Oh, I should've done a better job introducing you guys. He's a detective over in the—"

"The fuck do I care," Ian growled, grabbing my bicep and rushing me down the hall several feet in the opposite direction, toward the back door where it was quieter, before knocking me into the wall.

"Ian, are you—"

He took my mouth hard, just leaned in and kissed me, nothing gentle about it, claiming, possessive, and hungry. He slipped one hand to my hip and the other around the back of my head, sifting his fingers through my hair as he held me still.

I opened for him, allowing the feasting, craving it, having missed him all day, wrapping my arms around his neck to hold him to me, wanting him closer, under me, under my hands, in bed. Pressing close, I moaned softly, which he must have liked, if the way he parted my legs with his thigh was any indication.

"Fuck," he moaned like he was in pain, breaking the kiss but not stepping free of my arms, instead bumping his forehead against mine so we were sharing air.

"What's with you?" I asked, curious.

"Where the fuck is my head?"

I smiled and kissed his nose. "I hope right here."

He lifted his head and then winced before he took my face gently, reverently in his hard, callused hands. "Oh, love, what happened?"

Him calling me his love never failed to drench me in heat and make my pulse leap. It was one of those things: a gruff, growly, beautiful man being vulnerable and using an endearment that was all mine—it was enough to make me want to drop to my knees for him right there.

"Miro?"

I swallowed hard against the lump in my throat. My mouth had gone dry. "One of the guys hit me with his gun."

"How many stitches did you—"

"Just five."

"Jesus Christ, when the hell was this?"

I had to think. "Before I got a new job."

"A *what*?"

"It's a long story."

"I need to hear the—for fuck's sake, Miro," he husked, grimacing as he smoothed his hands down the sides of my neck, turning my head back and forth. "You've got bruises all over you. Where the fuck was—"

"It happens, you know that."

He shook his head. "I wasn't there."

"It's okay," I sighed, so happy he was with me now. "It's not—"

"And what the hell are you wearing," he snapped, yanking on my shirt. "Since when do you own anything purple?"

"It's Sharpe's," I replied, chuckling. He sounded more upset about the shirt than my injuries. "I think I look great in it."

"I don't… like it," he assured me, scowling.

"Well, I'm not crazy about this one that you've got on either."

"What?" He was confused. "Why?"

"Little tight, don't you think?" I teased, smiling at my sexy man.

A breath escaped before he kissed me again, just as hot and devouring as the first time, tugging on the shirt so he could get his hands under it, smoothing over my ribs, my abdomen, and down to my belt buckle while he rubbed his tongue over mine, stroking, taking more and more until I was trembling and boneless in his arms, ready for whatever he wanted. Always with Ian, my response to him was the same, the instant flare of desire followed by the devouring flame of arousal that could only be sated one way.

"Come home with me," he rumbled, and when I caught the glint of gold out of the corner of my eye, I made a noise I wasn't proud of. "What's wrong?"

"Nothing's—" My voice cracked, and I had to concentrate to get it to work. "You picked up your ring," I almost whined.

"Course," he said gruffly. "It was ready today. I went and got it right after work."

When I first put the ring on his finger, we realized we had purchased it just a bit too big, but we figured it wouldn't be an issue. That was before the weather changed from a bit cold to arctic, the way Chicago winters did, and the ring started sliding off everywhere. When it fell into a plate of kung pao chicken, Ian had winced and said maybe it was time to get it sized. He'd dropped it off two weeks ago, so I'd been missing him wearing it since then, but now it was back on his hand where it belonged and where I wanted it to stay.

"I'll never take it off," he promised like he was reading my mind.

"Yeah?" I asked hoarsely.

"Yeah," he said before he kissed me again.

I'd forgotten about the ring with everything else that was going on, but he hadn't, and the thought that he made a special trip out of his way to make sure he had it on the first day he could made my knees weak. Sometimes, stupidly, I wondered if I was as important to Ian as he was to me. But always, inevitably, inexorably, he proved to me I was paramount in his mind. It had been like that since the night in the truck in the rain when he told me he was leaving the Army because *I* was the adventure he wanted.

"So?"

My gaze met his.

"Can we leave already?"

"Love to," I said, grinning at him. "I just gotta get my phone from Eli."

He pulled my phone from his back pocket and passed it to me.

"Got everything covered, do you?"

"Always," he assured me, slipping his hand gently, tenderly, around the side of my neck before drawing me close for another kiss.

CHAPTER 4

ABOUT FIVE months ago, the Thursday a week after Thanksgiving, Ian and I went to the court building over on Randolph Street, down to the lower level where the marriages and civil unions were performed, and sat outside the door in the row of chairs with Carl Embrey, who was wanted for money laundering and bribery in Las Vegas. We had gotten the marriage license and paid the ten-dollar administrative fee on Tuesday and planned to get married the day after, but weren't able to get away from a fugitive pickup gone sideways. I wasn't waiting even one more day, so when Ian insisted we take Embrey back, I put my foot down.

"Fuck that," I said, turning in the passenger seat of the 1987 Buick GNX we were driving around in. I loved it and even asked Asset Forfeiture if there was any way I could go to the auction when it was put up. The marshal in charge was condescending, but worse, his boss called Kage, who asked if I was high.

"This is a nice car," Embrey commented, leaning back and wiggling on the leather seats.

I ignored him. "I want to go now," I told Ian, checking the Hermès Cape Cod watch Catherine had sent me.

Normally her gifts were not so extravagant, but I'd scared her due to my most recent run-in with Hartley, and so she bought something that conveyed the depth of her love. She later told me I should consider it both my Christmas and birthday presents, but since I got pajamas soon after, I was thinking she forgot how much she spent. Not that a neurosurgeon noticed, and with her husband being a composer—he did film and TV scores—it wasn't like even an Hermès watch would put a dent in their budget.

"It's three fifteen already, babe," he told me, turning the wheel like he was going to head back to the office with Embrey. "We can do it tomorrow early. We'll come before lunch."

I took a breath.

"Okay?" He sounded nonchalant, like if it didn't happen today, tomorrow was just as good.

"Ian."

He turned to look at me and did a double take when he saw my face.

"My honeymoon is already tabled because Janet had the baby. I will not put off being married to you even one... more... day."

He fixed his eyes on me, flicked them back to Embrey, who had smartly gone quiet, and then returned his gaze to mine.

"Unless the when of it really doesn't matter to—"

"No," he said hoarsely. He whipped us out of the parking spot on the street, directly into oncoming traffic on Harlem Avenue, before flipping a U-turn and flooring the gas pedal. That got us moving pretty damn fast considering the car could hit sixty in about five seconds.

"Jesus Christ!" Embrey gasped from the back seat.

I called Kage.

"Jones," he said like he always did, like I made him tired.

"We're gonna be about an hour late getting back, boss. We're stopping to get married."

A beat passed. "I'm sorry?"

"Married," I repeated. "We're doing that now."

It took him a moment to respond. "Okay."

When I got off the phone, I was smiling.

"Happy?" Ian teased as he wove in and out of lanes of traffic.

"I am," I sighed deeply, putting my hand on his thigh.

"No, no, don't do that," he cautioned. "I need every brain cell and all my reaction time for this drive."

"Yeah, leave him alone," Embrey muttered from behind me.

I could not wipe the huge grin off my face.

We made it across town in fifteen minutes—which was an Ian Doyle personal best, helped quite a bit by the Buick—and he parked while I went to sign us in. Ian got back to me fast, jogging down the long hall, and I noticed that because we'd been out of the office the whole day, we were both dressed in cargo pants, boots, T-shirts, and heavy hoodies, him wearing a shoulder and thigh holster, me with just the shoulder one, both of us with our badges on chains in the middle of our chests. It was not how I imagined it; us in suits was how it went in my head, with boutonnieres and rings. As it was, none of those things would happen, because I wanted us married *right the hell now*. I had a terrible habit of insisting on things, only to realize it wasn't the right choice after the horse left the barn.

Ian sat down beside me and took hold of my hand.

I lifted my head to tell him we could wait, but the smile he directed my way rendered me mute before he passed me a small box. Opening the lid, I found two thick gold comfort bands.

"You had these?" I ground out, lifting my head.

"Been carrying them around for a week," he said, leaning in to kiss me. "You're not the only one who wants to get married."

And that fast, what I wanted, and when I wanted it, was no longer a bad thing. "No?"

He chuckled. "No."

Fifteen minutes later, after couples went in and out—some looking like they were facing a firing squad, others bursting with happiness, some with family and friends trailing in after them, others alone—I was not surprised to turn and see people making a hole for Sam Kage.

He looked like he always did, polished, strong, like the rock you built on. It made sense he was there, and when he got close, we both stood up.

He offered me his hand when he reached us.

"Thank you for coming, sir."

"Of course," he said like it was expected, and then I realized he was in the lead of a surprising parade of massive proportion.

Behind him were Aruna and Liam, Kohn and Kowalski, and the three boys—men—Ian and I watched over: Josue, Cabot, and Drake.

"How did you do this?" I asked as Kage shook Ian's hand at the same time Aruna fluttered into my arms and her husband squeezed my shoulder.

"I called the judge's clerk and asked him to make sure you two were called last, and then I had Kowalski and Kohn pick up your boys, and I sent Sharpe and White to get Aruna and Liam."

"You weren't actually going to get married without me, were you?" Aruna, one of my oldest, dearest friends, asked me.

"Course not," I lied as she pulled her iPad Mini out of her bag. I was suddenly looking at the faces of three other women.

Besides Ian, I defined four other people in my life as family: Min Kwon, Catherine Benton, Aruna Duffy, and Janet Powell. Aruna was in Chicago with me, but Min was in her office in LA, Catherine was in scrubs at Mount Sinai Beth Israel, and Janet was in her office in Washington DC. They were all beaming at me and waving before Aruna turned it so they could see the others.

Kowalski glowered, but Eli gave them his patented flashing grin, and then on cue, I saw Sharpe and White coming toward us, followed by Ching and Becker with a guy in handcuffs between them. The man was bleeding, and Ching was wrapping the knuckles of his right hand with what looked like gauze. Everyone moved out of the way as Becker shoved their prisoner down beside Embrey. Two uniformed CPD officers came last, and they took up position, one on each side of the two men in handcuffs. Kage thanked them for being there, and they nodded, glancing over to us and, I was certain, wondering what the hell was going on. They didn't dare question it, however. That was the chief deputy US marshal standing there.

I hugged everyone, and when we were called in, I made the walk with one hand in Ian's and the other in Aruna's.

We didn't need witnesses, I knew that, but it made my heart swell and my eyes fill with everyone being there, even Dorsey and Ryan on FaceTime on Eli's phone.

It was fast, all of ten minutes. The important part was not the words but that it was official, and when it was over, Ian belonged to me. Sliding the ring onto Ian's finger settled my heart in my chest, grounded me, and fused him into my life forever. He was what I somehow thought he would never be: my husband. Even when he asked me to marry him, even when I said yes, I never thought we'd make it before the judge and have things legal and binding between us. But now I could see my whole life with him in it with such absolute certainty that I was, for a moment, overwhelmed. He was mine, and it was done, and as my vision blurred, he kissed me to a round of clapping and cheering. I put my face against his shoulder as I shuddered, and he held me tight enough to keep me from flying apart with happiness. It was, without a doubt, the greatest day of my life. I could not ever remember being happier.

Now, some months later, following Ian out of the club, seeing the resized ring back on his hand sent a tremor through me, and I had to clutch at him for balance.

"You all right?" he asked. I could hear the concern in his voice.

"Yeah, I'm great," I assured him, lacing my fingers with his.

He took me out the back so we wouldn't have to walk through the crowd, and on the street, bouncing along beside him, I asked how he'd known where I was.

"Kohn sent me pictures of you all night."

I turned to walk backward to face him. "What?"

"Yeah, he's an ass."

"Are you kidding?" But I knew he wasn't, and I understood Eli's game. He'd been on my phone sending Ian pictures so he could see all the fun he was missing out on. The man was an evil genius, and I needed to thank him.

"No, I'm not kidding," Ian snapped, puffed up and pissed off and utterly adorable.

"Did I look good?"

"Yes. Very." He bit off each word, which was even cuter.

"Drunk?"

"What?"

"Did I look drunk?"

"Yeah. Your eyes get all glassy."

"Oh yeah?"

"They get dark and wet."

"Which you like."

He grunted.

"Ian?" I fished, wanting to hear the words.

"Which I like. Yes."

"So you were worried that I'd run off with some sailor out on leave or something?"

"Not a sailor," he said, annoyed, petulant. "More like that guy—what's his name?"

"Daley."

"The fuck kind of name is that?"

"Irish, honey, just like yours."

"Like mine my ass."

I turned around and draped an arm around his neck, leaning on him, hanging, giving him some of my weight. "Don't be jealous."

"Me?"

I scoffed.

"The hell do I have to be jealous about?" His voice was low and a bit savage.

"Absolutely nothing," I mollified him, kissing his cheek.

He chuckled. "Listen, tomorrow night we're having dinner with the supervisory deputy."

"For what?"

"He wants to talk to me formally about the command position of SOG."

I stopped walking and let him go, and he rounded on me, hands on my hips.

"What?"

"So he really wants you to take it."

He nodded.

"Which means what?"

"Which means that you'll be suited up in Kevlar every day," he said, grinning.

I thought of Aruna.

It was the weirdest thing. I was standing there talking to Ian and my brain went blank, except for her.

The Saturday before, while Ian and Liam went shopping for our now-regular dinner with our friends—Ian was going to make some scary-sounding casserole—Aruna and I took her daughter, Sajani, now three, and Chickie Baby, my dog, for a walk. She had decided she wanted donuts, so we were on our way to Firecakes when she asked me if Ian and I ever wanted kids.

"Kids?" I asked, a bit horrified, scoffing to cover my discomfort. "Me? You think I should be somebody's father?"

She turned, looking hard at me, as though taking my measure. "I think if you wanted to be, you'd make a wonderful father, because you know what it's like not to have one, and so because of that, you would be the best one you know how to be."

"Or, because I have a few abandonment issues of my own, I might be really smothering and drive my kid away," I advised honestly, feeling sorry for myself in that fleeting moment. It never stayed; I was too happy with my life, with the people I had in it. But still, I had missing pieces that came from not having a family when I was young and knowing beyond a shadow of a doubt there was no one in the world who cared. That all changed in college when I met Aruna and the rest of my coven, and then with Ian.

But I was already a bit too possessive of Ian and could only imagine what that would look like if focused on a child.

"It's different than you think it is, and besides, you parent already."

"What're you talking about?"

"I'm talking about the boys." She meant Cabot and Drake and Josue. "You nurture them constantly."

"That's different," I allowed with a shrug. "They're all grown-up."

She snorted. "They are *so* not grown-up."

"Yeah, but—"

Her phone rang then, and as she pulled it from the back pocket of her jeans to check the caller ID, she scowled. "Okay, this is Catherine, but just think about it, all right? Either way you go—have a kid, don't have a kid—it works." She finished with a smile that told me I was adored before she answered quickly, hitting the speaker button. "Hey, Miro's here too. What's the word on our girl?"

"She seemed fine when I was there," Catherine said from the other end. "I stayed three days, and she was mad at first that I showed up because he called, but then she let it go and was happy to have me visit."

"I missed something," I said. "What're we talking about?"

"Janet," Aruna said on a sharp exhale. "Ned thinks she's got postpartum depression happening and he called Catherine, so she flew there to check her out."

"As a doctor or her friend?" I asked.

"Yeah, see, that's what she said," Catherine sighed. "So you know her, she was annoyed that I would jump on a plane without talking to her first and finding out if Ned was full of shit or not, but once I was there, visiting, she was good."

"And did she seem depressed to you?"

"I have to say that the only thing I saw her depressed about was how Ned's mother was hovering," Catherine explained, and I heard the sharp edge to her tone. "And admittedly, the woman is a bit intrusive. She was holding Cody and was worried that he was dehydrated, and I assured her that he was not."

"Uh-oh, I can hear your claws coming out."

"Well, she was all 'And are you a doctor?'"

I chuckled, and Aruna nodded and smiled.

"And I said, 'Why, yes, ma'am, as a matter of fact, I just so happen to be.'"

"Did you snarl or just speak?" I teased.

"I fuckin' snarled, are you kidding?"

I knew she had. I didn't have to be told.

"Fuckin' cow, how dare she suggest that Janet, who we all know has wanted to be a mother probably since she herself was born, would not be totally on top of that kid's every need. It's insane. I mean, Janet's already made arrangements to start telecommuting so she can work from home once her maternity leave is over, for fuck's sake."

I glanced at Aruna. "She swears a lot for a doctor."

"No shit," Aruna agreed.

"No shit," Sajani repeated, which sent me into hysterics.

"Was that Sajani?" Catherine asked, which made the whole thing even better.

"Oh goddammit," Aruna groaned, looking down at her toddler, who was clapping her hands, realizing she'd done something great.

"That's it, add to her vocabulary," I laughed, lifting Sajani out of the stroller and putting her down beside me so she could walk the rest of the short distance to the bakery with her little hand on Chickie's head.

It was an adorable sight, the werewolf and the tiny little girl.

"Well, anyway, I think Janet's all right, but we should go visit again soon. It was good we went when Cody was born, but I feel like she's a bit alone there. She doesn't have girlfriends or boyfriends around, and she has more trouble than Miro does making friends and trusting people."

"Hey," I groused.

"And next time when I say *all*, I mean you too, Miroslav," Catherine scolded.

"What? Babies freak me out."

"I don't care. How're you going to take care of your baby when the time comes if you don't start practicing now?"

"Since when am I having a baby?"

"Ohmygod, that's so funny, I was just telling him that he'd make a great father," Aruna told her, wincing as she heard Sajani say "shit" again.

"It's true, you would," Catherine agreed. "You're a natural caregiver. You're way more maternal than me."

And it was that, my two friends telling me how I would be with a kid, and the job change earlier in the day, as well as what Maureen Prescott had said, that prompted the response to Ian.

"Do you really think that's the best use of me?"

"Use of you?" He was confused; it was there in his scowl and the instant crossing of arms. Ian wasn't aware of it, but whenever anyone questioned him, he went instantly into his battle stance, bracing, feet apart, shoulders squared, chin up.

I shrugged. "I'm not a kick-the-door-down kinda guy, right? I'm more the 'Can I come in so we can have coffee and talk?' guy."

"Yeah, but what does that matter? You go where I go."

"Oh?"

"Is that not right?"

"Well, no, not necessarily."

His eyes widened.

"No, not like that," I said quickly, realizing with the amount of alcohol in my system, this was perhaps not the best time to talk about this. "I mean, we'll always be together, just maybe not at work."

"The hell is that supposed to mean?" he yelled. "I quit being a soldier for you!"

The accusation hurt, and I took a step back, but more than that, I was annoyed because I'd thought we were done with this. "No, you quit being a soldier for you."

"No," he argued, and I could feel the temperature of his voice drop by several degrees. "I quit because of our partnership at home and at work, so no, you don't get to say now that you don't want to be with me."

"You quit to be home, and you quit because you knew you could still help people as a marshal, but those two things aren't inseparable."

"What?" he asked irritably.

"I'm your home, yes?"

"I already told—"

"And your job can be done with or without me as your partner."

"That's *not* what I signed on for," he asserted, glaring at me, the muscles in his cheek working. "And I told you this would fuckin' happen."

"The hell are you talking about?"

"You're sick of me being around, and you wanna get rid of me. You miss your time alone, and you wish I was off in some desert somewhere."

The gasp was involuntary, it was like he'd hit me.

He looked startled, like he just figured out what came out of his mouth. "Wait," he began, moving forward, reaching for me.

I deflected, brushing his hands away, and when he moved again, I backed up several more steps, needing the space. "Make no mistake," I said, hearing the freeze in my voice. "I do not want you anywhere but home with me every night. But you want to be involved in the high-profile cases. You like going in first, with SOG, like SWAT. And you like to lead. I know that. I'm not asking you to change that about yourself."

"Then what the hell are you saying?"

"That we don't have the same skill set, and you know it," I replied, shivering in the cold March air now that I was out of the club.

"The fuck are you doing?" he said, releasing a frustrated gust of air.

"You're being an ass," I told him. "How dare you say something so stupid to me, and if you really believe that you quit being a soldier for anyone but you—"

"Miro—"

"And if you're gonna blame me for not doing what you love, then you should go back to doing it, and we'll figure something else—"

"No," he barked, rushing forward, taking my face in his hands, holding tighter when I tried to lift my head free. "I'm sorry, all right?"

Only Ian made *sorry* sound like he was doing me a favor and why was I being such a dick at the same time. It was impatient and growly, and fuck me, but I found it utterly endearing. He was not, as a rule, in touch with his feelings. They wandered all over the place, and trying to get them all together so he could speak definitively about them was like herding cats.

"Are you?" I gave him the out because the way he was touching my face felt really good, and something about the hold was rough and tender at the same time. I had no doubt Ian loved me fiercely and truly and with just a trace of scary possessiveness that was very hot.

"You know I am," he grumbled, letting me go, scowling. "I just want to be home with you, not off wherever."

"Okay," I said, grinning. "Then think before you speak, jackass, because you sound a bit muffled when you talk out of your ass."

"I just—if I'm not your partner, who's gonna watch out for you, and look what happened today just because I was across town!"

He was getting worked up again, so I reached out and cupped his cheek, feeling the rough stubble under my hand, seeing the laugh lines around his eyes and dragging my thumb across his bottom lip. "Baby, it's the job. Even when you're right there, I can still get hurt, yeah?"

His growl as I dropped my hand was adorable, and the urge to kiss him in the middle of the sidewalk became almost unbearable.

He closed his eyes a moment, raking his fingers through thick hair that had grown out quite a bit in the last few months. Normally for the Army he kept almost a buzz cut, but now it was longer, still high and tight on the sides, but longer on top so there was more texture and more to pull. My own hair never went back to its former pomp after I let it grow out during Ian's last deployment. So now it fell below my ears in a tousled, layered mess I was honestly surprised Kage had not insisted I cut yet. Either he didn't notice or didn't care, but either was fine with me. Watching Ian tug at his, though, made me think about bed.

"Ian," I began, sounding breathy, needy, my voice almost a rasp. "Can we talk about the rest of this tomorrow?"

"Miro—"

"In the morning," I pleaded, looking him up and down, hearing my exhale, feeling the tremor run through me.

He glared at me. "I'm not going to—"

"I drank a lot."

"So what? You can handle your liquor better than most people I know."

"Aww, that's nice," I placated, stepping in close and kissing the side of his neck, ending with a bite before stepping back. "But I want to get in bed with you now, and my brain is pretty much completely occupied with that."

He coughed softly. "So you're asking me to table our discussion about life here so we can go home and have sex."

"Yes. Exactly."

He ran his eyes over me from head to toe. "Yeah, okay, let's go."

It was nice he had it just as bad as me.

CHAPTER 5

As SOON as we walked through our front door, after I turned off the alarm and hung up my coat, I took off my ankle holster and my gun and passed them to Ian. He ran our Glocks and his SIG Sauer P228 upstairs—the Glocks to the safe, the weapon into the top drawer of his nightstand. Until Craig Hartley was apprehended, I couldn't imagine Ian not being able to roll over and be armed. Also, as a soldier, whether he was on active duty or not, being prepared had been drilled into him. Being anything less than ready was simply not an option.

I checked my text messages, thanked Aruna for keeping Chickie Baby, our werewolf, for the night, and saw I had one from Kage that told me and Ian to report to his office the following morning. I turned to yell for Ian, but when I did, I found him frozen under the arch that led from the kitchen to the living room. It was new, Ian having made the slight home improvement himself. Now that he was no longer constantly deployed, he had a lot more time to devote to fixing up our Greystone.

"You all right?" I asked. He was frozen in place, and his color was strange, off, a bit pale, waxen, like he was sick.

"Jesus, Miro," he said, sounding strangled, like he'd swallowed down a sob. "Your face."

It took me a second, but my mind jumped to where he was. Under the club lights and in the darkened street, apparently the stiches and bruises appeared bad, just not like they did in our kitchen. At home where I was sitting on the counter, Ian walked into the room and nearly puked.

"We both know you've seen a lot worse than me at this moment," I said, laying my phone on the counter, my entire focus on Ian.

No sound, just him wincing as I saw the weight of guilt pressing down on him.

"I'm fine. You can see I am," I threw out, trying another tactic.

The stricken expression on those gorgeous chiseled features of his didn't change.

Shit. "Oh, come on. I've been drinking all night. It doesn't even hurt," I said, giving him a game smile, trying my damnedest to lighten the mood.

It wasn't working. It was there on his face how twisted up he was inside.

"I swear I'm fine," I said, my voice gravelly as I opened my arms to him, seeing clearly the fear flickering there behind his eyes. "C'mere."

He rushed to my side and stepped between my dangling legs, wrapping his strong arms around me before crushing me to his chest.

"It's okay," I soothed as he buried his face in the curve of my neck and shoulder, inhaling as he shivered.

"It was just bad timing," I explained. "You—"

"I wasn't there," he whispered, and I could hear that he was ashamed and miserable and sad, and none of that was conducive to me getting laid.

"Hey."

He lifted his head to meet my gaze.

"You know what would make me feel better?"

"A warm bath?" he offered, the sadness still all over his face.

"No, stupid, you," I said, smirking.

The scowl I got made me laugh. Clearly I was not amusing. But the moan I got when I bent and kissed him, full of aching need, let me know how he really felt. Cheesy or not, acting like a doofus or not, he wanted me.

Pressing my advantage, I slid off the counter onto my feet, hands on his belt as I began walking him backward toward the stairs.

"Couch," he whimpered, taking a step that way.

"Shower," I countered, spinning him around and steering him toward the steps. "I'm all sweaty and gross, and you came home and changed but didn't shower, I'm guessing."

He grunted.

"Yeah, so, let's go get clean, Doyle."

Most nights, the loft—the half floor with our bed, master bathroom, and closet—was not an ordeal to get to, but at the moment, Ian didn't seem like he was in the waiting frame of mind.

"Now," I ordered, my tone rough and low.

He moved fast, checking to make sure I was following before he started up.

I was right behind him, admiring the way his pants clung to his tight, round ass, and reached out to take hold of him.

He stopped, gripping the railing on the left, and I moved up behind him on the same step, my chest sliding up his back before I kissed the side of his neck.

"I—you," he began breathily with almost a whimper, "didn't want that guy at the club, did you?"

Amazing when everything gelled into place and you had the *aha* moment that explained what was going on.

I got hurt, then Eli sent Ian pictures of me having a great time all night, getting wasted, dancing with strangers, and then when he finally got to me there, I was holding off a guy in the hallway outside the bathroom. From his perspective, I had instilled some questions. And not that he truly believed something so ridiculous, but he was human, after all.

I slipped my arm around his chest, clutching him tight, and he let his head fall back, surrendering. "You know better than that," I said, dipping my head and taking a gentle bite of the skin between his neck and shoulder.

He jolted as I sucked and licked, moving slowly, insidiously, up behind his ear and letting my warm breath touch everything I had just made wet.

I smiled against his skin, pressing another kiss there before turning his face to me so I could take his mouth.

A whine slid out of his throat as I rubbed my tongue over his, opening him up, making him mine as he turned in my arms to face me, never breaking the kiss, wrapping his arms around my neck, ensuring I couldn't get away.

Ian used to tell me, when we were just friends, that he was often told he was a terrible kisser. I never knew that to be the case. Every one of Ian's kisses had the same drugging, mind-numbing effect on me as the first one, and I didn't see that ever changing.

Rucking up the henley, I got my hands underneath, mapped skin and muscle, and was ready to put him facedown on the stairs as he broke the kiss to gulp some air.

"I guess you have to breathe, huh?"

He nodded and kissed me again, but I made it quick, leaning free seconds later.

"No, come—what're you doing?" he husked.

"Shower now," I commanded, manhandling him, uncoiling his arms, spinning him around and shoving him forward up the stairs.

"I'm going," he muttered, flopping on the bed to loosen the laces on his boots just enough to get them off before standing to work on his jeans.

Watching Ian get naked was always a treat—miles of battle-scarred olive skin stretched over powerful carved muscle, his long and cut gorgeous cock, the heavy balls, and his perfect ass—him walking away always pulled a groan from my gut.

He stopped before walking into the bathroom, hand on the doorframe as he looked back over his shoulder at me.

"You could come in here with me and make sure I don't miss anything."

I pretended to think about it and then started yanking off my clothes. When I was done, I noticed he hadn't moved, instead watching me intently.

"What're you doing? Go turn on the damn water," I ordered.

"My husband is crazy hot," he murmured, tipping his head. "I learned my lesson."

"And what's that?" I asked, starting toward him.

"That letting you out alone is really fuckin' stupid."

"No," I promised, reaching him. "You're all I see."

Cupping my neck, he eased me closer into a kiss and then opened for me, moaning greedily as I palmed his cock, stroking him idly before walking him backward into the bathroom. When I bumped him up against the wall between the toilet and the shower, he trembled with the chill on his skin.

I broke the kiss and stepped back so he could move. "I'm sorry, that was dumb."

"What?" He was out of it, pupils blown, lips swollen from me mauling them and the skin of his throat mottled with bites.

"I need to be gentler," I remarked, wincing because his olive skin showed off every mark.

"No," he whispered, hands on my hips before he reached lower for my hardening cock. "Don't be gentle, that's not what I need."

"But that's how you need to be treated," I soothed him, taking another kiss because I couldn't help it, my brain and body sending mixed signals. I wanted to show him how precious he was to me by taking my time, but I also wanted to grind into him until we became one person, one thing, and that made my blood race.

"Miro," he began but stopped himself, instead leaning sideways to turn on the water. Only then did I realize how flushed he was.

"Ian?"

He shook his head.

"Tell me."

"It's stupid," he said gruffly, stepping into the shower.

I followed him in, closing the glass door behind me as he leaned into the water.

Something was wrong, and as I grabbed the loofah and the sandalwood and bergamot shower gel he loved and got it all sudsy, I made sure to kiss over the scars on his back.

He braced his hands on the wall and let his head hang down as he waited for me to take care of him.

"Needy bastard," I teased, soaping him up, getting everywhere, under, inside, my fingers gentle as I cleaned from the top of his head to the bottom of his feet.

"I am," he agreed, groaning as I cleaned his cock.

"No, you're not," I said playfully, hanging the loofah up for a moment as I grabbed his shampoo and went to work massaging his scalp, digging my fingers into the base of his skull, working out the knots of tension.

"I'm sorry I wasn't with you tonight," he sighed, letting me turn him under the deluge of water, and I smiled over his gasp as the water sluiced down his back and inside where I wanted it. "I promise you I'm not stupid enough to do it again."

"Enough, already. What's with you?"

Straightening, he met my gaze. "I just—I don't want you to think I take this—us—for granted, because I know what I have."

I kissed him, and he parted his lips instantly, sucking on my tongue as I leaned him back into the water, tipping his head, breaking the kiss and letting the heat ease all the remaining tension out of his beautiful body.

Once he was out, I took my own shower, much faster than his, and he was still drying off when I got out.

"I'm in some weird headspace or something," he said, leaving the bathroom with me right behind him, heading for the bed. "I'm relaxed but not tired."

"That's good," I told him, smirking, staring at his ass.

"What're you—Miro!"

It was his own fault. He was walking too slowly, so when he got close enough to the bed, I shoved him forward and he tumbled down onto the comforter. He was chuckling as I pounced on him, rolling him easily to his back, and I realized that between my hunger for him and the alcohol in my system, the need to be inside him was my only agenda.

"You know, we never talk anymore," he teased.

I growled, and he chuckled until I took hold of his already leaking dick and squeezed and stroked until I got the delicious whimper I was after.

Ian bowed up off the bed, forgetting he was being playful, and I curled forward, pulling the head of his long, beautiful cock into my mouth.

"Miro," he rasped, hands in my hair, tugging, pushing up, trying to bury himself, the hitching of his breath and the gasps and whimpers letting me know how much more he needed.

I sucked hard as I took him all the way to the back of my throat in one swallow, letting him feel the wet heat a moment before lifting, working my tongue over his head, dragging it over every inch and then lowering, slowly, drawing out his pleasure until my lips were at his base and I lifted my eyes to meet his gaze.

"Fuck, lookit your face," he mewled, jolting under me, his breath catching, causing me to smile because I was doing that to him. "Killin' me."

I lifted my mouth free, grinning before licking over the still-leaking head.

"Jesus, Miro, when you smile like that—just suck my dick." The hoarse request, guttural, up from his chest, was very sexy.

I waggled my eyebrows.

"Awww fuck, please," he begged, the tone plaintive, strangled.

Leaning forward, I swallowed him to the root again before slowly, purposely sucking hard, making the suction so strong he caught his breath, and then laving and licking around and under the head, nibbling the side, tracing the thick vein before repeating the same slick, hot, downward slide that left him buried in the back of my throat.

"Holy God, your mouth should be illegal," he moaned, hand tangled in my hair, holding tight, making sure I couldn't pull away or stop.

He lifted his right leg, bending at the knee, giving me access, and I slipped a finger into my mouth beside his cock and got it wet and dripping. As I bobbed my head, causing his breath to stop and start, I gently, tenderly, slid my finger into his ass.

"Oh, you—fuck!" he roared, pulling away like I'd burned him, rolling fast to his stomach, head down, fisting the blankets in his hands as he lifted his ass in the air.

I had found recently that with being married came new depths to my sex life. It was like the ring signaled he could ask for all the things he really wanted but had maybe thought, without the commitment of marriage, might freak me out. It was ridiculous, very behind-closed-doors kind of thinking, but I was thankful because it was another layer of trust Ian shared only with me.

"Miro," he husked, opening his legs wider, shivering with anticipation, "now."

Ian loved being rimmed, and I more than enjoyed doing it to him, and though I knew it got him hot, I'd had no idea he could come simply from my tongue in his ass. It was, he'd confessed once while we lay in bed, hot and dirty and not something he ever even imagined he'd like before the first time I spread his cheeks and speared inside of him.

The revelation went hand in hand with knowing that while Ian loved to fuck me, loved holding me down, pushing inside, feeling my satiny heat hold him like a vise—more than that, he craved me in him. Being taken and used, having me pound his ass, turned Ian inside out. And he was gibbering, a word now and then making sense, but mostly just there, ready for me, waiting and wanting.

I pushed down on his ass, flattening him on the bed, and then bent over to kiss my way down his spine.

His aching, frustrated groan made me grin as I kissed and nibbled and licked. There was no way I could not worship the beauty that was Ian Doyle. His heavily scarred back, the corded muscles rippling under his warm, sleek skin, was a work of art. When I pressed my chest to his bare back, he growled at me, and I nipped his shoulder.

"Worship me later, fuck me now," he snarled, turning his head, thrashing under me but knowing better than to try to flip me to my back. I had more leverage from where I was, and he didn't actually want me to move, anyway.

"Something else you want first?"

"Miro," he rasped.

Lifting off him, shifting sideways, I watched the decadent sight of Ian lifting to his hands and knees, head hanging between his shoulders, waiting for me like some gorgeous, erotic piece of sculpture.

"Look at you," I said, rolling off the bed and walking to the nightstand, where I retrieved the lube, staring at him, all carved and chiseled muscle, face flushed, biting his lip as he stared at me with dark, narrowed eyes. I couldn't even see any blue there, just blown pupils and need. He was trembling with it.

Climbing back onto the bed, I dropped the lube and then ran my hands down his sides, tracing ribs, over his flanks, squeezing his powerful thighs before sliding my hands up the backs, higher, to his ass.

"God, the feel of your hands on me is—please just fuck me, never mind the—Miro!"

I gently bit his right cheek before kissing the small of his back, then licking over the top of his crease.

"Miro, honey, love," he ground out before I speared my tongue into his hole.

He yelled my name then, and I had to hold him down as I feasted, licking and pushing deep and then rimming him, loving his taste, the way tremor after tremor raced through him as he tried to push back onto my tongue.

He rocked against me when I slipped a saliva-coated finger inside of him, then two; his decadent groan and the way he pleaded for more made it impossible not to comply.

I could do it for hours just to watch him come apart, to hear the noises he made, full of longing, yearning, and watching my fingers disappear inside of him made me ache to have him, fill him, hold him still and press inside until I hit his core.

I reached for my cock, bumping my hand on the back of his thigh.

"No," he wailed, lifting his head, turning to look over his shoulder. "I want that now, please, fuckin' Miro, just—fuck!"

"I wanna keep doing this. It's getting me off," I croaked, my voice thick, husky. It was hard to speak with how hot I was, how ready, how aroused. And like always with the discovery of how responsive Ian was, it hit me that I was in control, he had already surrendered, and the most important thing was him, not me. "I wanna make you feel good."

"Listen!" he snarled.

I focused on his beseeching expression, the vulnerability there in his eyes, and stilled.

"I need you—close." His voice was punctuated by staccato breathing, like he couldn't get enough air. "Miro."

I sat back on my haunches. "Roll over."

He complied quickly, flipping over and then reaching above his head, slipping his hands under the headboard, the space between that and the mattress allowing it, readying himself for me, to take the thrusting. He showed no hesitation, no trace of feeling self-conscious, knowing I'd never tease him for what he wanted or needed because that was sacred, a trust between us.

Grabbing the bottle of lube, I slathered some on my cock, coating it longer than necessary because watching him watch me was a big fat turn-on. The desire on his face was just gorgeous to see.

"Hurry," he pleaded, and I arched over him, dick in hand, lining it up with his ready, saliva-slicked hole, his muscles having succumbed to my ministrations so that the slow press inside his body was a sensuous, easy slide.

He wrapped his legs around my hips, wanting faster and harder, but before he could wedge his heels into the back of my thighs like he did when he wanted it rough, I changed positions, slipping my arms under his knees, curling his back, lifting his ass up off the bed as I drove down into him.

His hands scrabbled on the sheets, looking for purchase, a grip, no longer able to hold on to the headboard in the position I had him in, needing to brace himself, push up as I thrust down.

"Oh fuck yeah, like that," he mewled, head back, eyes tightly closed as he arched under me, needing more.

He was slick and tight and hot, and I got lost in the feel of him as I used my arms and legs to hold him immobile, taking him hard, my body lost in a furious rhythm. At one time I would have worried about just letting go, about not checking. But I knew better now, knew when he wanted me hard and fast, that he was asking to feel me inside for hours after. Not hurting, never quite that, but close, a stretch, a tenderness in his body that he craved. It had been Ian's initial draw to me, and it remained, always, that I could hurt him but could never, would never, because he was my heart. The tears in the midst of us wrecking our bed together were a surprise.

"Ian?" I ground out, my voice scratchy, not sounding like me at all.

His eyes fluttered open, and I saw everything I'd dreamed of years ago when he was only a dream. He was so very mine.

"What's—"

"You'll only ever do this with me, yeah? How lucky am I."

It was me, I was the one who was lucky, and I was going to tell him, but I felt him tightening, contracting around me, heard him gasp as he bowed up off the bed, the murmured pleading for me to claim him, show him it could only ever be him, because he knew it in his heart but had to feel it in his body.

"Ian, you know I—"

"Show me," he murmured, gaze locked with mine.

I reached down between us and grasped his leaking cock, pumping my fist at the same interval as I shoved into his ass, relentless, not letting the pressure lessen even for a second, feeling him shudder and clench but too far gone to do anything but ride him. My name had never sounded better than when he yelled it hoarsely as he splattered my chest with cum.

I was seconds behind him, filling him up, pulsing deep inside, frozen as my orgasm washed through me almost painfully. There were those times when us together in bed was gentle, slow, or fast and dirty. This was neither. Ian needed to be claimed, marks upon him, and we were both sticky with cum, slick with lube and sweat, and utterly, utterly sated and spent.

When my arms gave out, he caught me and gathered me close, nuzzling my damp hair, kissing over my forehead, brows, eyes, nose, and finally taking my mouth. But the kisses weren't devouring and ravenous anymore, instead tender, deep, and possessive.

As he rolled me to my back, he gently eased off the end of my cock, the gush of fluid between us making me groan as Ian hovered over me, smiling wickedly.

"What?" I chuckled as he kissed over my jaw and down the side of my throat, pressing kiss after kiss there, sucking on my skin.

"You taste good."

I grunted, replete and happy, sliding one hand up and down his bicep, slipping the other over his ass, rubbing.

"Really? You can't leave my ass alone?"

I inhaled deeply, getting that musk of sex and sweat and traces of Ian's shampoo and the lingering scent of gun oil from when he sat on the bed and cleaned his Sig the night before.

"God I'm starving," he said into the soothing lull between us. "You wanna sandwich?"

I chuckled because he was adorable. Needs met, he was ready to go on to the next thing on his list. "I'm glad I rate before food."

"Well, yeah," he teased matter-of-factly, giving me a quick kiss before he rolled out of bed, fluid, boneless, with the powerful grace of a man in absolute awareness of his body because he depended on his strength and athleticism to keep him alive.

Lying there alone, just breathing, listening to him rattling around in the kitchen, I couldn't remember ever feeling more content.

"Do you want one?" he yelled up.

"No," I called, smiling as I heard him talking to the different deli meat in our kitchen, asking what kind he wanted. Ian was a big sandwich guy, so I always made sure we had stuff for him to make one.

"Is this cheese Ossau?" he asked.

"Yes, dear."

"You cut off the outside for me?"

"I did."

"And you cut it into thin slices?"

I laughed softly because he was pretty fucking cute. "I most certainly did."

"Such a thoughtful man," he said to himself.

A few minutes later, he rejoined me, carrying a bottle of water for me under his arm, one for him, and a monster sandwich, including a dill pickle and potato chips.

"Did you not eat at all?"

He shrugged, and since that could go either way, I let it go and turned back to the TV in the corner of our room that I had flipped on while he was downstairs.

When I lived there alone, there was only the one in the living room, but Ian convinced me that cuddling in bed together, under the covers, me asleep on him while he watched a movie, would be his third favorite thing in the world. Kissing was first, sex was second, and hugging and spooning rounded out his top three. After that it went to things that included deadly force.

I was just channel surfing, drinking water, and wasting time as Ian ate, finally giving up and switching to Netflix.

"No, don't do that," he said, taking the controller away from me and turning off the TV before he wiped his face on the paper towel, took a gulp of water, and put his empty plate down on the nightstand.

"Really? You're just gonna leave that there?"

"There's crumbs on it, Jones," he said, lying down beside me and nestling close, then gently biting my cheek. "Ain't gonna bother nothin'."

A part of it was his voice, the husky rumble of his, and some of it was his warm skin touching mine, but mostly it was just Ian, close to me, that sent a shiver of heat swimming through me.

"Hey, listen," he rumbled in my ear, reaching between my legs to graze his fingers over my flaccid shaft. "I was serious before. I don't want you to ever think I take you for granted, so let's not go out without each other anymore."

"I know you like to spend time with those guys from SOG, so it's okay if—"

"No, it's not. It's not okay because I like spending time with you best."

"Oh yeah?" I murmured as I rolled my head to look into the deep blue-black eyes of my husband. Normally they were lighter, clearer, but sex darkened them to midnight every time. "Well, I like being with you more than anybody too."

"Good," he said, pressing his face into the side of my neck, at the same time stroking my cock with a deliberateness that had all my attention. The motion had changed from something he was doing as an afterthought to something he wanted.

"Ian," I barely got out, unable to stop myself from pushing up into his fist.

"Yes, Miro?" he asked, his breathing rough in my ear as he kissed over my collarbone, grinding against my thigh, his cock having slowly thickened.

I slid my hand over his ass, letting my middle finger press between his asscheeks and then deeper until I heard the hum of satisfaction I was after. As I added a second to his tender opening, a shudder ran through his powerful frame.

"Pass me the lube," I ordered.

"No, I'm good."

"Ian, are you sure you—"

"Yes," he whispered, rolling to his other side.

I followed like I was glued to him, notching between his cheeks, the slide in easy, smooth, the stretch and give almost more than I could bear, needing to thrust deep and hard inside of him but instead willing myself to move slowly until I was buried to the hilt.

"Fuck, you feel good," I groaned, wrapping one arm under him and around his chest so he could feel me holding him, then sliding my other hand over his hip to take hold of his cock.

He bowed in my arms, pressing back into me, and my body took over, pistoning forward, plunging deep as I used my hand to wring his pleasure from him.

"Don't let me go," he cried out before he came over my fingers and wrist, just a few spurts, but enough.

His muscles clamped down on me, and I was done, mindlessly grinding inside of him, my body shuddering, the orgasm annihilating my control as I came for the second time with my man wrapped around me.

We lay there panting, trying to push air through our lungs, neither of us moving.

"Do you think I could ever do that?"

Nothing from him, only his stubbly cheek rubbing against mine. "Ian?"

"Sometimes when we're doing our thing, I feel like we're one person."

"Me too," I agreed. The way my skin was plastered to his felt so much better than good. "But you didn't answer the question."

"No," he whispered until his voice leveled out. "I don't think you'd ever let me go."

"That's good because I won't. You're stuck with me now, and I don't ever want to be in bed with anyone but you."

Deep, contented sigh from him. "Okay, yeah, so turns out I needed to hear that."

I knew he did. It had been simmering there below the surface since he saw me in the club. His bravado was a defense mechanism, and I knew that. He was everything in my life, but really, truly, I was the same for him. He feared losing me, and he had to stop because I was never going anywhere.

"There's only you," I vowed.

"I know," he rumbled, still not so great at discussing his feelings, better at showing me how much I was loved.

"I should pull out," I said after several long minutes.

He grunted his agreement.

"I wasn't gentle with you either time," I mumbled into his hair. "I'm worried you won't be able to walk tomorrow."

"You've never—hurt me," he gasped as I eased free of his still-clenching channel.

His hand was instantly on my ass. "Stay here. Don't get out of bed."

"We killed it, and we'll be cemented here by morning."

"I don't care, just—hold tight."

I wrapped him in my arms, my chest plastered to his back, the front of my thighs wedged to the backs of his, and the curve of his ass settled against my groin. "I don't want to squash you," I murmured into his nape. "You need to be able to breathe."

"Breathing is a secondary consideration."

I chuckled softly as he tried to push back against me and tightened my arms a bit so there was no more give.

His sigh made me smile. "I love you," I said because it was as true in that moment as it was over coffee every morning. He was my whole life, and as long as I had him with me, loving me, everything would be all right.

CHAPTER 6

IAN WALKED into the bathroom and set a mug of coffee down for me as I put product in my hair, raking my hands through it. I looked at him in the mirror and noted the crossed arms and scowl, the lines between his furrowed brows I always found sexy. I was getting the serious face, and so I took a sip of the French roast with the perfect balance of cream and girded myself for whatever he was going to say.

"Okay," I said with mock seriousness, "release the Kraken."

"This is not funny."

I leaned toward him anyway, wanting a kiss, needing it before I started whatever the day was going to be.

"No."

I froze, mid lean, mid pucker, and grinned. "No, what?"

"That won't work," he told me flatly. "You don't get to be adorable or irresistible or any of the things I normally find you."

This was news. "You find me irresistible?"

"And sexy and everything else," he concluded. "But right now that doesn't matter."

"Why doesn't it matter?" I really wanted to know, because him wanting me was always a very good thing, and he didn't cough up the vault of his heart often.

Ian still, after so long, was not the kind of man who revealed much about his own thoughts and feelings. It simply wasn't him. I didn't know if it had to do with his mother and how emotionally closed off she became after his father left, or the military, or whether it was simply him. But I did know things learned and seen when you were a kid didn't just *poof* into the ether when you hit puberty. Life lessons were just that: they stayed forever.

"We're not going off on a tangent," he explained, his tone, that fast, already irritated. "All kissing, touching, hugging, anything is off the table until we have this out."

I was crap in the morning before I had lots of caffeine in me, and he knew that. I had no idea why he was trying to—

"Drink more of that," he commanded, tipping his chin at the tantalizing cup of coffee. "Hurry up."

I took several sips because it wasn't scalding—it was drinkable, yet another truth he knew about me. "Okay, now, what are we having out?"

Arms crossed, legs braced, I got the picture. We were picking up where we left off last night in the street. This was us talking about our career paths.

"So we're going to discuss me not wanting to wear Kevlar."

He waited, those gorgeous clear eyes of his on me just as they were the night before. But now instead of blown pupils and the struggle to remain open, I had hyperfocus that was really a lot to deal with so early in the morning.

"And I get that this is serious, but why can't I touch you?"

"Because I can't concentrate if you do, and I wanna know what the hell is going on with you not wanting to be my partner anymore!"

And I got it, I did. He'd left the Army for him, not me, but still, being my partner, being there when I needed him at work in the capacity of being my backup, was also a big part of why he could give up being in Special Forces. So me telling him the path he wanted to take was not the one I felt was best for me was, to him, a betrayal of trust, hence the yelling. It all made sense; it was just a lot of volume in the space of the bathroom.

I left, taking my coffee with me. He caught up easily—he was not carrying precious liquid—and barred my path.

"Talk to me."

"Then sit while I find something to wear."

He grunted but let me pass, and I took several sips before leaving the cup on the nightstand to go rummage through my closet.

"Now," he insisted, taking a seat on the bed to watch me.

"Kage and I went up to Custodial to speak to—"

"No," he stopped me. "Go back to you getting hurt and go forward."

Ian was a details guy; he liked to know all of them. It was not a surprise that me starting midstory wasn't going to work for him.

"It all started with seeing Wen Li yesterday," I began. "She was placed in a home that pimps out little girls."

He didn't say anything, so I glanced over my shoulder and saw the stunned expression on his face.

"It's true," I sighed, turning to face him. "You should have seen them, both girls with bruises, both of them—" I couldn't tell him they both had STDs, both jumped at every loud noise, recoiling from every man who came near them except me. When Han saw me walking into her room, she'd hyperventilated with happiness. "It was horrible."

"And where are they now?"

"With their aunt in San Antonio."

"Where the hell was the aunt this whole time?"

It was a long story, so I hit the high points for him, running down the connections.

"Well, good," he sighed, "at least they're safe now, but what the hell does this have to do with you not working with me?"

"Because what happened to those two girls, no one looking out for them, has been happening to a lot of the kids in Custodial."

The realization of where I was going with this spread slowly across his face. I saw the dread appear as he furrowed his brows and clenched his jaw, and then, of course, he crossed his arms over his wide, muscular chest.

"Fuck no."

"Wait."

He stood up. "No fuckin' way, Miro."

"Why?"

"You'll be taking care of kids."

"Exactly."

"Yeah, that's not gonna work."

"And why's that?"

"You know why."

"Clearly not," I said indignantly.

"Don't do that," he cautioned. "It's not the right choice for you, period."

"It's not for you to say."

"Oh no?" he said dramatically.

"Just—"

"You can't do that. It's not a good place for you."

"Kage seems to think it is."

"Well, Mills is the one who—"

"We both know that Kage eats Mills for lunch, and besides, I don't know how much longer he's even gonna have a job. I wouldn't get too cozy with him."

"I don't give a shit about Mills," he snapped, starting to pace. "Or me. I only care about you, and you in Custodial is a very bad idea."

"What's your problem with Custodial?"

"That should be obvious."

"No," I answered irritably. He'd never doubted my abilities before; I was at a loss to understand why he didn't think I was up to the challenge of working with minors. "It's not. Explain what you're thinking."

"Can you not see that you're gonna get hurt?"

"How? I get a paper cut or something?"

"Don't be an ass," he hissed, the anger bubbling in his voice.

"I'm not trying to be. I'm really trying to figure out what you're talking about."

He took hold of my arms, staring into my face. "You will get hurt because you'll get invested with the kids like you always do, and when things go wrong—again, because they always do—you're gonna be devastated."

I absorbed that, rolled it around in my head a second, him thinking I would be emotionally devastated if something were to happen to one of the kids. And while he was right—yes, it would hurt—that was part of putting yourself out there in any kind of relationship, be it personal or professional. It didn't in any way change the need to act. "Are you serious?"

The answering growl told me he was.

"For crissakes, Ian," I sighed, cupping his face in my hands. "Of course I'm gonna get hurt, but that's part of it, right?"

"No," he retorted, visibly choked up, easing out of my hands and taking several steps back. "You were a foster kid, Miro. You remember what it was like to have no one and be homeless—how are reminders like that good for you?"

"They're not," I agreed. "But they also make me damn empathetic, right?"

He shook his head. "That's not our deal."

"Deal? What deal?" I rasped, frustrated because it was like pulling teeth. He was being so closed off.

"You're my partner."

"Yeah, and you're mine," I reminded him. "I'll bet you right now that Kage expects you to go with me today to start talking to the kids."

"Which is fine for today," he said pointedly. "But that's it."

"I'm the *interim* director."

His scowl was dark.

"Speak."

"You have to tell Kage to find someone else."

"Oh? Just tell Kage?"

"Yeah."

"Ian, I—"

"No. If you tell him you can't because of being in foster care yourself, he'll listen."

"But that would be a lie."

"I don't care. I don't want you to do it, so whatever you have to do to get out of it is fine with me."

"And what if it's not fine with me?"

He shook his head.

"Ian, you—"

"No," he insisted, and I could hear the hard edge of anger in his voice. "I won't let you do this to yourself. This is bullshit."

"You can't be serious," I pressed, certain he would snap out of feeling like this at any second because it was so illogical.

"Oh, I'm dead serious," he countered, and I heard how dug in he was, how he was so sure he was right.

"Ian, come on, this isn't like you."

"I have a say now," he reminded me implacably. "We're not just partners. We're married, and my opinion means something."

"It always meant something!"

"Yeah, but now there's weight too. If I say no, it's no."

I loved him, but he was being ridiculous. "That's not how marriage works!"

"I think that's exactly how it works," he ground out hoarsely, the emotion there in his voice as he swallowed hard, trying to breathe through his anger.

I had to figure out why he was actually mad. What was it he was so scared of? Because this wasn't about control—Ian didn't want power over me, but right now, at this moment, he was absolutely terrified. I just had to figure out of what.

"Are you listening to me?"

Ian was a natural protector, and the person he most wanted to keep safe was me.

"Honey, you can't stand between me and the world for the rest of my life," I explained, trying to keep my voice level so he'd hear me and not bristle. "And I wouldn't want you to."

"Well, clearly I do since you're not using your head."

Deep breath because, holy shit, did he want to have a knock-down drag-out or what? He was ready to throw down with me right there. "I know exactly what I'm doing."

His snarl of frustration told me he was far angrier than I originally thought. "Listen, I know you have a natural drive to create families wherever you go."

"What are you talking about?" I had him; he was it, my whole family. There wasn't anyone else besides—

"I'm talking about the girls. You made a family there."

"I didn't even have one before—"

"Cabot, Drake, and Josue spent Thanksgiving with us last year, and they were right back again at Christmas."

"Are you kidding?" I asked, surprised the boys were being thrown in my face since from seeing them all together, it seemed he liked them. "What the hell was I supposed to do? They have no one but us and... I... we—"

"Just—"

"I thought you liked having them over here!"

"I did! I do!" he shouted, back to pacing. "They're all good, but think about it for a second. What're you gonna do when you realize that you can't bring home every kid that's in Custodial to live with us?"

"I already know that."

"Are you sure?"

"You're being really fuckin' snide," I advised him, feeling my blood start to boil with how condescending his words were.

"I don't care. The fact of the matter is that every kid that we've ever been in charge of, you've brought into our home."

"There've been extenuating circumstances."

"Won't there always be?"

"A little credit here, please."

"Don't gimme that shit. This isn't about credit or anything else but *me* knowing that *you* always think there's something else you can do."

"Are you listening to yourself?" He made no sense. "I haven't even started yet. How can I know shit about what I can or cannot do?"

"Again, this goes back to your desire to create families—which is great, it is—but I don't want one. I don't wanna be anyone's father, I don't want to adopt, I just… I don't."

"Have you lost your mind? I don't wanna be a father either."

"That's a lie," he retorted.

But it wasn't.

Even though thinking back on what Aruna had said made me start to wonder about what kind of father I would be, I still wasn't ready to say I wanted to be a parent. She had faith and she knew me well, so there had to be some truth to her belief I had paternal ability in me somewhere. But that didn't translate to fatherhood. And did that mean me being a caregiver meant I was there for a child, or was I there for mentoring, for guiding kids who didn't have someone in their corner? I didn't have the answer, but certainly I would never push a choice on Ian. I would never presume that because I wanted something, he had to as well. Our marriage was a partnership first, and in it, to me, he was first always, so to hear him think I could want something he didn't, push him to do something he didn't want—that hurt.

I was stunned, and the hurt must have shown on my face.

"You know it is," he said raggedly, reaching for me but stopping himself. "You're ready to be a father."

"Ian," I said, taking a breath so I wouldn't say something wrong. "I—"

"You know what the worst part of this is?" he asked, heat in his tone. "I don't think you even realize that you already are a father."

"To *who*?" I asked sharply.

"Well, for starters, to Josue and Cabot and Drake."

"Oh, for fuck's sake, Ian, I—"

"No, you come on! You have any idea what it's like for me to watch you bring home strays? I mean, Jesus, Miro, why do you keep doing that? Where's that compulsion come from?"

"From a place of caring? From being a decent human being?"

"Don't gimme that," he snapped. "We're not talking about having Sharpe over after he and his girl broke up, or babysitting for Liam and Aruna, or something like that. We're talking about you not being able to separate yourself from people you meet on the job."

"I had no idea this bothered you so much. I can stop having the boys over so you—"

"I'm not talking about the boys!" he yelled, arms flailing, flushed now, his voice shredded with emotion. "I like the boys! What I'm talking about is the precedent that you've already set."

"I—"

"You have to nurture others. It's part of who you are, and it's one of the reasons I love you, but I thought that at home, I would be enough, but I'm not."

"You're more than enough," I gasped, blindsided by his admission. He was everything! My whole life walking around in one person. How could he believe for a second he was not?

"I don't mean… it, like… shit—what I mean is that you have to take care of more than just me. You have to take care of everyone."

"But that's not true."

"That's bullshit, and you knew it was the second it came out of your mouth."

I shook my head because I wasn't sure how to make him hear me.

"Listen, I don't fuckin' care about this right now, we can figure the kid part out later—"

"Ian, I'm not dying to be a father or—"

"Again, this is not my immediate concern," he said, his voice rising ominously but not yelling, back to pacing. Apparently he was done shouting. "What I do care about is the fact that you are not going to work in Custodial WITSEC, and that's final."

I crossed my arms, watching him move back and forth like a caged animal. "Is that right?"

"Oh fuck yeah," he warned, his voice all steely and honed.

"And why not?"

"I forbid it."

I wasn't certain I'd heard him right. "I thought you said you didn't drink last night," I challenged, half of me pissed he thought his word had suddenly become law, half of me mollified by knowing all of his bluster had to do with being scared to death that I would get my heart eviscerated every single day. It came from a place of love, but he was being an ass, and I had to get him out of protective mode and back to the rational man I knew.

"What?"

"I thought you said you—"

"I had two drinks to your nine or whatever," he retorted, the judgment there in his cutting tone. "And what the hell does that have to do with the discussion we're having right now?"

"Because clearly you're drunk," I apprised him, trying for playful, hoping maybe that would work.

"What did you say?" His voice went way up.

"*Forbid me?*" I repeated, shaking my head like he was nuts. "The hell is with that?"

"Miro." He huffed a breath like I was trying his patience to no end, jolting to a stop in front of me. "Are you serious?"

"Yeah, I'm serious, and don't treat me like an idiot."

"Then please, love, stop acting like one," he said softly, lulling, his tone, everything, shifting to coaxing, wanting me to hear him, to listen, and using the depth and resonance of his voice to soothe me.

"Ian—"

He shook his head. "You're not listening to me, and you're hearing it like an attack, and it's not," he said, shivering with the emotion, his hands trembling as he took a deep breath. "Please just listen to me."

I took a step closer, but he took one back, hand up to keep me away from him as he turned and walked to the bed and sat down before lifting his eyes to me.

"We're made different. You need more than just me to take care of, and I get that, I do. So when the boys trickled in, as Cabot and Drake got closer because we're all they've got—I was okay with that. When you added Josue last year—again—made sense. But now you're talking about going beyond the occasional witness pickup to being a surrogate father to hundreds of kids. I just don't see how that ends well."

"It won't be like that," I assured him, walking over to take a seat beside him. I got close, but I didn't touch him, unsure if he would want that.

There was resignation now, almost like he was grieving, and honestly, that was worse. The fight in him had drained away, leaving only defeat. I almost preferred the yelling to Ian ever being hurt, and especially by me. "I think you're being really naïve."

He was killing me. "Ian—"

As he turned to face me, the sadness in his eyes made my stomach hurt. It hit me then that he was absolutely terrified.

"I'm not gonna leave you."

He nodded, but I could tell from the response, automatic, that he didn't believe me.

"Ian—"

"You have to imagine, for a second, what does *our* family become if you keep trying to add to it? And if you work in Custodial, will I ever see you again?"

"I—"

"No, you really need to think about this now," he stressed, holding my gaze. "What does you working there do to us?"

It would be the same as what I did now. Yes, the things I did would be different, the people I saw, what I dealt with on a daily basis, but it would still just be me being a marshal. I shook my head. "I truly think you're making too much of this."

"No, I'm not. I don't want anything to come between us. I picked you; I want you. If you persist with this, then you're telling me that I'm not enough."

"That's ridiculous," I bit off because, all of a sudden, this felt like blackmail. If I didn't follow him to SOG or wherever else, then he was going to question my commitment to him? It was ludicrous! I was in love with him, but I knew where my strengths lay, and they were not in kicking down doors and arresting people. "Ian, you need to—"

"No, think about it. I want to do a job. We can stay like we are, investigators working for Kage, or we can both go to SOG. Either way, those jobs stop at the end of the day. If you're in Custodial, does that stop?"

He was basically telling me what *he* thought I should do with my life. It was arrogant and hurtful and blind... but I knew it was coming from a place of loss. Ian had lost his father to divorce, his mother to death, had just made a huge choice to leave the Army, and now, if he didn't have me—his husband—then what was left? So I had to reassure him while sticking to my guns at the same time.

"Of course it stops."

"No, I don't think so. I know you. You're going to be thinking about the kids, about saving them, about fixing things for them all the time."

"Ian—"

"I left the Army to be here with you, home with you, and be your partner at work. If we're not partners anymore and I don't get to see you because you're going to be putting in ridiculous hours, then what was the point? Tell me what the point was."

"The point was that we're together, and you're home and—"

His phone buzzed on the nightstand, and after a few beats of pained silence, he got up and walked around the bed to check it because we were required to. After reading the display, he picked it up and answered. "Morning, sir."

I watched him listen, saw him furrow his brows as he slowly drew himself up, all the rippling apprehension that had drained away back in seconds, the strain easy to read on his scrunched-up features. In the past I would have thought he was about to be deployed, the call coming in to get his gear and head for the airport. But Ian had dropped his retirement packet, so he no longer went out on missions, just had to do his drills one weekend a month and two weeks' AT in the summer. But the rigid stance I saw couldn't be military, and so had to be something else.

"Yessir, we'll be right there," he said and then disconnected the call and turned to me.

"What?"

"This discussion isn't over, but Kage wants us downtown now."

I nodded.

He charged back around the bed, and I stood fast so that the second I could reach him, I reeled him into my arms. Wrapping him up tight, I pressed my face against his shoulder and simply inhaled, loving the fresh, clean detergent and fabric softener smell of his clothes, along with the trace of lime from the shampoo he used, and the vetiver and cedarwood from the skin balm he smoothed over his face every morning.

There was a truth here I needed to be smart about. Nothing was more important that Ian. I made him a promise the day we exchanged rings, and that was bigger than anything else. Remembering how it was when he was deployed, how I was, how lonely and untethered it made me, how I ached for him body and soul, made it even more obvious.

"I thought wherever I go, Miro goes. It was never a question." Ian sighed, leaning his head on mine, holding me as fiercely as I was him. "I know that was an assumption, but—"

"No," I insisted, even though I knew that in a way, he was right. It was an assumption, and truthfully, a wrong one. Because we didn't have to do the same job to be together, and in that respect, he needed a reality check. We had completely different strengths, and what I was good at and what he was good at might not work on the same team. But there was one absolute, and I needed him to know. "I won't sacrifice us for any job, Ian. I swear to you I won't."

"I don't think that's a promise you can keep," he murmured before kissing my cheek and resting his forehead against mine so we were breathing the same air.

Taking the job or not had just become a much bigger decision than I ever imagined.

BY THE time we got downtown to the Federal building, I was stewing. It had occurred to me while Ian drove that, had he been with me when I got hurt, and had he seen Wen at the hospital and then gone to Cullen's office with us, maybe he would have said something right then. And if he had spoken up when Kage was thinking about me in the director's role, then perhaps Kage would have rethought his position, and none of this would have ever been an issue. Not that I didn't want to help kids, not that this wasn't the place for me, but maybe Ian could have stopped the whole cycle from starting.

On the other hand, had he done that, I might have died of humiliation right there, assuming Kage even let Ian get a word in, which was a stretch. I couldn't imagine Kage letting anyone but that individual make decisions for himself.

The fact of the matter was, because Ian wasn't there, he was coming late to the party after I had already given my word, and now everything was a huge fucking mess.

I slammed the passenger-side door to the truck and started toward the entrance to the building without looking at him. Ian caught me easily, grabbing my bicep and spinning me around to face him.

"What?"

He scowled instantly. "Tell me what you're thinking."

I shook my head. "It won't fix anything."

"Why're you pissed at me?"

Really, the balls on the man, holy shit. "No," I said, slipping around him to again head for the underground entrance.

"No?"

"I am not doing this when we're about to go up in the goddamn elevator."

He caught up to me easily, cutting in front of me, and when I went to walk by him again, he barred my path and put his hands on my hips under my John Varvatos suit jacket.

"I'm not stupid," he said huskily, staring into my eyes. "I know if I'd been there yesterday that I could have said something to you—or even Kage—before this went down."

Easing free of his hold, I stepped back and crossed my arms as I regarded him. "I was just thinking about that, and really, you would've said something to Kage when he was in fixer mode? Is that what you're telling me?"

He was thinking about that, I could tell from the squint.

"When he gets all barky with the orders, and when he snaps all his words?"

The grimace was telling. No one I knew said a word when Kage turned into a steamroller. None of us had the balls.

"I'm just scared, all right?" he rasped, voice cracking. "We just locked this thing down, and I don't want anything to fuck it up."

"I don't either, but you know how you've been saying that you want us together at work?"

"I do want that."

"Yes," I agreed, "but your actions don't really convey that, right?"

"How do you mean?"

"Ian" was all I said.

He was quiet a moment before I got the grunt that told me he'd figured it out. "I have been spending a lot of time with SOG instead of backing you up."

"Which is fine."

"Except not yesterday."

"That was a one-off. Doesn't happen every day."

"Yeah, but here I am telling you I want us to stay partners, and… I can see where I'd come off a bit hypocritical."

It was one of Ian's best qualities, his own self-awareness, given a little time.

"But SOG needs me," he countered, still scowling. "They need us."

"They need somebody to take charge, I'll give you that, but I actually think you're more qualified than is necessary, and I'd be no help to them at all. Think about me there. Can you even see it?"

"Yes," he said, crossing his arms as I dropped mine.

"Really?" I asked, taking hold of his biceps. "Ian?"

His growl made me smile. It was impossible for him not to see my side of an argument, had always been that way. He just needed time. And not that things were fixed—they were not, he was still scared—but I saw the thaw in his icy gaze.

"Yeah, well, maybe you can do some thinking for yourself."

"Oh?" I taunted. "Can I?"

"You don't have to be all—I mean, I can see where I could've come off like a dick."

He wasn't sorry, he wasn't apologizing, but he had put himself in my place and saw himself from my perspective, and really, it was impressive.

"When you scare me, though, I can't think."

And I knew that too.

I held his gaze, marveling as I always did over the color. Every now and then, I was still amazed I had fallen in love with my best friend and that he'd fallen for me right back.

"I'm just—"

"Worried," I offered, moving him back and forth a bit because I really wanted to shake him violently until he saw the truth of the situation. Because yes, I could be a bleeding heart, and most assuredly I was going to get hurt... but it would be okay because I had him to go home to every night. Wasn't that the whole point of a marriage, of a union, to begin with? Having a partner who could strip away all the bullshit from your day, make you feel loved, help you enjoy life, and create a sanctuary that let you breathe? "But won't you be there to pick up the pieces?"

"Yes."

"Isn't that what you signed on for?"

He nodded.

"Well, then."

He searched my face a moment before leaning in and brushing a light kiss over my lips. It was fast, barely there, and then he took hold of my hand to tug me after him. Ian being possessive of me after we had any kind of disagreement was a usual occurrence, and since I liked it and it gave him comfort, I followed along behind him without another word.

Once the elevator hit the lobby, we had to move to the back of the car, and as more and more people crammed in, I found myself wedged into the corner with Ian in front of me, his broad, muscular back pressed to my chest as he stood there solid and strong where I knew he wanted to be, between me and everyone else. I would have grabbed him and hugged him if we'd been alone, would have let my head fall between his shoulder blades, would have simply kissed the back of his neck if we weren't at work. And it hit me that was true for any two people who worked together in a professional setting, and there was something sweet and secret about our situation. As the elevator climbed floor after floor and became less and less crowded, I couldn't help but give Ian's hand a quick squeeze before he stepped away from me.

At our floor, we stepped out, and I immediately saw Kage was in the middle of the office—at Ian's desk, actually, perched on the edge of it, addressing the room. Five men stood off to the side, and I thought at first glance I didn't know any of them until I looked closer and saw that I did.

When I first met Josiah Redeker in the terminal of the Vegas airport, I thought he looked like a guy who ran a bar or belonged in a motorcycle gang. I'd been binge-watching *Sons of Anarchy* while Ian was deployed, so that was probably why that thought tumbled into my head. But as I got to know him over the course of a couple of days, I realized that under the carelessly kept surface was a man with laser focus and the ability to adapt quickly to any given situation.

He, like Ian, could go from complete stillness to an explosion of motion in seconds. There was also the whiff of loner that came off him, a sort of wandering cowboy quality complete with a gleam of danger in his dark eyes that was terribly appealing. There was no denying his masculine beauty, and I completely understood why his partner had it so bad. The fact that Bodhi Callahan was not standing beside him concerned me. If Redeker was in Chicago alone, the fallout must have been bad when Bodhi confessed his feelings. The last I knew, I thought that was the plan, but perhaps that was wrong as well. I hadn't followed up, so maybe they had just gone their separate ways. And maybe not. Maybe I was reading way too much into him being here alone, and nothing had occurred at all. I was going to find out, though, just as soon as possible.

When Ian and I stepped into the bullpen, all five men turned to look at us, and when Redeker saw me, his face broke into the wide smile with the deep lines—not dimples, as they creased the length of his cheeks—I remembered well from my short time spent with him. I raised my hand, and he gave me a nod back.

"Who's that?" Ian asked close to my ear.

"Josiah Redeker, out of the Vegas office," I replied softly, not wanting to disturb Kage, who was saying something about changes. "I worked with him and his partner, Bodhi Callahan, when I transported Josue."

Ian grunted, and we both looked at Kage, who had stopped speaking.

We were just inside the circle of desks on the outer edge, but I had no desire to move closer, especially with Kage being quiet as he scanned the room. Normally that meant he was deciding something as he stood there, and like in school when you didn't know the answer, not making eye contact never helped. But being right in front of him was not the best idea either.

When the elevator dinged, Eli came into the room, followed closely by Maureen Prescott. She and Eli had not come together; that was clear when Eli stopped walking, noticing her behind him. Prescott said something to him quickly and touched his arm briefly as she scooted around him to join Kage at Ian's desk. At the same time, Elyes stood up from her desk right outside Kage's office and joined him and Prescott. They were all quiet for a moment, and only then did I see Prescott holding what looked like a large organizer with one of those Velcro closures, and Elyes had two smaller ones, as well as a handful of lanyards.

"Okay," Kage said. He took a breath before rising to his towering height and crossing his arms, which always made them look like tree trunks. "In the last twelve hours, there have been some big changes here at the office, and because of those, this department will be impacted."

Everyone was silent; nobody moved. Nobody even took a sip of morning coffee, which was amazing since we were a huge caffeine-fueled group.

"The only one I've spoken privately to is Becker," Kage said, looking over at him, giving a slight smile that somehow conveyed warmth, even being no more than a faint softening of his eyes and a curl to his lip that was gone before he turned back to all of us, "as he is the only one who's being promoted. The rest of you will receive your new interim assignments, and they will be assessed in ninety days."

Still quiet.

"As our department grows, so does our reach into the community, and we need to be able to work seamlessly with other law enforcement. The task force opportunities will only grow as we educate and are in turn educated by other agencies. For that reason, I've added a deputy director position here that we haven't had before—haven't needed before now—that will coordinate this new interagency cooperation."

Poor Becker. Really, God, poor fucking Becker. I couldn't imagine the horror of being the guy who had to talk to Chicago PD and the Illinois State Police, the FBI, Homeland, ATF, and of course, the DEA. I got chills just thinking about being the poster boy of interagency clusterfucks. It made sense he'd choose Becker, as he was without a doubt the one of us who was the most unflappable, the most grounded, the guy who rowed the steadiest boat. But still, to be the center of the storm, the one who had to keep tabs on everyone, who coordinated who went where and how and what and when, required a level of professionalism and patience, organization and quiet, steely command I certainly did not possess. Becker was the best choice for the job.

"So," Kage said, taking a breath, "as of today, Christopher Becker has been promoted to supervisory deputy of the Northern District of Illinois."

It took a second for the words to sink in because that was not where I thought he was going at all. And didn't we already have a supervisory deputy?

"Holy shit," I gasped, stunned and sucker-punched but also very thrilled for my friend, who so deserved the promotion. Just working with Ching all those years should have gotten him some kind of commendation.

I started whooping and clapping along with everyone else, and anyone who wasn't standing did, as did Becker, who smiled, nodded, and gave us a wave before flipping us all off. It was totally him.

He then turned to Kage, who walked over to him and offered this hand. The two men shook, with Kage squeezing his shoulder and Becker taking deep breaths.

"I won't let you down, sir," he promised as Kage passed him a new badge, new credentials in the small trifold wallet, and a lanyard we were all supposed to wear inside the building and never did.

"I know that," Kage assured him with a true smile this time, patting Becker's shoulder before releasing him and stepping back.

We rushed Becker then, Ching first, hugging his best friend and partner tight and whispering urgently.

All I heard was Becker's reply: "Nothing changes with us."

"No," Ching agreed, pounding his back and then letting go so the rest of us could hug him, one after another.

After he and Ian embraced, when my husband went to draw back, Becker clutched at him, holding him there. "I promise to give you all the support you need, Doyle."

Ian looked up at him, appreciative but also confused. "Why do I need support?"

Becker shrugged and then gave him a pat before letting him go.

"Settle," Kage ordered, and we all went quiet. "Darren Mills has been reassigned to the Warrants division here and will be reporting to Becker as of today."

He didn't say the words no one ever wanted to be associated with: demotion, reclassification, reassignment. I noticed the grimaces on everyone and felt it too, the stab of guilt that came with the relief that it wasn't me.

"As supervisory deputy, you carry a gun, but Mills does not in his new capacity," Kage said, enunciating the "not" at the end so Becker, along with the rest of us, were clear. "I had him turn in his firearm last night, but if he comes in with his spare for *any* reason, he's to be placed immediately on administrative leave." He finished with a pointed stare at his new supervisory deputy.

"Yessir," Becker acknowledged solemnly.

I glanced over at Becker, and his look of pain was unmissable. That was going to be a barrel of fun right there.

"Moving on," Kage said quickly, facing the room. "The commander position that has been vacant in SOG will be filled by Wesley Ching."

I was stunned, and clearly, when I turned to Ian, so was he. But Ching was a former Marine, a gunnery sergeant with years of combat experience, and he'd been a marshal a lot longer than the rest of us, except for Becker. So the surprise wasn't that Ching couldn't do the job, never that, it was just that Ian, with his Special Forces background—he was an ex–Green Beret, for fuck's sake—was, in my mind, the more likely choice.

But… if I were Kage, maybe that's the choice I would have made too. As hotheaded as Ching seemed, as dangerous as his reputation was, as badass, he was still, on a whole, more by-the-book than Ian. He didn't charge in; he assessed, he made a plan, and he always, always had Becker's back. There wasn't a time I could recall when Becker couldn't turn around and find Ching right there. The same could not be said for me, yesterday being a prime example. Ian went where he thought he was most needed, which was not always where the group consensus agreed he should be.

Before anyone could congratulate Ching, though, Kage lifted his hands to stop us. "I have more of these to get through," he explained, and so we all stayed still except for Becker, who had his hand on the back of Ching's neck, squeezing gently as Ching stood, looking dazed but with a trace of a smile lighting up his normally stony expression.

Elyes slipped over to Ching, passed him an organizer and a lanyard, and then moved quickly back to Kage's side.

"That has a new department designation on the lanyard," Kage said to Ching, "but your badge remains the same."

Ching nodded as Kage continued.

"When he returns from vacation, Jer Kowalski will take over the director position of Judicial Support. That department has come under scrutiny lately, and I need someone I can depend on. I have no doubt that he will do an exemplary job."

"Without a doubt," Eli agreed, and I could tell from his voice the comment was bittersweet. He'd miss his partner.

"Beginning today, Miro Jones will take over as interim director of Custodial WITSEC."

Even knowing it was coming, I was still floored by the faith my boss had in me. And when I looked at Ian, expecting him to be shooting daggers out of his eyes, instead I saw resignation.

"Ian?" I said under my breath.

This was my moment, and the question was, would he be supportive or not? Would he ruin it or not? Because yes, he had concerns, and we were arguing and trying to come to some kind of compromise, and the road was about to get ten kinds of rocky, but… taking care of kids, caretaking, nurturing, there was just no way that wasn't right up my alley. He knew that, didn't he? If he knew me and knew what I needed and who I was, then couldn't he put aside what he needed for what I—for what... I... for me. Just me.

It hit me like a bullet to the brain, what I'd been missing, what Ian had been saying all morning.

Holymotherfuckinghell, how goddamn blind was I?

"Miro?"

Jesus Christ, could I be any stupider?

"M?"

Oh, fuck me.

"Love?" Ian whispered, standing next to me beside Kowalski's desk, which I guess technically wasn't his anymore because he was leaving, and that was just one of many things that would be different and strange, and since it didn't seem like Kage was anywhere near done, that meant there would be more strangers coming and more friends leaving, and it felt like everything was moving faster and faster and....

Oh God, oh God, oh God. Life-altering change along with deep, soul-sucking revelation equaled panic attack. I could see the spots in front of my eyes, and the room seemed to be rocking back and forth... back... and forth.

It was funny but, while being shot at, facing life-and-death things, I felt no panic, no hysteria. But anything to do with Ian—like *at all*—and I was a fucking basket case.

Why was that? What was it about Ian that made me go fetal with doubt?

"Miro," Ian said, low and gravelly, "try and breathe."

But yesterday my life was one way, and today....

I thought I'd just be upstairs from the guys I worked with and still see them all the time, and Ian would still be my partner both on and off the field, and I'd still be trying to figure out what Kowalski's first name was, and Eli and I would hang out, and I'd see... and I would spend time... and....

People were leaving me and—how in the hell had I let myself get so close to all these guys? The girls were one thing. I knew they'd always be there, all four of them like rocks in my life, and then Ian— that was why he had to stay home with me, be home with me, because the idea of losing him was just.... I couldn't, and now he'd been trying to tell me he was feeling the exact same way, and I—

Because he'd chosen me, us, our life, yes, but that didn't mean he couldn't change his mind back. It wasn't like he had just one choice to make. He had unlimited options if, for instance, he stopped caring about having me in his life. And no, that wasn't likely, but it was possible. He'd picked me, but he could pick the Army again if I fucked this up, if I showed him over and over again that he was not the most important thing in my life.

I thought that once we were together in the same place each and every day, that would be it. We'd be perfect. But the fact of the matter was, if you didn't want what you had once you got it, then that didn't work either. It wasn't enough of a solution.

What if Ian decided he'd made an impossible choice to be with me, and he couldn't live with it and wanted to go? Or, again, if he made the wrong choice and wanted to go? Then either way, he'd leave, and I'd be alone. Worse than alone: without him.

A wave of dizziness nearly put me on my knees, but Ian was there, right there, grabbing hold of my arm, keeping me steady and on my feet.

"Okay," he soothed, his voice like honey as I held on, probably too tight, clinging as the surge of emotions rolled through me, ridiculously scared he was going to walk out on me.

I was not some kind of ingenue alone in the world. I was strong. I'd been alone before, I could remake my life from scratch if needed. I could. No doubt. But the issue was not if I could; the issue was I didn't want to. Ian was it. Ian was the one, and losing him would make me different. I didn't want to know what I would look like without him.

The epiphany was a whopper, and I'd been blindsided to boot.

"Jones?" Kage said my name irritably, but it was like he was far away at the other end of a long tunnel, and I could barely hear him.

There were no words. I had none for him.

"He's just overwhelmed, sir. It's a big deal," Ian said quickly, and I heard it clearly because my hearing came back in stereo, even though my vison stayed blurred.

"He'll do fine," Kage declared like he was giving me his blessing, and suddenly Prescott was there at my shoulder, passing me a thick black organizer with the marshals' star on the cover, and the lanyard I'd be wearing into people's homes that had my employment photo on it, which was even more horrible than the picture on my driver's license.

Still holding on to Ian, I realized Kage's attention was elsewhere, and I felt the relief Frodo and Sam must have experienced when the Eye moved off them, because I could breathe a bit more, even though I was still right there on the edge of hyperventilating.

"Hey."

Turning to Ian, I saw a trace of a smile before he took a deep breath in and then blew it out, softly, slowly.

I watched him intently as he did it again.

"What is this, Lamaze?" I teased, my voice cracking, going out on me.

He repeated the process, and the second time, I mimicked him, which was clearly what he was after, and finally pushed some air into my lungs.

"What's wrong?" he whispered, his eyes locked on mine.

"I'm a piece of shit," I husked, "and I don't deserve you."

"Oh?"

I growled softly, wincing, feeling worse by the second. "You left the Army for me."

His smile was wicked as he shook his head. "No, you were right. I left the Army for me, because I wanted to be with you."

"But you stopped doing something you loved for me, and I was just about to *not* stop doing something for you, and what about commitment? What about our wedding vows?" I choked out, reeling with everything running through my head.

Oh, I was seriously going to stop breathing and have a full-blown panic attack after having a goddamn revelation in the middle of the bullpen about how I had been just as selfish and singularly focused as Ian.

Everyone was clapping again as I bent over and braced my hands above my knees.

Ian put a hand on my back, began rubbing comforting circles there before leaning down so he could speak into my ear. "It's not the same thing."

"How?" I gasped, taking shallow breaths. "I needed you home; you changed your whole life. You need me with you; I'm saying no. It's the same."

"I was on the other side of the world. You just might miss dinner sometimes," he clarified, chuckling softly, speaking into my hair.

"Why're you being nice to me now?"

"Because you just saw things from my perspective, and that's pretty great."

"But nothing's fixed," I claimed miserably.

"Yeah, but nothing's completely busted either."

"You're being very glass-half-full right now instead of empty."

"I know, right? Lookit me with the growth and shit."

God. "We won't work together anymore," I reminded him, trying to breathe around my fear.

"No."

"And that was half the point of you staying home, wasn't it? I mean, Kage was going to give me a new partner because you were gone so much, and neither of us wanted that, and you made a point of—"

"Maybe you should sit down, huh?"

"When this meeting is over, I'll go tell Kage that—"

"No," he insisted. "You won't tell Kage a damn thing."

I took a breath. "You're the most important thing."

"I feel the same."

"Which leaves us where?" I asked, catching my breath, then swallowing hard.

"We'll figure—"

"Are you okay?" Eli asked, moving in beside me, hand next to Ian's on my back. "You look like you're gonna barf."

"I'm having some issues."

"Well, yeah, you—"

Kage started talking again. "As of today, Eli Kohn will be the new director of the Public Affairs Division, the new face of the Northern District."

I straightened up like I'd been zapped by a Taser, looked at Kage a second, and then turned to look sideways at Eli. To say he looked gobsmacked was an understatement.

"Now who's lookin' barfy?" Ian asked Eli with a smirk.

Eli opened his mouth, but no sound came out.

"As that post has stood vacant for the last six months since the retirement of Gordon Eames, Kohn will not be interim, but the direct replacement to the post."

Deer in the headlights all the way.

Eli accepted the organizer and lanyard from Elyes as Kage assured him he'd do a fine job. "I have every faith in you," he finished. "You'll represent the office well."

"Thank you, sir," Eli said, his voice sounding like dried leaves.

We were all standing there looking shell-shocked.

"And finally," Kage said in his deep rumble, "Ian Doyle will take over as deputy director and, going forward, will be the main point of contact in all interagency dealings. He's the go-to guy for issues with anyone outside of this office."

Oh. Holy. Fuck.

I turned to him, and Ian was *gray*. I'd never actually seen anyone do that. All color drained from his face—I had no idea that could actually happen. "Gobsmacked" didn't do his expression justice anymore.

"I think I know what we're gonna do after work today," Eli ventured.

Me too. Drinking. Lots and lots of drinking.

"Jesus, Doyle, you look like ass."

Ian sat down hard in Kowalski's chair, and I stepped in close, hand on his shoulder, squeezing gently.

"That makes no logical sense," Ian whispered like his brain was offline.

I was at a loss myself. I could not imagine anyone being *less* ready to be a liaison than Ian. But at the same time... Ian was very similar to Kage in a lot of ways. Meeting Kage, hearing him bellow, seeing his size, and being the subject of his glare, you wouldn't guess he was unflappable under pressure and the rock we all clung to.

So maybe, just maybe, Kage saw the same in Ian.

Still, the announcement made my chest explode with a flock of flapping birds. I couldn't even take one more surprise today. Not. One.

Kage then cleared his throat and indicated the back of the room with an open hand.

"With the changes I've just implemented, we need an additional six men here in the investigator office, and we have five—oh, four—here today."

Attention shifted to the men standing along the back wall close to the exit. Our floor was set up so there was glass at desk level to the ceiling and concrete block from desk level to the ground. There was no door that let out of the bullpen. The only door that could be closed was the one to Kage's office.

When Kage was promoted, he was supposed to move to the chief deputy's office, one door down from where we were now, but he'd stayed in the supervisory deputy's office. I wondered what would happen now.

"Joining our team are Senior Investigator Josiah Redeker, from the District of Nevada," Kage announced, and Redeker lifted his hand, "Deputy Marshal Gabriel Brodie, from the Southern District here in Illinois, Probationary Marshal Leo Rodriguez, who moved here from New York, Probationary Marshal Sen Yamane, from LA—" Kage paused as another man came in, all smiles until he saw Kage furrow his brow. "—and Deputy Marshal Eric Pazzi, from the Northern District of California."

We all remained quiet as Kage took a breath.

"We arrive on time here in Chicago, Pazzi."

"Yessir," he said quickly, grimacing.

"There will be one more joining us in the next few days, but at the moment, I'm still awaiting transfer paperwork."

Ian put a hand on my shoulder, drawing my attention.

"All the transfers meet me in the conference room. Everyone else remain here so I can give you your—yes?"

A man I had not seen since the past fall stood in the bullpen doorway, and even though seeing him shouldn't have signaled alarm in me—he was just an FBI agent, not some harbinger of doom—I still jolted. After a moment two more joined him, all in trench coats, and Special Agent Tilden Adair, who I knew, the one in front, opened his badge to reveal the familiar FBI credentials and pulled them for Kage.

"I'm Special Agent—"

"Tilden Adair," Kage finished for him. "I remember. What can I do for you, Agent?"

He gave Kage a nod as he put his wallet away. "We have a situation, Chief, and we need Marshal Jones."

"And what situation is that?"

He coughed. "I have three dead men in an art gallery in the West Loop."

"Which has what to do with Jones?"

I knew what the answer was before the words were even out of his mouth. There could be no question, not really. The FBI only came looking for me, to me, for one reason.

"We believe it's Craig Hartley," Adair announced, and everyone in the room turned to look at me.

I read it on the faces of the new guys, the surprise and then shock that turned fast to sympathy. They all felt bad for me, and even if they didn't know the whole story—and how could they, only my most inner circle did—still, they were sorry. Because when you had a serial killer kidnap and torture you and then pay you house calls and save your life… it was weird and twisty, and there was a blurring of good and evil there.

In the beginning, when Hartley had put a kitchen knife into my side, a singular emotion could be dredged up when his name was spoken, and that was fear. But over the years, as he had escaped from prison and found his way back to me twice, now what could be fished from the depths of my soul was still panic and dread, but also humiliation, gratitude, and rapport. So when Adair spoke, the jolt of terror was followed almost instantly by resignation.

"Believe or know?" Kage growled.

"We know," Adair said before turning quickly, grabbing Kowalski's garbage can, and vomiting, I was guessing, both his breakfast and morning coffee.

I turned to look at Kage, who looked over his shoulder at Prescott. "You might need to start this morning without Jones."

IT WAS a field trip, but not everyone went. Kage was sending Becker in his place, and since Ian was the new liaison, he was going, which was good since, one way or another, he was going with me. Before I could follow Ian out of the room, Kage called me over.

Stepping in front of him, I was surprised when he took hold of my shoulder.

"Listen, make sure you let Kohn talk to any reporters that are there. If you have to vomit, do it like Adair and not at the scene, and if the Feds or anyone gives you any trouble, sic Doyle on them because that's what he's there to do, corral the interagency bullshit."

"Yessir," I agreed, smiling slightly over the vomit part. Leave it to Kage to remind me of something ordinary like throwing up to somehow inject normalcy. I appreciated it more than I could say.

He nodded and tipped his head toward the door.

"Thank you, sir," I said and pivoted and darted to catch up to Ian.

I could tell, as I walked out of the office, that some of the guys were unsure about me. It was weird, I would guess, to be that close to someone they'd read about or even seen on the news. My name had been in print in conjunction with Hartley a lot over the years. The Wikipedia entry on him had my marshal picture, and while the whole thing with Hartley cutting out my rib wasn't in there because it was not common knowledge, there was still the part about him kidnapping and torturing me. There were also some lurid bits about what he'd done to the women he'd killed, as well as Special Agent Wojno, and his picture from the FBI Most Wanted list. The fact that he had eluded the FBI on a number of occasions was also in there, and the opinion that, while dangerous, he was not a rampaging psychopath.

The men I rode the elevator down with cast surreptitious glances at me, wanting, I knew, to ask about Hartley. I had been asked about Hartley since he first became a suspect and was still unsure how to answer. The big question, why I was still alive, was one I certainly had no response for. Only Hartley could say. But as I stood there silently, back against the cold steel as we descended toward the parking garage, I could feel how thick the tension was around me. Adair himself was eying me warily.

"Listen, Jones, it should only be you coming with us. This is an FBI inves—"

"You heard Kage," Becker interrupted. "You get me and Doyle, Kohn, and four others, and that's how this is gonna go. If you don't like it, you can have your boss call mine, and maybe Jones will—"

"Yeah, all right," Adair agreed with a grunt, clearly annoyed. "Just don't turn this thing into a circus."

"That's hysterical, coming from you," Ian retorted, his voice a sarcastic drawl. "You're the ones who shared what happened to your agents with the press before Thanksgiving last year. That was fuckin' brilliant."

Becker bumped Ian, and he crossed his arms and exhaled sharply. Apparently the new liaison needed to calm the hell down. Ryan and Dorsey were there to show Rodriguez and Brodie, the new guys Kage sent with us, how we ran things, and both of them were suddenly staring forward, trying not to make eye contact with Ian. I understood. If it were me, I wouldn't have wanted to deal with him either. He looked like he was ready to tear someone's head off, the way his jaw was set, clenched with the muscle working in his right cheek, how flat and cold his eyes had gone, and the rigid battle stance. The whole soldier mantle was drawn tight around him, and he was bristling with seething menace.

Gently, quietly, I put a hand between Ian's shoulder blades before sliding it up into his hair. He closed his eyes for a second, and when he opened them back up, he looked better, settled, grounded, and as he took a breath, I saw him relax a bit. He wasn't calm, but he was better. Nice to know just my touch could do that.

We took the gigantic Chevy Suburbans that normally went out only for fugitive pickups or if the whole department was involved in a task force. The last time we all went on assignment as a group was before Halloween last year, when our Most Wanted included a child predator. Now, loaded up with Becker driving, we moved out, following the Feds to the gallery.

No one said a thing during the ride, only Ian's hand on my thigh, where no one could see, keeping me calm. I wasn't scared—Hartley wasn't there waiting for me—but there was that anxiety over what had been left for me to see.

Once we reached the street and parked, we all piled out and waited for Adair and the rest of his team to join us.

"So how do you know it was him?" I asked when Adair motioned for us to follow him.

I remembered him because of his looks. I had never met anyone with black eyes that were so striking under heavy black brows, framed by long, thick lashes in his pale—like alabaster-white—face. He didn't look sickly, but you could see the blue veins under the skin of his throat and hands.

"He—" Quick breath, and I took a step away from him because he'd already shown his stomach was iffy. "—signed it, and there's an inscription on the wall."

I stopped walking and looked at him because that hit me as all kinds of wrong, and I felt it physically, the tremor that shuddered through me, but also, and more importantly, instinctively. Because while Hartley did leave messages, he didn't sign his work; it wasn't his way. He wasn't prideful in that respect, and that was part of the point of knowing who you were chasing. He made you *have* to get to know him, which I did.

"We would have kept this from you, Marshal, but even though you're not involved with our ongoing pursuit of Craig Hartley, you are, in fact, tied to him until he's back behind bars."

"Right," I concurred as Ian slipped a hand up my back, resting it on my shoulder for a moment before letting it slide off. He couldn't very well hold my hand, but I could have really used the contact.

The Sanderson Gallery down by the Loop was only fifteen minutes from the office. CPD was keeping a crowd back. I saw the yellow tape up, and then inside of that, as we closed in, the spray of what I thought was probably blood on the front windows.

"Is that what I think it is?"

"Yeah, it's blood."

"Is there more inside?" I asked Adair, already knowing the man I knew was not responsible for whatever horror was behind the door. The last time I saw Hartley, I got the feeling murder was no longer in his repertoire. He did it to sort out something horrible in his head, to make a statement about who was weak and able to be seduced, and who was not.

There were women who came forward afterward, horrified it could have been them if they had, in fact, decided to cheat on their husbands. There was one woman who implied murder was what an adulteress deserved. I had roared at her at my desk, sent her scurrying from the bullpen because it was such shit that I couldn't stand to look at her. But all of that, the women Hartley killed, the way he did it, the people he murdered during his last escape and the man he dispatched to save me… none of that was ever rage. He was methodical, steady, and… what, tidy? There was never a mess, never blood splatters and over-the-top shows of power. It wasn't him, and as my stomach turned into a block of ice, a feeling of dread sank over me.

What the hell was going on?

"Jones?"

"Yeah, sorry. So is there more blood?"

"No, that's all there is, period, and it only belongs to one of the men. There's no more blood anywhere than that in the gallery."

Which was more like Hartley, but still not likely.

I kept pace with everyone, and a part of me wished it was just me, Ian, and Becker, and maybe Eli. I didn't like the new guys seeing how closely I was involved with a psychopath.

The cop at the door gave us booties to cover our shoes and gloves for our hands, and then one by one, we entered the gallery.

It was a beautiful space, with an open-beam ceiling, polished hardwood floors, and industrial lighting. The exposed brick wall along one side would have made it feel warm, but it contrasted with a lot of glass and chrome and modern furniture that made the room seem cold. Of course the three dead men hanging from the moveable walls added to the morgue vibe of the place.

At Becker's direction, all of us, as well as the agents, fanned out so they could take in what I was sure the papers would call a horrific tableau. They liked saying shit like that.

"This is new," Ian said to no one in particular, scanning what was clearly a presentation before pointing to the words *For Miro* done in beautiful flowing cursive. "What is that?"

"Paint," Adair answered with a cough. "Like I said, the only blood in here is on the front window."

"So where do we think their blood is?" Ian continued.

"We have a—oh, here," Adair said quickly before gesturing to the other side of the room, where a man stood surrounded by several others. It looked like a trench coat convention. "Kelson! Here!"

I expected him to be talking to one of the older men, but a younger one I hadn't noticed stepped out from the circle and strode, almost strutted, across the room, followed closely by two others.

"This is our behavioral profiler, Kol Kelson, from Langley."

Kelson had to be older than he looked because, if I had to go on a guess, I would have said twenty-three, twenty-five tops. He was about five nine, thin, with lean muscles, golden-brown skin, delicate features, and honey-colored eyes. He was easily one of the prettiest men I'd ever met in my life.

"Oh, Marshal Jones," he said reverently, rushing forward, hand out, eyes wide, staring at me like I held the secrets to the universe. "I wish we could have met under better circumstances, but really, it's a pleasure."

"Likewise," I muttered, shaking his hand as he put his other over the clasp.

It was eerie. I felt strange, like the air in the room was slowly being sucked out, and I was starting to have that prickling, uneasy feeling where my clothes felt too tight and my skin started to itch, and there was a cramp in the back of my neck.

"What do you think of your love letter?" he tossed out nonchalantly, almost arrogantly.

"I'm sorry?" I snapped, pulling back my hand, glaring at him because these were men he was talking about, people who were now dead, and his callous disregard made me want to punch him in his smug elfin face.

"Did you not tell him?" Kelson asked, squinting at Adair.

"No, I-I thought you would want to."

Kelson's face brightened. "Thank you, that was thoughtful."

He made me uncomfortable. I felt that quirk of something I didn't like. Kelson was... *off* somehow. His reactions didn't match what was happening. He should have been horrified like the rest of us, sickened, but instead he was enthralled. And I wasn't stupid; I knew people processed trauma differently. At her grandmother's funeral, Catherine could not stop laughing until I finally took her out of the synagogue to the car, where she dissolved into a deluge of tears. But this wasn't that. This was Kelson hopped up on adrenaline, and I had to figure out why.

After taking hold of my bicep, he walked me closer to the three bodies, letting go once we were within touching distance of the wall.

The three panels were arranged as a trifold, like those pieces of posterboard kids bought to stick their projects to when they presented them to the class. Each man hung on a separate moveable wall.

The man on the left was turned on his side, facing the middle, stuck to the wall with what looked to me like fishing line, posed as though he were running and throwing roses in the air. Each petal was glued down, and a small mound of petals lay on the floor in front of the wall. The man on the right had his left hand on his chest, and in his right, he held out a bouquet of roses. Another mound of petals on the floor. The man in the middle faced front, holding a human heart, presumably his, in his cupped hands, along with several roses, as though offering it to whoever was standing in front of him. It was horrifying and stunning at the same time.

"Jesus," Ian said, his breath rushing out as he stopped beside me, his hand on the small of my back, not caring who might see him touching me.

"Marshal Jones." Kelson almost sang my name.

"Do we—" I coughed. "—know who these men are?"

"Yes," Kelson said, "and that's why Hartley dedicating them to you is interesting."

I waited, irritated he wasn't just telling me, instead making it more dramatic than it needed to be.

"These are three of the FBI's Most Wanted."

"Are you kidding?"

He shook his head. "No. And from what the forensic team has been able to determine already, one of them has been dead for a month, and the other two between one and two weeks."

"So he hunted these guys down and killed them."

"Yes."

I stared at the dead men because this was getting further and further from anything Hartley had ever done in his life.

There had been copycats over the years, and the second I thought it, the idea took hold because, really, the man I knew was not some kind of vigilante. And honestly, if he were going to make an overture of love toward me, he would have probably kidnapped me, gutted me, and filled my cadaver with flowers. That was more his speed—the statement, not this. I had no idea what was going on, but the longer I stood there, the more alien the scene became.

I had visited nineteen scenes where Hartley had killed a woman, and each was reverently arranged in a way that if you didn't touch them, you would have sworn they were alive until you saw the other side of their body or their face or really looked at what they were holding—one woman had a suitcase filled with her own organs—or sitting on. Another woman was lounging on a chaise, arranged so that's what you saw, ease and grace, the drape of her body over the expensive piece of furniture, but when you walked around to the other side, her torso was hollowed out and filled with various toys, stuffed animals, and dolls. It turned out her company employed child labor in China, and the toys represented the playtime, the childhood, stolen from the kids. Horrifying, yes, but not the act of a man killing for any other reason than making a statement. The bodies in front of me were not that.

"Who are they?" Becker asked Kelson.

"The middle one there, missing his heart, that's Emile Stigler. We had Interpol looking for him because he was supposed to be in Brazil."

I turned to Kelson. "Do you think he was actually there?"

He nodded. "I do. I don't know if Hartley killed him there and transported the body, or if he brought him back to the US and killed him here—we have no way of knowing."

"No," Adair chimed in, joining us. "We can't guess when the killing was done or how without an autopsy. What we can say for certain is that the top three men on the FBI's Most Wanted are now here, dead, apparently as a gift."

"It's more than that," Kelson said, studying me, scrutinizing me. "May I be frank?"

"Go ahead," I granted, crossing my arms, waiting, realizing that normally my skin would be crawling with just the feel of being so close to something Hartley had done. But I wasn't getting that. It was horrifying, yes, but the longer I stood there, the less I felt like this was his doing.

"It's like he's courting you."

I heard Ian catch his breath, so I turned, gave a subtle shake of my head that had him squinting with confusion, and then returned my attention back to Kelson.

"Courting me? That's ridiculous," I said, shooting that down with a quick shake of my head. "Where are you getting that?"

"From Kelson. He's one of our top profilers. We brought him in because no one knows Hartley better," Adair explained, gesturing at him.

That would have made sense if I weren't there, if I didn't know better. And while there was no surge of pride like I had knowing no one knew Ian better than me… still, I was absolutely confident Kelson was out of his depth with Hartley. "Since when?" I prodded.

"I'm sorry?" Adair asked, clearly annoyed. It was in his tone and his scowl.

"Since when does your guy know Craig Hartley so well?" I asked flatly. "I've never heard of him, and I've certainly never met him before today." The fact of the matter was, when they needed to talk to Hartley, to have him answer questions—they asked *me* to ask him. It had been like that since he first tried to kill me and I saved him from being shot by my partner at the time. Cochran Norris had wanted to put a bullet in the serial killer; I wanted him rotting in jail. I won the argument and nearly died in the process, and now, these many years later, I would have loved to *not* be his favorite law enforcement officer, but that ship had long sailed. So what Adair was saying was total crap. I was the authority on Prince Charming and always would be.

"Kelson is the—"

"No one knows Hartley like me," I advised him solemnly, and my words sounded hollow and pained because it hurt to say, even though it was the truth. "So I ask again, where are you getting this whole courting crap?"

"It's not crap," Kelson almost snarled, and I saw it then, the anger. It was there in the glint in his eyes, the flush on his cheeks, the flared nostrils, and the thin line of his lips pressing together so tight the muscles in his jaw corded. More words clearly wanted to come out, and he was mustering all his strength to stay silent. I had too many years of talking to people not to see the signs. Ian's hand on my shoulder was not a surprise.

"You have no idea what you're talking about," I baited him, hearing my own breath, my vision tunneling down to only Kelson.

I swore I could hear the click of my watch on my wrist as I looked into Kelson's eyes, which he narrowed in cold fury. It was almost possible to taste the hatred in the air between us.

"Gun!"

The fact that nothing changed in Kelson's eyes as he pulled his Glock told me something scary. His focus was solely on me; no one else mattered. He wanted me dead.

Had Kelson done his homework, he would have known better than to try to hurt me while Ian was standing right beside me. He also would have learned that, being a Green Beret, Ian had no delay in his reaction time. So he yanked me out of the way before Kelson even figured out what was happening.

"No!" Kelson howled as Ian hurled him to the ground and pinned him there with a knee in his back while Becker trapped Kelson's hand under his right foot. I was on the ground, dragged to my knees by Eli, and I distantly noted the Magnanni punch-trim cap-toe oxfords he was wearing.

It was weird, and I'd had it happen before. When Hartley was cutting my back open to remove a rib, I watched blood splatter his Cole Haan brogue medallion double monkstrap brown shoes. They were images I held on to and again, in this moment, I had focused on the mundane.

"I have a pair like that," I told Eli, turning to look at him.

"I have a pair of Magnanni calfskin chukka boots that are really comfortable," he offered since we were just shootin' the shit and all. "You should get some."

I nodded.

"Miro!" Ian snarled.

I snapped my head up and faced a glare that should have stopped my heart. Me being in danger had scared him to death.

"I'm good," I told him.

"I'm going to—"

"Freeze!"

The federal agents drew their weapons in rapid succession, a chain reaction that made no sense because the threat was already dealt with.

Ian turned to face them, and I realized that in the confusion, the Feds assumed Ian had attacked Kelson without provocation. I didn't want to get shot accidentally, so I stayed on the ground with Eli as the FBI held guns on us.

It was one of those insane standoff situations.

I thought it would be Becker's voice that boomed out, or even Adair's, so I was surprised when it turned out to be Ian.

"Put your guns down," he ordered, his voice deep and thunderous. "Your man attacked a deputy US marshal. His gun's on the floor and— Adair! Call off your men!"

"Stand down," Adair yelled, using both hands to signal everyone to lower their weapons as he moved closer to us, holstering his own.

"Eli."

He looked up at Ian.

"Take him."

He moved quickly, changing places with Ian, his knee now between Kelson's shoulder blades as Ian stood slowly and put up his hands, not offering any threat to Adair or his men but clearly in control.

"Fuck," Adair growled, clearly flustered and embarrassed by the fact that his men weren't listening to him. "Put your goddamn guns away now!"

And then, finally, looking at Ian standing there with his hands up, the rest of the marshals poised to act, Adair's men all slowly, one by one, holstered their guns.

"For the record," Eli said snidely to Adair as he dragged Kelson to his feet, "if any of us took that long to lower our guns once the chief deputy gave us a direct order, we'd be suspended for days or weeks and then demoted."

Adair muttered something under his breath.

Becker passed handcuffs to Eli. None of the rest of us carried them; we carried zip ties in our TAC vests—which none of us were wearing at the moment because the plan was that we were looking at a crime scene, not apprehending anyone.

"I guess with my new position, I'll carry cuffs again," I mentioned to no one in particular.

Once the room took a collective breath, Eli spun Kelson around to face me as Adair moved up beside me.

"No," Ian barked, snapping his fingers, making sure Kelson, Adair, Eli, anyone close by was looking at him, not me. "We have no idea what's been contaminated at this crime scene because of him."

Which was true.

"So we're going to have CPD take this over until we figure out what's going on. Everybody clear out."

I saw Becker nod, and I thought, but wasn't sure, I saw a faint smile. "You heard him," Becker said, his voice carrying throughout the room. "Everyone get back to the office but me and Doyle."

Instantaneous movement, a far cry from what had happened with Adair's men.

"Dorsey, secure Kelson—"

"We'll take him," Adair barked, reaching for Kelson.

"No," Becker cut him off, signaling to Dorsey, who moved fast, taking custody of Kelson. "We clear this attack on Jones first, and then you guys can have him and take his brain apart."

Adair opened his mouth to argue, but clearly, between Ian and Becker, he was outmanned.

Dorsey moved with the speed and confidence of a man who'd performed his job a thousand times, hand on Kelson's bicep as he led him toward the door, Ryan walking behind him. They'd been partners so long they even walked with the same stride.

"Rodriguez and Brodie, you guys go with them; you're their backup."

"Yessir," both men said quickly, and as they all headed for the door, I saw Rodriguez grab Brodie's barn coat when Brodie was about to walk into one of the agents. Brodie gave him a smile and moved quickly to match Rodriguez's stride. I hoped Ian or Becker saw that. It was nice when new partners started out even being thoughtful of each other.

"Eli," Ian said, and I saw then how his eyes flickered over to me. He wanted to go with me; it was taking a lot for him to accept that he needed to stay there. But I wasn't in imminent danger, and we all had jobs to do. "I need you with him like a shadow, yeah?"

"Absolutely," Eli agreed quickly, reaching out to give Ian a quick touch of reassurance.

Ian nodded, swallowing hard before stepping in front of me. "You lose Eli for any reason, I'll assume that you want to be single."

My gaze met his, and I saw how steely his was, how level.

"Do you understand?"

"I do."

"And you will answer your phone when I call," he said flatly. "Do you understand?"

"Yes."

"Okay." He took a breath. "I'll see you soon."

He turned away from me without another word, pulling out his phone as he moved, and I was suddenly faced with Becker.

"We'll head back to the office, Jones, so you and Eli can make a plan for the day. It looks like he'll be going with you to meet some kids."

I glanced over at Eli in time to catch his look of horror. Oh yeah, he was thrilled he got to babysit me, I could tell.

CHAPTER 7

WHILE KELSON sat in one of our six holding rooms, Ryan and Dorsey manned the office. Kage, who was in the process of moving down the hall and giving Becker his old office, was meeting with Adair's boss and his boss's boss—the Feds had an organizational chart that was hard to follow—as well as the police superintendent and the deputy mayor.

Eli and I stopped on the way back to the office for coffee because I was frozen inside, plus something to eat because, as he said, "You look like you're going to pass out."

"How'd you know?" Eli asked as we sat in the drive-thru at Starbucks.

"That Kelson was wrong?"

He grunted.

"It's a sad truth, but no one knows Hartley like me."

"Do you think he had anything to do with that?"

"No. That kind of vigilantism has never been him."

"But he's still out there somewhere killing people."

I shook my head. "I disagree. It's not him anymore, and I don't know how to explain it other than it's like the killing he did, that's out of his system."

"But you can't say that for certain."

"Yeah, I can," I sighed, leaning my head back. "I think if the Feds just let him go now, he wouldn't be a threat anymore."

"Willing to stake your life on it?"

I thought a moment of what I knew of Hartley. "Yes."

"No shit?" He was startled and turned to me instead of ordering, stunned.

"I need a red eye, so tell her," I said, pointing at the speaker. "And get me a scone."

At the window, Eli was still so flustered when she told him they were out of blueberry scones, and did he want something else, that he started saying things they didn't even have. Once they agreed on a chocolate croissant, he tried to give the cashier a hundred-dollar bill she clearly wasn't about to break. I leaned across him and passed her my phone instead.

"Thank you," she said, shooting Eli a look of pure distaste.

When he pulled away, I patted his thigh. "Calm yourself."

"You realize that right now you sound as psycho as Hartley."

I turned to him and laughed. "Really? Just as psycho?"

He had to pull over so I could drive when he realized he'd compared me to a serial killer.

Once we were back at the office, Kage told Eli to get his ass back to the crime scene so he could keep the reporters off Ian and Becker.

He didn't want to argue, but he didn't want to leave me either.

"Redeker," Kage barked, and Redeker rose from Kowalski's desk, which was apparently going to become his, and crossed the room to me. "You're with Jones today."

"Yessir."

Kage pointed at the door, and Eli moved fast, talking to me over his shoulder. "I'll tell Ian as soon as I get there."

"I'll call too," I told him before turning back to Kage, who had left without another word. "Okay, I guess that was all," I said to no one in particular before pulling my phone from the breast pocket of my suit jacket to call Ian.

"Are you all right?" he said instead of hello.

"Yeah, I just wanted to tell you that Kage sent Eli back to you so he can talk to the press and do all that," I explained.

"Then who the hell is—"

"Redeker."

Silence.

"He's good, Ian, I swear. You'd like him."

He gave that grunt I knew so well, the one saying he was deciding what to do.

"I'm not helpless anyway, right? I carry a gun, Hartley's always been the biggest threat to me, and honestly, we both know whatever that was this morning had nothing to do with him."

Back to silence.

"He might not even be in Chicago."

Quick clearing of his throat. "Lemme talk to Redeker."

"No," I said gently. "Just… stop. I'll be fine."

"Turn on the GPS on your phone."

"Ian," I sighed. He knew as well as I did using the tracking software on our phones to keep tabs on each other was prohibited by the marshals service. It was probably the same for the FBI or DEA or ATF. No one wanted a cloned phone to find an undercover agent or a marshal on a task force ready to serve a warrant. If Kage ever caught either of us with it on—I didn't even know how severe the ramifications would be.

"Fine," he growled, "just—please." Unspoken: *Be careful, come home in one piece, don't do anything stupid, and take care of yourself.*

"Yes, dear," I agreed. He was silent, and so was I, and in that moment, the fear of the changes being made and how we were going to cope and even if we should… drowned me. "Ian—"

"Just focus on the day, all right?" he said sharply.

I took a shaky breath because he sounded ice-cold, which meant he was pulling away, turning his emotions off, both of which were bad for me, for us.

"Focus on the job, all right? Be safe."

I had no choice. I would keep busy so I couldn't think. It was all I could do. "Yes."

He hung up, and I faced Redeker. "Listen, I'm sorry that—"

"So your boss—"

"Your boss now too," I corrected because I was a smartass.

"Jesus."

"Sorry, but technically he is *our* boss."

"Who is? That's what I'm confused about. Who am I reporting to?"

"Becker," I told him as he walked with me to the Custodial office. "Kage is Becker's boss—which is weird for all you new guys because he hasn't been all that great about giving up command."

"You think he will now?"

"I think now that it's Becker, who he trusts… yeah."

"That's good, then."

"I think it will make things around here easier."

"So Kage, he gets stuck with the suits a lot?"

"Yeah."

"And Becker and Doyle, they have to deal with the on-site crap?"

"It's brand-new for both of them, but yeah, they'll both be there until the scene gets turned over to CPD, and then I'm thinking they'll come back, and Becker will decide who's going to be whose partner and have them report to him. I'm thinking Ian will have to go around to all the other offices and meet people. He'll have to create the database of who's where and who to talk to, and—that just sounds horrible to me."

"Yeah, that job with all the red tape and the million different ways of doing things—I mean, what's the SOP for a task force?"

"Is there one?"

"No, but there should be, right? I mean, if everyone is coming to work with the marshals, then the marshals should lead. It should be our rules."

"Have you ever seen those enforced?"

"No," he answered implacably, "but I've never been in an office big enough to have a deputy director either. You gotta figure *our* boss can have that now since he's got a man under his supervisor to take over making sure every other agency complies with how we do things, not the other way around. Most offices don't have someone like Doyle to take over that piece, and there aren't enough hours in a day for the supervisory deputy to deal with it all."

"Huh," I said, ending that discussion.

"Huh?"

"Yeah. That's all interesting, but I wanna be done talking about that because there's more important stuff I need to know."

"More—what?"

I rounded on him before we went in. "So what the hell?" I snapped.

His glare came fast as he crossed his arms. "Why're you yelling at me?"

"That is *so* not yelling."

"What's with—"

"Speak."

"I have no idea what you're—"

"Don't be stupid. Where's your partner?"

"I haven't been assigned one yet."

I crossed my arms, mirroring him, and waited, hoping he saw the irritation on my face.

He groaned loudly, showing me his annoyance. "He's in Vegas."

"Why?"

"You know why."

"If I did, I wouldn't be asking."

He winced. "We had words."

"And then you ran away."

"I did not run away," he said much too defensively.

"Listen, I'm not trying to get in your business," I lied to his face. "I've just seen your dynamic up close, and it works. He's careful, and you're kind of a cowboy."

His glare was back. "When did he tell you that I grew up on a ranch in Wyoming?"

Pivoting, I ignored him and went into Custodial's office, and six pairs of eyes were on me as Prescott came out of what was, in fact, now my office.

"Are you okay to be here?" she asked me solemnly, and I saw the worry in her gaze. Unlike with Kelson, I could read emotions in *her* eyes. "I would be curled up in a ball in the corner of a room."

I gave her a game smile. "I've had Craig Hartley in my life longer than some people have been married. It's no big deal."

She gaped as she stared at me.

"And even if it was, being scared doesn't help anything."

"True," she granted. "But are you sure you want to start in with all of this today? I mean, Jones, you've had one hell of a morning."

"Compared to being kidnapped and tortured by the man, it was a walk in the park."

Sometimes I forgot being honest could be dicey. Now and again people got freaked out by how normally I treated things that were not so easy for others to deal with, like, for instance, serial killers. But truly it wasn't that I was so used to the idea of a nightmare of

Chicago's past being a part of my life. It was that on a day-to-day basis, I didn't think about him. I didn't worry I was being stalked; I let go of that fear years ago. I never thought Hartley was the type to walk up behind me in a crowd, pull the trigger, and blow my brains out. If he was going to kill me, he'd make me squirm first like a worm on the end of a hook. I knew that firsthand.

"I… don't—I can't even begin to imagine what—"

"We really need to get out and see the kids," I told her. "We need to get interviews started today, and I want to meet my team."

She was staring at me, trying to figure me out, searching for the correct response. But there wasn't one, and I saw her pull herself together.

"May I please meet everyone?" I asked to give her something to think about besides Hartley.

"Of course," she agreed as people got up from their desks.

I ORDERED the entire office into the field to get the home visits done as quickly as possible because I was more than worried about the kids who'd been in former Director Cullen's care. In theory, six people in three teams of two, along with me and Redeker, could make a serious dent in the home visits even on the first day. Maureen insisted I call her by her given name and that she could do visits as well, but someone needed to man the desk in the department, and she still had Cullen's paperwork to sort through. She finally agreed that since she knew what red flags to look for, she was the logical choice to remain.

"I've assigned you one of the top social workers I know, and she'll join you at the first home. I emailed her over your schedule for the day."

"Thank you," I told her.

"No, thank you, Marshal. Already—just in the care you're showing, in your zeal to get started and not waste any time—you're a vast improvement over Sebreta Cullen."

Anyone would have been a step up from mediocrity. I just wanted to make a difference in the lives of the children as quickly as possible.

"Why Custodial?" Redeker asked as he drove us toward the Fuller Park neighborhood on the South Side. "Don't you want to move up?"

"I want to help take care of kids," I told him, watching the world go by outside the Ford Expedition delegated for the use of the director of Custodial WITSEC. It had government plates and was painted metallic gray instead of black. I was excited, and Redeker was confused until I explained about the first-come, first-serve way the marshals' office found cars at our disposal. He was horrified when I told him about Ian and me in a carnation-pink Cabriolet.

"Maybe you should be a foster parent," Redeker suggested after a few minutes of silence.

"What?"

"Being a foster parent would let you get out all those feelings of wanting to take care of people, and you could still work your job."

But making sure that a lot of kids were in good places, not just me nurturing one, seemed like a better fit for me. I wasn't sure I could be anyone's father because while I knew I was a caretaker, could tell from how I wanted to shield Josue, Cabot, and Drake and direct their lives, put my two cents in even when it wasn't asked for, I also knew just because I could didn't mean I had to.

Some people were made to be parents. For others, it grew out of their love for their partner, the desire to share more with them. Some people who were parents shouldn't have been, some too selfish, while others simply wanted to heed the call of the open road or the sea, to travel, to be free, to lead, to create change, or a million other pursuits that did not include parenthood. Being a father wouldn't complete me. It wouldn't make me whole; I already was. My dream was to be the best man I could be, the best friend, colleague, uncle, and most of all, husband. Loving Ian took all the parts inside that had been cold and dreary and made them happy and warm and light. But it was hard to explain. How did I say to Redeker that, for me, the natural progression of my marriage was not to a child because already my heart was content? I had Ian, I had the girls, I even had the boys. I was full up. People could look at me and say, "You would make a good father," but that didn't mean that was what I wanted.

"Do I have to be a father?"

"What?"

"I mean, am I broken if I don't want to?"

He glanced at me. "What're you talking about?"

"People ask women who don't have kids all the time, when are you going to have a baby? This happens to my friend Catherine on an almost daily basis. She's a doctor, and her husband's a composer, and they're both at the top of their game, you know, but still it's like they're judged because they don't have kids yet, and her most of all."

"Which is a shitty double standard," he advised me.

"It is because it's like she's less of a woman because she's not a mother."

He grunted.

"That's crap."

"Agreed."

"But it's the same for me because if I'm never a father, does that make me less?"

"I think people are a billion times more judgmental of a woman not having kids than if a man doesn't."

"No, I know, but still, people look at Eriq—that's my friend Catherine's husband—and whenever he plays with a kid or holds a baby, people say, oh, what a good father he'd be, he should have kids."

He nodded. "I've heard that too."

"Right? But see, maybe that ten or twenty minutes is all the nurturing any of us has in him."

"Very possible," he said. "Is that how it is for you?"

"I dunno, but I am certainly not ready to be anyone's father. I can't even fathom that level of responsibility.

"Yeah, join the club."

We were both silent for a bit as we passed gutted, rotting buildings with broken windows and piles of garbage, small crowds of men clustered on stoops and in doorways, and the husks of abandoned cars and the ubiquitous graffiti.

"So, is that a yes on the foster parent thing? I mean, that's helping, right? You don't have to adopt the kids, just give them a secure place to be for a certain amount of time."

I cleared my throat. "I was a ward of the state myself, so I'm not sure I'd make a great parent, foster or otherwise."

"Why not?"

I shrugged. "I think maybe certain people are made to be parents, and other people aren't."

"I get that."

I turned to him. "Do you wanna be a dad?"

He thought a moment. "Yeah, I think so."

"Huh."

"Why huh?"

"No, nothing, I just thought, with how you are, that being a parent wouldn't be on your list."

"'With how I am'? The fuck is that supposed to mean?"

I gestured at him. "When I met you in Vegas, there was some hard living you were doing, according to your partner."

He grunted.

"You're saying that was a lie?"

"I'm saying that people change."

It was true. Ian and I certainly had.

"Don't you find that in life?" Redeker asked.

"I do."

"So then I'm telling you things are different for me now."

"And what brought on this epiphany?"

He shook his head.

"I'm guessing something to do with Callahan?"

He exhaled sharply. "I needed a fresh start. I can't be what anyone needs unless I get my shit together."

I was starting to get an idea of what had happened. "You ran away from him."

"I've never run from anything in my life."

Uh-huh. "So you thought, what, I don't want to fuck up his life, so I'll just go?"

"Is there going to be a social worker going with us on these visits, or are we doing them alone?" Redeker asked, completely ignoring the question I'd put to him.

"That won't work."

"Whatzat?"

"Changing the subject."

He ran a hand through his thick hair. "I don't—this isn't for you to fix, Jones, or for you to make me examine and do whatever. This is my deal with… it's my life, yeah?"

It was, but I'd been where he was and lost so much time not diving into the deep end with Ian. I could see things so much clearer than he could, and if he'd only hear me out, then he wouldn't be haunted like he looked now. He was missing his other half, but he was too bullheaded to know it. But was it my place to make him think about Callahan or what he was missing or… what…?

The ring caught my eye.

He was still yanking on his hair with his left hand, which bore a silver ring that was somehow familiar. It was shaped like the tentacle of an octopus, wide and tapering, both masculine and delicate at the same time. Then it hit me: the last time I'd seen Callahan, the same ring had been on *his* hand. But now it was with Redeker, entwined around his middle finger, and it was doubtful he was even aware of it. Instead, he wore it naturally, just as he did the love of his partner, without any awareness at all.

So he had Bodhi Callahan's ring on his left hand. I needed to shut the hell up because one thing I did know was that everything happened for a reason, and even if he had no idea what was going on, I suspected his partner most certainly did.

"I just—"

"No, you're right," I amended, smiling for his benefit. "I'll shut up."

He checked my face, trying, I was sure, to get a read on me.

"And just so you know, there will be several different social workers," I informed him.

"Okay, good," he rumbled as he pulled up in front of an apartment building and parked.

"You're getting around pretty well already," I praised him.

"Well, you know, GPS, it's a thing, but I've been here a week already, so some things are starting to make a little more sense. Though some of the streets I've been on—there are potholes that you could lose an axle in, and I swear I was driving down Milwaukee Avenue, and I'm pretty sure it turned into, like, two different streets or something, and some of the intersections here… I pray to God I'm never first because I would have no idea where to turn."

I chuckled. "You're used to living in a city on a grid."

"Yes, I am."

"Yeah, no," I teased before getting out of the car.

We were there to check on Ernesto Ramirez. He was placed in witness protection after he saw his father, an elementary school science teacher, killed in Tucson, Arizona. The reason Ernesto was taken into WITSEC and not simply foster care was who pulled the trigger. Troy Littlefield was a hedge fund manager supposedly lost at sea two years prior after an accident on his yacht. Ernesto's father, Manuel, knew—everyone did—that the story had been splashed all over the internet, so when he recognized Littlefield, he snapped a picture and ran. Unfortunately Littlefield was not alone. His men caught Manuel, and Littlefield shot him, only realizing the little boy was there when Ernesto gasped. But it wasn't as easy for the men to catch a speedy, skinny eleven-year-old, and Ernesto got away by running straight to the police. That was a year ago, and the trial was still being scheduled, so Ernesto was in our system.

As I stood with Redeker outside the door, I took a quick breath, terrified of what we were going to see.

"Good morning," a woman greeted me cheerfully through the opening the chain would allow. "May I help you?"

We both lifted our credentials so she could see them, along with the stars hanging from chains around our necks.

"I'm Deputy US Marshal Miro Jones, and this is Deputy US Marshal Josiah Redeker. Are you Monalisa Verone?"

"I am," she said sweetly, closing the door to take the chain off and then opening the door wide.

The aroma tumbled out of the hall as she stood in her doorway, and I whined. I tried to stop it, but whatever it was smelled incredible. My stomach growled at the same time. It must have sounded pitiful.

Redeker looked at me like I'd grown another head.

She chuckled. "Come in and have some empanadas, Marshal, before you pass out."

She introduced her mother, Conchita, who was cooking and appeared very pleased to see us. The only person happier to see us was Ernesto. He shook our hands as I sat beside him at the small kitchen table.

"That woman was so mean to me, Miro," he said, using my name as I directed him to. "And she never paid Mrs. Verone, and it's really hard for her to get all of us stuff for school if she only uses what—"

"Wait," I stopped him. "Go back to the not paying Mrs. Verone."

He nodded quickly. "She always said that the paperwork was lost and needed to be refiled."

"Ma'am," I said, "are you receiving the appropriate subsidy payments for Ernesto being here?"

Monalisa waved her hand. "Don't worry about it, Marshal, I—"

"I'm worried about it," I told her. "You're supposed to be compen—"

She grabbed my hand so fast it startled me, and she squeezed it. "Mrs. Cullen told me that if I pushed about the money, she would remove Ernesto from our home, and I—"

"No," I assured her. "I won't move him, and I will get you what's owed, and whatever is back-owed. Do you have paperwork for me?"

Monalisa's mouth fell open.

"*Mija*," Conchita snapped. "Go get the nice man the paperwork that you filled out over and over so he can get you some money and some health insurance."

Oh shit. "Not that either?" I asked Conchita.

"Not yet," she said, pinning me with a pointed stare.

Redeker snorted. "Tell me who to call, Jones."

When Tori Macin from DCFS got to the apartment, the harried-looking social worker was stunned to find I had already scanned and sent paperwork out to her office.

"So you—you just took it upon yourself to do that?"

I squinted at her as Conchita passed her an empanada.

"Thank you so much," Macin said quickly before turning back to me.

"Have you worked with the marshals service before?"

"I have," she told me, "but only with Sebreta Cullen," she amended. "And I will say that that was only in her office. She never came out in the field."

I grunted.

"So you're saying that this is how fast this is *supposed* to work?"

"The marshals are a government agency," I reminded her. "And so we're at the mercy of the same bureaucratic red tape bullcrap that you are, but these are federal witnesses as well as children, so they go to the top of the list."

She glanced over the paperwork I submitted. "How are you getting health care for the entire family?"

"It's considered an environmental standard," I explained. I'd been doing WITSEC intake paperwork for years. I knew how to work the system and in fact knew a few loopholes the others didn't. I couldn't count the times I'd been asked how to do something where benefits were concerned. I was especially vigilant about allowances for kids. "You cannot place a single witness into an environment where anything is out of the ordinary for said witness. So if he has full insurance, then the rest of the family must as well."

"Wow" was all Macin could manage.

"If you put him in a home where everyone had to get around by car because the distance to school was too great, then we'd get him a car. Ernesto cannot stand out to anyone for any reason. Do you understand?"

"I do now," she said, the awe clear in her voice and on her face as she stared at me. "It's amazing what can get done when you have the right people in position."

"I think—oh," I said, laughing, having been startled by Monalisa and Conchita grabbing me at the same time.

"I can quit the second job," Monalisa sighed happily. "Thank you, Marshal."

"Let's do some direct deposit paperwork now," I said, taking my third empanada and handing Redeker his second.

By the time we left half an hour later, Monalisa had the first payment for Ernesto's care in her bank account and temporary health insurance cards on her phone. As she hugged me, I told her the real ones would be mailed. It was a good start for the morning.

Unfortunately Redeker and Macin and I were in for a frightening status check in the next home out in Skokie. Kendra Paulson's foster parents hadn't seen her for a week, and they hadn't reported it because they were certain she just ran away as, Mrs. Paulson said, "girls like her do."

"What kind of girls are those?" Macin asked her pointedly.

"Like you," Mrs. Paulson spat. "Black."

Macin pulled out her phone.

"What are you doing?" I asked.

"I'm calling the police, Jones," she explained, visibly annoyed at my question.

"You don't need to do that."

She opened her mouth to protest but stopped as Redeker pulled out his cuffs.

"We're full-service ride-along," I informed her.

Her face brightened as Redeker cuffed Mr. and Mrs. Paulson before he called the office and got ahold of Sharpe.

"Is this legal?" Mrs. Paulson asked.

"Yes, ma'am," Redeker told her snidely. "You get arrested for neglect of a minor in the great state of Illinois. Now where is Kendra's room?"

She appeared utterly flummoxed, and her husband was too drunk to have any idea what was going on.

Kendra's room had a broken window, mouse and roach traps on the ground, and no radiator. I could only imagine how cold it got in there in the dead of winter. While Redeker and Macin remained with the Paulsons, I searched the room. I checked the ceiling, behind the pipes, but found nothing. And then it hit me, and I walked back out the living room.

"Did the school call you?"

"What?" Mrs. Paulson snarled.

"Did the school call you?" I asked again, enunciating each word.

"No, why the fuck would they do that?"

I looked at Macin. "Let's go. Redeker will stay here and wait for Skokie PD, and then he can join us at... lemme look," I said, opening the binder I'd carried in with me.

"Denning," Macin offered. "The school is Denning."

"Is it close?"

"Fifteen minutes away," she informed me.

We were out the door in seconds.

THE SCHOOL had no idea there was an issue because Kendra had not missed a day. When we pulled her out of class to talk to her, I saw a bruise on her jaw.

"Is that from Mr. Paulson, or Mrs.?"

Stunned, she stared at me like I was speaking Greek.

"Kendra?"

"Mr. Paulson," she answered quickly.

I saw Macin make a note of that.

Kendra was tall for her age, with big brown eyes, expressive dark eyebrows, and a silver nose ring. Her afro had natural highlights in it, and I liked the sprinkle of freckles across her nose.

Quick clearing of her throat before she checked my face, as though making sure I was for real. "So what, you took over for Mrs. Cullen?"

"Yeah."

"You're the new her."

"Well, I'm me, but yes."

She coughed. "And you'll believe me when I tell you that the Paulsons are terrible, awful people?" She was testing my resolve, sounding bored, but the way she was chewing on her bottom lip gave her away.

"I will," I replied implacably.

She was startled and uncrossed her arms before sitting up in her chair. "No shit?"

"No shit."

"And you?" she grilled Macin.

"I believe you too," she assured her.

Kendra looked back and forth between us. "Where've you all been?"

"I'm sorry," I apologized. "We were late. It won't happen again."

She nodded. "This is a mindfuck, man."

"I suspect it is."

She grunted. "Okay, so I've been living with my girlfriend Robyn and her family, and they said I could stay for as long as I like."

"Oh yeah?" I asked.

"Yeah. They really like me. I'm a good influence on her."

Macin had questions, but I cut her off. "What if you guys break up?"

"Nah, man. This is the real deal. Some people still find their soul mates in high school, no matter what you see on TV. Don't be so jaded."

"Really?"

A second grunt from her.

"Listen, I'm not arguing with you, what do I know?" I said, getting up. "Let's go talk to your soul mate's mother."

"Was that sarcasm?"

"Surely not."

And her smile, from nothing to brilliant, was a joy to see.

"Okay, Miro Jones, let's go."

MACIN DIDN'T like it. I explained to her I didn't care. Kendra liked it, and after losing her folks and being let down by the marshals' office, I was ready to go on faith.

Redeker caught up with Macin and me an hour later at the home of Melinda Shelby, who had a very big house and who was very, very excited to have Kendra come live permanently with she and her husband, their daughter Robyn, and her other two sons. She was crying as she held on to my arm.

"You don't understand. Last year before Robyn came out to us, she was so scared, and there were drugs, and she almost flunked out of school, and we were fighting all the time, and we—we thought we were going to lose her. I thought, this is how my family ends, you know? But then over the summer, it's suddenly all about Kendra and how she's a lesbian too, and can we still love her, and—I mean, of course we love her, why in the world would her sexual orientation matter?"

"Good job, Mom," I said, patting her on the shoulder.

"And this is crazy," she continued, smiling, "but Kendra and my husband—two peas in a pod. They both like to fish and play *Call of Duty* and make crepes and garden…. I mean, those horrible people she was living with, they have no idea what a sweet girl they have there."

I nodded.

"So yes, please, whatever I need to do to sign up to be her foster mother, let's make that happen as soon as possible."

Macin was pleased after that.

The next three were close: one in Des Plaines, one in Parkridge, and then one in Harwood Heights. Two of the kids were doing well and, while happy to meet me, were in good homes, while the third, Jason Knowles, was not where he was supposed to be.

After Kendra, our routine was to go directly to the school and pull the kids out of class. It was better than waiting to see them at home, and we got honest answers. When Jason was not in school, we went to his house.

When I knocked, a woman came to the door but only opened it a crack. I didn't get the delicious aroma of wafting food like at Ernesto's home; instead I got vomit and sweat. Her right eye looked fearful, and she was clearly trembling. I shifted the folder to my left hand and lifted my badge for her to see. The credentials wouldn't get the door open, but the star would.

"Ma'am, I'm Deputy US Marshal Miro Jones, and this is my partner, Deputy US Marshal Josiah Redeker. May we come in, please?"

She took a heaving breath and then lifted her finger to her lips, asking for silence.

I nodded quickly.

So carefully, so quietly, she closed the door just enough to remove the chain and then slowly opened it back up.

The living room was right there, and it was strewn with clothes, smashed dishes, food, empty beer bottles, and vomit. It wasn't the room that made my stomach turn, though, but the woman herself. Standing there in only a tank top and panties, she was battered and bruised, her lip and nose bleeding, her left eye swollen on the way to closing. Finger-shaped bruises dotted her throat and, as I looked down her body, her thighs. Redeker turned to the coats hanging next to the door, grabbed a long sweater, and passed it to me. I held it up, and she turned around and let me help her put it on. It was difficult—I could tell her left arm was broken.

"Where is he?" I whispered.

"In the bedroom," she whispered back.

"Is he armed?"

She nodded.

"Is Jason home?"

A tremor ran through her, and she took a shuddering breath. "No. I made him take my little girl to school on the bus this morning because I needed to get them out of the house."

I nodded, watching as she winced just standing there. "Did he rape you?"

Quick nod.

Turning to Macin, I tipped my head toward the door.

Quickly she took the woman's good arm and led her away.

"He's big," she told me before allowing Macin to move her.

"Oh, I hope he's stupid enough to fight," Redeker growled as the two of us drew our guns and headed toward the bedroom.

What the man was, was drunk. Very drunk. Sawing-logs-on-the-bed drunk. Blood streaked the sheets. Redeker went to the bathroom, grabbed toilet paper, took the gun out of the man's hand, and stood with it by the door as I got on my phone and called it in.

He was probably only about six feet tall, but since the woman he'd beaten up was all of five feet, he seemed "big" to her. Redeker was bigger, and both of us had quite a bit of muscle on him, but he was beefy compared to his tiny, delicate wife.

We stood there, watching him sleep naked in the middle of the bed. I noted the blood on his upper thigh, knowing it wasn't his.

"I bet you if I punched him in the gut, he'd barf, and then we could watch him choke on it," Redeker suggested darkly.

"True," I agreed, hearing the sirens wail in the distance. "That would be fitting since this seems so anticlimactic."

"I bet you the wife knows he's coming home drunk, been out all night doing God knows what, so she gets the kids out of the house, makes him breakfast to try and placate the fucker, and then he comes in, maybe even eats for a bit, then beats the shit outta her, makes her hurl up her food, and then rapes her."

I turned to him, wincing, sad to hear him so easily make assumptions about what went on. There was only one way people knew those kinds of things: experience. "You sound like you know this scenario."

He shrugged. "My old man, he was like this, except my mom left me and my sister alone to fend for ourselves."

I cleared my throat. "You protected your sister, huh?"

"Oh hell yeah."

"Were you in foster care?"

"No. My dad had a sister, and one weekend she drove up in her red Firebird, packed up me and my sister, put us in the car, and drove clear to her ranch in Wyoming."

"How old were you?"

"I was five. Lisa was four."

"I like this aunt."

"So did we. She was our angel."

"She still alive?"

"No. Cancer."

"I'm sorry."

He nodded.

Moments later I heard movement in the living room, and then CPD came through the door—six uniformed officers, all looking grim, obviously having seen the woman in the hall.

Redeker and I walked out as we heard an outraged yell.

"I really wanted to shoot him," Redeker grumbled.

"Me too."

MACIN HAD no idea in the world how Eric Durant and his wife, Carmen, had qualified to be foster parents. Carmen wasn't a problem, but Eric had a record of battery, more than a few drunk-and-disorderly citations, and my favorite: mob fighting. I hadn't come across that one in a while.

We sent Carmen to the hospital, and right about the time she left in the ambulance, Jason came running down the street, clearly in a rush to get up to the apartment.

"Jason," I called.

He pivoted to face me, and I saw the panic on his face.

"She's on her way to the hospital," I informed him. "We're going there too. Do you want to ride with us?"

He bolted over to me and reached for my hand when I offered it.

"I'm Miro Jones, and I'm from the marshals' office, and we need to talk so we can figure out what you want to do."

He took a breath. "I want Carmen and her daughter, Anaj, to be safe."

"They will be."

"Are you sure?" He sounded scared. "Can you promise that?"

Could I? I had no power over Carmen and her daughter's situation, only Jason's. "I can promise that Mr. Durant is going to jail."

"Because of the gun, right?"

"Yes."

He cleared his throat. "My dad was a lawyer, and he said that using a gun to coerce someone else is a serious charge."

"Coerce, huh?"

He smiled just slightly. "I remember all the words he used."

"You wanna be a lawyer like your dad?"

"I do, yeah."

"Good. That's real good."

He exhaled long and loud.

"Jason?"

"Yes, Marshal?"

"Do you want to live with Mrs. Durant and her daughter?"

No answer.

"It's okay, yanno," I assured him. "No one's gonna be mad at you, especially Mrs. Durant. I can tell you've been a big help to them."

"She always makes sure the two of us are safe, but it's like—I mean, he's like a bomb, and I just… I'm not—"

The kid never knew when an eruption was coming. He was forever living on borrowed time. It had to be terrifying for him.

He shook his head, biting his lip like he was embarrassed.

"It's okay," I soothed him. "I promise you Mrs. Durant and her daughter are not your responsibility."

Tears welled up in his eyes, and I slid an arm around his shoulders. It took a moment, and then I had a sixteen-year-old boy sobbing all over me.

"My mom always said that it was our responsibility to take care of people who didn't have all the blessings we had."

His parents were killed in what was made to look like a home invasion but was really his father's close friend and business partner, Charlton Stewart. Apparently he'd been skimming from their employees' retirement fund and from their clients, and Jason's father was a day away from finding out the truth. It would have been the perfect crime, but Jason came home early, saw his godfather, and fled. The people Stewart was giving the money to were not happy, and thus, WITSEC for Jason.

When Jason turned twenty-one, he had a hefty trust fund coming his way, but nothing, even the death of his parents, could change that he had to wait. It ended up lucky for him, though, with all the people who came after Stewart, and in turn Jason's parents' estate, to recoup their stolen money. The estate was picked clean but for the trust fund. I couldn't imagine what it was like for Jason to go from private schools and country clubs to the inner city. Cullen, of course, saw a black boy and nothing else. She never considered for a moment how new and different the transition had to have been for him.

"Marshal?"

"Yes?" I said softly, rubbing circles on his back as his face stayed down on my shoulder, his arms wrapped around my waist.

"Can I go live somewhere else?"

"Yes, you most certainly can," I sighed. "Let's go upstairs and collect your things, all right?"

He cleared his throat as he leaned back to peer up at my face. "You're sure it's okay? Mrs. Durant won't think I abandoned her?"

"No, buddy, I promise she won't."

He shuddered, and I could see he was relieved. "Maybe, uhm.... I've been staying at my friend Mark's house a lot, and his mom said I could visit any time."

"Where do they live?"

"In La Grange," he told me. "I met him when he came to my school for a science fair."

I nodded, and he smiled sheepishly.

"We're both big nerds."

"Nothing wrong with that," I assured him. "Let's go upstairs and get your stuff."

He was more than ready to do that.

MRS. APRIL Takashima, Mark's mom, was very excited about the idea of keeping Jason. Her husband, a high school science teacher at a Montessori school in the area, was also thrilled by the prospect. And their oldest had just left for Yale, so they even had a bedroom open. The money for taking him in would be welcome, but more importantly, Jason was an excellent influence on Mark, who was, April told me, a bit of flibbertigibbet.

I nodded because she was very serious when she said it. Like not being able to focus was the worst thing she could think of.

As Redeker, Macin, and I walked down the long row of stairs that led from the Takashimas' front door to the sidewalk, Macin explained it didn't work like this.

"Whatzat?" I asked, rounding on her at the bottom.

"This doesn't just happen," she blurted, and I wasn't sure if she was excited or irritated. It sounded like a bit of both. "You don't just snap your fingers and abracadabra, new life."

I was confused. "But that's exactly what WITSEC does."

She shook her head.

"You lost me."

"You don't move kids in one day! You don't trust people you haven't vetted to enroll kids in school, to just take them in and—who *are* you?"

"This is Custodial WITSEC," I explained. "I have the authority to make any decisions I deem appropriate for the continued safety of my witnesses."

"Well, yes, but—"

"This is all within the scope of the marshals service," Redeker reminded her.

"I know that, but—"

"I don't understand, then," I said.

She gestured at me. "You don't just *poof* foster parents into being."

"What?"

"The Takashimas," she explained. "It should take months to decide if they are a suitable fit for Jason. We have to run background checks and financials and—"

"We did all that," I apprised her. "You saw me and Redeker on the phone."

"I know! How the hell do you guys have access to someone's whole life that fast?"

I looked at Redeker, who only shrugged before returning my focus to her. "We're United States marshals, ma'am. We don't wait for anything."

She just stood there shaking her head in disbelief.

"We all missed lunch," I announced into the silence. "I think we should have a late one. Who's with me?"

"I saw an Indian place," Redeker chimed in. "How's that sound?"

She looked back and forth between us. "Things don't happen this fast."

"You keep saying that," I apprised her. "But in my world," I said, hand over my heart, "in his," I continued, placing my hand on Redeker's shoulder, "they do. They always have."

"Maybe in other areas, but not where kids are concerned."

"I don't see the difference."

"I know you don't, but you should because sooner or later you're going to bump up against a situation you can't wave your magic wand over."

I scoffed at her.

"Marshal, I promise you, there are not fixes like this in the real world."

"We're not Child and Family Services," I reminded her. "You get that, right?"

"I do. Of course I do. But you're still a government agency!" she maintained, willing me to understand the point she was trying to make, which I suspected was that there were miles and miles of red tape I was skirting.

"We are, and normally we move slower too, but this is witness protection," I clarified, "and we don't work through regular channels for that. We don't have to."

"We move fast," Redeker said, giving her his lazy cowboy grin. "I mean, it's life-and-death, after all. You can't dick around with people's lives, especially kids'."

She still looked like she was at a loss.

"C'mon, Indian food, my treat," Redeker said, taking her arm gently and leading her to her car. He drove her car—she was that out of it—and I followed in the Ford.

Kama Bistro was on South La Grange Road, and once we were inside, Macin took a breath and calmed down.

"I just had no idea that kids could be rescued like that," she conceded. "I've been a social worker for three years, and I've not seen anything like what I've seen today."

"I don't know what to tell you. That's what has to happen in WITSEC. We make quick decisions and hope they're right. It doesn't mean we always make the best ones," I amended. "But that's why we check and double-check and triple-check to make sure that everything we think we did correctly actually stays that way."

She nodded.

"Eat, you'll feel better," I said, smiling.

"No," she protested, "you misunderstand me. I'm not upset or—I'm just going to get spoiled if I keep working with you. I'll want it to work like this for all the kids, not just the ones in WITSEC."

"It should work like that, and I wish it did. But it takes vigilance, right?"

"It does."

"We're not perfect. Look at Cullen. Kids died on her watch. We have one in the morgue right now that we're trying to get to the bottom of. Sadly everything that happens with kids in the foster care system is only as good as the people administering those services."

"It takes a village and all that," Redeker said, smiling up at our server as she approached the table.

After we got our drinks and the appetizers came out, masala fries and chicken lemon tadka, Redeker asked her where we were off to next. Macin just put her head in her hand and looked at him.

"What?"

"I'll go anywhere with you guys."

It was nice to hear.

CHAPTER 8

WE WERE on our way to see a kid who lived in Brookfield when Kage called and ordered me and Redeker back to the office. We waited with Macin until Ryan and Dorsey showed up, taking over for me just for the rest of the day.

I watched Macin's gaze roam over Mike Ryan from head to toe as he closed in on us. I thought she might like hanging out with Ryan better than me and Redeker. Though if I thought about it, I wasn't sure Redeker wouldn't be interested in her. Just because I knew Callahan was into him—and really, he into Callahan—didn't mean Redeker couldn't also be interested in Macin. What was clear, however, was Mike Ryan was her idea of pretty.

"So are you two going to be changing the lives of kids today too?" she asked Dorsey, tearing her eyes away from Ryan with difficulty.

"Well, yeah," Dorsey assured her. "We're marshals, ma'am. We can do whatever we want to keep a witness safe."

She rolled her eyes, and he shot me a look.

"She's not used to things getting done so fast."

"Ah," he said like that explained everything.

It took an hour to get back to the office in traffic, and while Redeker tried to find a station he liked—not being into the hard rock Ian was—I called the man I loved.

"You all right?" Ian answered on the second ring, sounding frantic, voice higher than normal.

"Can you stop asking me that?" I teased. "I just wanted to hear how you're doing."

"I'm fine," he said dismissively. "Tell me how you are."

"Well, Redeker and I have officially freaked out the nice social worker."

"Why? What'd you do?" It sounded like he was afraid of the answer.

"Apparently the marshals service moves a little quicker than Child Protective Services."

A moment of silence. "Well, yeah, I would think so. It's life-and-death with us."

"Yeah, but it is with CPS too."

"And I know that," he agreed, "but with vigilance on the part of the social workers and decent foster families, a lot of those kids will make it out of the system in one piece, right?"

"Taking into consideration those two factors—yeah," I allowed.

"But with Custodial you're talking about kids being hunted and killed if the person they're testifying against gets ahold of them."

"Right," I obliged, "and that's the part that the social worker riding along with me and Redeker has never seen in action."

"Got it."

I coughed softly. "You know, I'm doing pretty well today."

"Why do you sound surprised? You're great with kids," he said, defending me.

I smiled into the phone. We argued all morning, back and forth, and then simple statements like that told me exactly what Ian's true feelings were about my capabilities. He'd have me sighing like some schmuck in a rom-com if I wasn't careful.

"I *am* good with kids, but I can see the difference between this being my job and what the commitment to being a parent is."

"You're beating a dead horse here, you know that."

Perhaps, but I needed Ian to hear it, that I knew what I could truly do. "So off topic: guess who had homemade empanadas today?"

"What?"

I cackled.

"Empanadas?" he whined. They were one of his absolute favorites and hard to find—the ones he truly loved, not greasy, not super flaky, just the perfect in-between.

"I might have eaten a few."

"And you, what, didn't snag me one?"

"Didn't wanna be a glutton," I taunted.

"You know I was worried about you, you dick."

He still was, but it was good to laugh, even though he hung up on me.

"I dunno if your relationship with your husband is all that healthy," Redeker said after a few minutes of silence.

But it so very much was.

IT WAS after four when we made it upstairs to the bullpen. I was surprised by all the suits there, and Becker crossed the room to me with Adair and three others in tow. He excused Redeker, told him to check in with Ian on the other side of the room for his partner assignment, and then turned to me as the men clustered around.

"We're in the conference room, Jones."

I nodded, looked around him for Ian, who gestured me over to him.

"One sec, I'll meet you in there," I told him, brushing by the others to follow Redeker over to Ian.

"I'll be right with you," Ian said to Redeker as he took hold of my bicep and led me a few feet away. "You still doing all right?"

"I am. Like I said, it's been busy but good."

"Yeah?"

"Yeah, I mean, we got some kids moved out of some bad situations, saw some others that were fine. All in all, for a first day, I'll take it." I grinned.

He smiled back, lifted his hand like he was going to touch my cheek, but remembered where he was and lowered it. "Mine's been… different."

I snorted.

"Hey," he said, glaring. "I'm a billion times more patient than I thought I was."

"Oh?"

"You have no idea."

I took hold of the lapel of his suit jacket. "You're coming to the conference room?"

"I will. I'll be right there."

I nodded and then turned to rejoin Becker and the others.

Kage was standing by the whiteboard at the front of the room when I walked in, and he pointed at a seat at the end of the table across from three empty places. When I sat and Adair tried to take the seat beside me, Kage told him to take the next one down. Two others tried, but Kage kept it open for Ian, who was the next to last one in the room. He moved quickly, crossing the room, moving the chair closer to me, bumping my knee with his as he sat. There were twenty people in the room when Becker held the door open for one last man, then came in and closed the door behind them.

"Everyone," Kage began, "this is Andrew Ryerson, assistant director of the Criminal, Cyber, Response, and Services Branch of the FBI."

Ryerson moved to the front of the room beside Kage and stood there looking over all of us before he turned his attention on me. He was a handsome man, I was guessing midfifties, with traces of gray in his hair—less than Kage, who had lots of silver streaks in his hair now but somehow made that look good: fatherly, debonair, and classic. Ryerson had a thin, drawn, pinched face with no laugh lines. His suit was immaculate, it fit perfectly, and he looked like he belonged on a magazine cover, not in front of a room full of rumpled men who'd worked all day. Kage was the only one who looked just as good, though standing up there next to him, Ryerson looked almost fragile.

"Marshal Jones," Ryerson addressed me.

"Sir."

"I'm going to be frank with you, Jones, and skip all the jargon and the posturing because I'd like us to all get to the heart of the matter as quickly as possible," he said, voice strained, clearly exhausted but still professional. "Is that acceptable?"

"Yessir."

He took a breath. "This morning it was made painfully clear to us that Special Agent Cillian Wojno was not the only leak in our office connected to the escaped felon Craig Hartley," he explained gravely. "After only a cursory look into profiler Kol Kelson's personal correspondence, it appears that he's been communicating with Hartley since he escaped from federal custody before you were taken two years ago."

I never stood a chance. The thought threatened to drown me.

Hartley was brilliant all by himself, and on top of that, he'd had not one but two corrupt federal agents working for him. The deck had been stacked against me from the beginning, and the worst part was he wasn't paying either of them.

Wojno was dead, killed by the man who had blackmailed him into service.

Kelson was still a mystery. I had no idea if some sin he'd committed had ruined him and put him in Hartley's path, like had happened with Wojno, or if he had been willingly seduced to the darkness. Either way, the FBI, which should have had a hand in protecting me, had done the exact opposite. I was used to it at this point, to their failings, but it didn't make the admission any better.

"Through Kelson, Hartley was given direct access to FBI databases containing private information such as your home address and—"

Ian scoffed loudly.

"Doyle," Kage warned.

"Stop," I muttered.

"Sir," Ian replied to Kage, his voice a mixture of consternation and a sharp, serrated edge. Anyone who knew him at all could tell how disgusted and furious he was.

Kage answered with a scowl because he was, I knew, angry. But in a different way, not protective and possessive as Ian was. His feelings about Hartley and the FBI were more righteous indignation than the simmering fury Ian had been holding on to since last November.

"Is there an issue I'm not aware of?" Ryerson asked sharply.

"No, sir," I answered before Ian could.

"Yes, sir," Ian nearly snarled, not caring in the least that I was trying to build a bridge, not burn one down.

"And what is that, Marshal?" he challenged Ian.

"Well, I just wanted you to know that we are well aware that Craig Hartley knows where we live since he was just fuckin' there!"

Ryerson processed that in silence before he turned back to Ian. "I'm sorry?"

I cleared my throat so Ryerson would focus on me and took that opportunity to lean on Ian. He needed to feel how close I was, the warmth of my body, the reassurance I was right there. We didn't talk about it, but between what we had been going through with Ian being deployed all the time and Hartley popping up out of the clear blue sky multiple times, we had been on the verge of walking away from everything. But Ian had decided I was the most important thing in his life, and Hartley and I were on a new path that did not, I was fairly certain, include me being dissected, even if I inadvertently tumbled into a trap.

"Marshal?" Ryerson barked.

"Craig Hartley was just in my house last November," I explained clinically, not letting him hear what that encounter had done to me. "So there's not a question of *if* he knows where I live—he absolutely does."

The FBI guys in the room made startled noises, sounding scared, maybe even sick, as did the new marshals in our group. And I understood. I probably would have been freaked out too, hearing the news for the first time that a serial killer visited my colleague. If it could happen to me, maybe it could also happen to them. It had to be sobering, terrifying to think about.

"Perhaps you didn't have time to read Jones's file on the flight in," Kage suggested, his voice rising over the others, his arms crossed, looking at Ryerson like he was a total tool.

"No, I—" He gestured at Adair, who was sitting on the other side of Ian. "Please."

"Bottom line is," Adair began, leaning forward in his chair so he could see me around Ian. "We need to take you into protective custody, Jones. It's become an issue of—"

"No," I told him flatly. "We already tried protective custody, and it didn't make a bit of difference. Hartley knows everything about me, from the fact that I got married four months ago to the fact that he's the one who saved my dog."

"He did what?" Ryerson asked, floundering, looking as flummoxed as the other members of his team and the newbie marshals. Again, I understood. Hartley was a psychopath, and yet he kept my dog alive? What in the world was going on? "The hell are you talking about, Jones?"

"My dog was shot, and Hartley saved him," I answered, bumping Ian before leaning away from him. "So I have to say that if he wanted me dead, I would be. You should really focus your efforts on somebody else."

Ryerson blurted, "But we cannot guarantee your safety if—"

"I don't need my safety guaranteed," I told him. "He won't hurt me."

"You can't know what—"

"Ask Kelson," I argued. "He'll tell you."

"He's not speaking."

"Then bring him in here, and I'll ask him. He'll talk to me."

"And how the hell do you know that?"

I exhaled deeply. "He's got a hard-on for Hartley, and I don't know why, but he does. You all think that was Hartley this morning in that gallery, and I think you're wrong. I don't think any of that was Hartley's doing, but I have no idea what's going on with your boy."

"He's not our—"

"Just—no one knows Hartley better than me, so Kelson will want to talk to me."

Ryerson studied my face for a moment, checking to see if he was looking at resolve or just bravado, but he must have decided I wasn't full of shit because he turned to a couple of his men and commanded them to bring Kelson into the briefing room.

Minutes later Kelson was brought in, in cuffs, Rodriguez and Brodie flanking him, and they put him in the chair across from me between the two of them.

All eyes were on the disgraced profiler as he stared at me, his eyes that same flat, cold lifelessness as before.

"Go ahead," Ryerson directed.

"So," I said to Kelson, "they think Hartley wants to hurt me. I say no. What do you say?"

The silence went on for several moments before Ryerson began speaking.

"I told you, Jones, he—"

"No," Kelson agreed, cutting off his former boss. "Craig Hartley would try and take you, but not hurt you. That's why the gesture today."

I nodded, leaning forward in my chair. "You would've been in trouble if you killed me."

"Yes. He would have had me killed if I'd succeeded." And for the first time, I saw actual fear on his face, the worry in the twist of his mouth, the furrow of his brows.

"He never has to know," I said with a slight smile, whispering the last conspiratorially. I needed him on my side so he'd talk to me. This was the only in I had.

He had sounded sad, dead, but suddenly he snapped his head up, and a light infused his face. "You won't tell him?"

"Well, I hope *not* to talk to him soon, but no, I won't tell him."

"Thank you," he said breathily, clearly overwhelmed.

I shrugged. "And you know, even if he reads it on some secure email, he won't believe any other report but mine."

"That's true." His smile was really beautiful. "I—you're being very kind to me."

"Why shouldn't I? We're two of a kind, aren't we?"

He nodded.

"We both know Hartley well."

"Yes," Kelson agreed, sounding hopeful.

"There's not too many of us."

He leaned forward.

"I mean, how many more of us could there be?"

"You might be surprised."

"Would I?" I asked as though unconvinced, digging gently, not wanting him to notice me trying to excavate the truth.

He nodded, hands on the table, doing the same thing Hartley used to when I visited him in jail, straining to get closer.

"Hartley can't have that many acolytes."

"Not like us," he advised me, lumping us together. "But he has more friends in the Bureau. He's very seductive."

Gasps from all over the room.

"Do you know who?"

"Some, not all. I'm thinking that if I need some leverage down the road, pulling another name out of my hat will be a good thing."

"That's smart," I told him, nodding, then cleared my throat. "Did you kill those guys, or did you have someone else do it?"

He looked surprised, shocked, but even in such a short time, from this morning to now, I was getting a feel for him, and the camaraderie I had going worked for him just as it had, in a way, on Hartley.

"Come on," I prodded. "I'm thinking you had help."

He smiled slowly, the façade of disbelief stripped from his features as he smirked. "I did have help. I have guys on my payroll, just like he does."

I nodded. "Nice."

"He thinks I'm so helpless, but I'm not."

"No, you're definitely not."

Kelson puffed up, pleased with himself and me. "How did you know?"

"That it wasn't Hartley?"

His eyes were sparkling with excitement as he nodded.

I smiled at him, tipping my head. "It's not really him, right? The whole heart-in-hands thing is much more poetic. It was truly artistic."

"It was, wasn't it," he sighed happily. "He was right about you, Marshal. You do see things so very clearly."

"I try," I said, moving my hand, reaching for his.

He grabbed me quickly, and Ian shifted beside me, hand on my thigh under the table, gripping hard, nervous suddenly, not liking what I was doing.

Kelson clutched at my hand, covering our joined ones with his other as he searched my face. "This is the scary part now."

"I know," I soothed. "You did all that to create a diversion, right? You know your team has to run those guys down, see where they were, find out the stories, and while they're doing that, then you had time to do something else."

"Yes."

"It was a diversion," I said confidently.

"How did you know?"

There was a collective breath held in the room, and I could hear it and feel it even without the benefit of turning to look.

"What did you do?"

"Not me."

"No," I agreed, "because you were here with us. But you put something in play, had your men moving around the chessboard at your direction."

The honey-colored eyes got big and wide, and his mouth dropped open. "You are very good at this, Marshal."

"I've had lots of practice."

"Yes. He said you play the game well."

"But this isn't his game. It's yours."

Quick flashing smile as he squeezed my hand in his. "Yes."

"And you're sick of someone."

"I am."

"Someone you hate?"

He nodded.

"Who's been bugging you?" I said, looking up at Ryerson. "A thorn in your side."

Kelson gasped. "Oh my God, how did you know it was Ryerson?"

"You report to him, and you hate it."

"I do."

"Because you're so much smarter than him."

He nodded hard. "I am."

"But he's been there in your way this whole time."

"He certainly has."

I thought a moment, reached out to pat his hand, and then slipped from his grasp, leaning back to study him. "You lied about the names. There's no more guys in the Bureau reporting to Hartley. You would never let that happen."

Kelson clapped his hands. "Oh my God, Marshal, you are brilliant."

"You're not playing the long game for a reduced sentence; this is a short one because you want the hell out of here."

"Yes," he agreed. "Exactly."

"You want to be with Hartley, but you had to do something to prove your loyalty, and in the process, also punish your boss, show him up for being stupid. Show everyone what went on right under his nose."

His eyes were glazed over; he looked drunk. "Yes. All of that."

"So you did what he couldn't," I went on, feeling Ian slide his hand off my leg as he pressed his shoulder against mine. He needed the closeness, and so did I. Just watching Kelson happily go insane in front of me was frightening. How people so lost themselves in jealousy and hatred, or in his case, madness, was ultimately so very sad. "With your men, with Hartley's contacts, you got three of the most wanted and killed them."

Kelson beamed at me.

"You showed up your boss, impressed Hartley, and used the diversion from this morning to do what?" I asked solemnly. "What was your plan this morning?"

"Punishment," he said robotically.

"Punish who? Your boss?"

He didn't answer, but he didn't have to. It clicked in my head, and I turned to look at Ryerson, who was sitting there shell-shocked after all he'd heard in the last five minutes. It had to be hard to find out a colleague, someone you saw every day, harbored such anger, such hatred for you.

"Sir," I said softly, "where is your family?"

He blanched.

Ian was out of his chair, heading for the door. Kage grabbed Ryerson's arm and hauled him after Ian. The room emptied in a blur, and Rodriguez and Brodie went as well, which surprised me, but they were new.

I knew why Ian and Becker and Kage had left. It was their job, and there was coordinating to do. Everyone else, they were just scrambling, and it left me and Kelson alone.

"Who did you take?"

"His wife," he answered.

"Why would you take her?" I asked, aware that we were alone but not afraid even for a moment. Kelson could hurt me if he had a gun or if he surprised me. Since neither was an option, I was good.

"Because *he* took women."

He meant Hartley. "But he seduced them. Is that what you did?"

Suddenly he could not hold my gaze.

"We both know you didn't," I baited him. "You don't have his charm."

"How do you know?" Kelson spat, the anger flaring fast.

"Because you're not using any on me," I advised, staring holes through him.

Hartley never missed an opportunity to try to seduce me—not sexually, never that, but instead to his side, to stand with him, to go with him, to be his man. I had no doubt that, even more than Hartley wanted to hurt me, he wanted me to simply be his to call. At the same time, the second I gave in, he'd value me less for being weak enough to be spellbound.

It was a fine line. How many people enjoyed the hunt, the chase, but lost interest once their quarry gave in? How many people liked the bad boys or girls, the ones who didn't care, but as soon as they had an epiphany and fell in love, suddenly they seemed weak and unappealing? For Hartley, people were like that. The second they gave in to him, he was done with them, which was when he changed them from women into art. He'd told me once that in death, he restored their beauty and grace, and even though he still showed what they had done, what kind of people they truly were, he still made them *more* than they were. The fact that I had never been bespelled by him did more to ensure my survival than anything else.

"You think I couldn't have had you?" Kelson dared me.

"That's exactly what I think."

"And Hartley could?"

"I've never known Hartley to use his charm on men," I pointed out. "Have you?"

He shook his head. "But he's not so good either."

"In what way?"

"I—the women he took were all whores. How hard could that be?"

And now the jealousy. So while he wanted to be in Hartley's inner circle, he also hated him a bit. I could hear it underlying his words. "None of the women that Hartley killed were prostitutes, so I don't—"

"They all cheated on their husbands!"

Ah. "That's true," I agreed. "But that doesn't make them whores."

"I think it does, and some would say they had it coming."

"I think you deserve a divorce for cheating, not death," I said flatly, scowling. Like murderers got to make judgment calls on others.

"Perhaps."

I took a breath, and he put his arms on the table and rested his
chin on his fists.

"What are you thinking about?"

"I'm really sorry I tried to hurt you this morning. I apologize."
Kelson appeared contrite.

"Apology accepted."

"He's right, you know. You're very easy to talk to."

"Thank you."

Kelson smiled.

WE TALKED for a long time, a couple of hours, and then I led Kelson
to the door. When I opened it, Eli was there.

"What're you doing here?" I asked, pleased to see him.

He shrugged. "The day's pretty much over, so I thought I'd
check on you."

I nodded. "Thank you. I'm driving out to Elgin because I don't
want him to hurt himself, and the Feds will just leave him here all night."

"I won't hurt myself," Kelson promised.

"Things change," I pointed out.

"True," he agreed.

"Let's go to Elgin," Eli said, chuckling. "I'll drive."

Leaving Sharpe and White manning the main desk, Eli and
I took Kelson down the elevator and put him in one of the Chevy
Suburbans we'd taken out this morning.

According to any GPS or any online directions, the trip from the
office downtown out to Elgin Mental Health Center by way of I-90
West should have taken forty-five minutes. I had never gotten there
in less than an hour. Since we were thick in the middle of rush-hour
traffic, I was sure it would take at least two hours one way.

Halfway there, Kage called, and I put him on speaker.

"Jones."

"Sir."

"Where are you?"

"On my way to Elgin with Kelson, sir."

And because Kage was a very smart man, he knew why.
Whether he thought so, Kelson was a suicide risk. Anyone totally

brainwashed by a serial killer could easily decide on a whim to kill themselves, or remember they'd been told to do so after speaking for a certain amount of time, or God knew what else. There were a hundred scenarios, but basically the result was Kelson had to be watched, and in one of the cells in the marshals' office or with the FBI, he would not get the observation he needed. Had it been earlier in the day, someone else would have transferred him to Elgin. But I knew the drill; I'd had dealings with more than one psychotic felon in my life. Hartley was the worst, but there were enough others for me to know what I was doing.

"Just you, Jones?"

"No, sir," Eli spoke up. "I'm here."

Deep breath. "Okay."

"The Bureau can deal with this tomorrow. I just want him dropped off tonight," I explained. "It was the only thing to do."

"Agreed."

I didn't want to ask. "Sir? Ryerson's family?"

"His wife is in stable condition in the hospital."

He didn't say where. It wasn't for Kelson to know.

"Does he have kids?"

"He does. They're all accounted for."

That was good. "And Hartley?"

"No sign of him beyond his fingerprints and DNA."

I wasn't going to ask where his DNA was.

"Ryerson is very thankful," Kage said. "He wants you to work for him."

"I work for you, sir," I told him. "I'll send you a notification when Kelson's dropped off."

"Good," he said and was gone.

"That man has terrible communication skills," Kelson said, shaking his head as he sat beside me.

"I would agree with that," Eli replied from the front seat.

I EXPLAINED to the doctor in charge at Elgin that I thought Kelson would be the model prisoner if he didn't try to swallow his tongue.

The last thing I heard him asking the doctor, as two orderlies walked him slowly inside, was if he could stay in Hartley's old room.

"He really likes you," Eli said once we were outside.

"All the crazy ones like me," I agreed, walking over to the grass next to the Suburban and losing everything in my stomach.

"I'm thinking it's lucky tomorrow's Friday."

I nodded as he passed me a bottle of water. My phone started ringing, and Eli answered because I wasn't sure if I needed to dry heave.

"Yeah, he's good. We're out at Elgin. Where are you?" He listened for a moment. "We're heading back now. I'll drop him off at—oh, okay. Thanks."

"Who was that?" I asked as I got into the passenger-side seat.

"Ian. He's got to meet with the Feds about some operation for Monday that Adair put him in charge of that Kage just signed off on."

"*Adair* put him in charge?"

Eli shrugged as he started the SUV. "Apparently watching Ian all day made him think he could handle it."

"How big an operation?"

"Six-agency big."

"Gang task force?"

"It sounds like a Homeland thing. They're looking for guns and explosives. ATF is in there as well."

"And Ian's spearheading the whole thing?" That was a lot to take the lead on for a guy brand-new in his position.

"Sounds like it."

Impressive after one day, but it made sense since it was Ian, after all. People looked at him and simply knew he could handle whatever was put on his plate.

"Maybe that's what Kage was doing, huh?"

"What do you mean?" I asked as he drove us out of the parking lot and out onto the street.

"Maybe Kage wants Ian to discover that diplomacy can be just as life-and-death as breaching a building with an automatic rifle in your hand."

I turned to look at him.

"What?"

"And me?"

"And you what?"

"What does Kage want me to learn?"

He shook his head. "It's not about you learning anything. It's about you finally using your skills where they'll do the most good."

"Explain."

"It's the kids, Miro," he said softly, kindly, smiling at me. "You're so good with them, and you care so much."

"What're you—"

"We all tease you about Cabot and Drake and that new kid, uhm...."

"Josue."

"Yeah, him. We all tease you, but that's who you are. You care. You go outta your way to make sure that kids are safe, and even their pets."

"I—"

"Remember that family that got moved last year, but their cat was at the vet, and they couldn't wait?"

The Parkinsons. Of course I remembered.

"So once the cat was cleared to travel by the vet, you flew the cat out to Palm Springs and delivered it to their door because it wasn't fair that they had to leave a member of their family."

"Yeah. So?"

"It was a *cat*, Miro."

I glared at him. "Clearly you've never had a pet."

He waved his hand dismissively. "You're a fuckin' bleeding heart, and how no one checked that on your way to becoming a marshal, I have no idea, but I seriously can't think of anyone better than you to take care of all the kids in Custodial."

"So you think Kage—"

"Picked the best guy for the job," he assured me with a smack on the arm. "Yeah, I do."

"Thanks, Eli," I said, choking up a bit because so far it had been a hell of a day.

"You're gonna do great."

I sighed. "I wish Ian felt the same. I think he's worried I'm gonna get hurt."

"Oh well, yeah, you're gonna get hurt," Eli said, shooting me a look like *of course*. "You're in the most heartbreaking job we got at the marshals service. There's no way you're not getting your heart diced up regularly from now on, but—that's only one side of it, right? You can't just dwell on the bad part. Who does that?"

Ian, apparently. "Right," I sighed, really loving him at that moment. "You have to think about the whole picture, and if you do that, I'm gonna be all right."

"Without a doubt," he agreed. "I mean, have you ever known Kage to be wrong?"

And I thought about that for the first time that day, just about him, about my boss and how his mind worked.

"Sometimes instead of being all twisted up about something, you just gotta have a little faith."

"Tell Ian, will ya?"

"I'll put it on my list."

IT WAS after nine by the time we made it back to the Greystone in Lincoln Park, and everyone was home, of course, so we ended up having to park a block away. We had assigned parking, but Ian had parked the truck in our spot earlier.

"I am suddenly dead-ass tired," I said.

"It's been a weird day," Eli agreed.

"Did your cousin go home?"

"You just thought about him now?"

"Yeah," I told him, not sorry even a bit.

"Yes, he went home. I took him before work. That's why I was a few minutes late."

I smiled.

"What?"

"Everybody left me and Kelson alone. What do you think Kage did to those guys for that?"

"Something horribly painful," he said, cackling.

"Asset forfeiture," I said and then I grinned as I saw a werewolf headed down the street toward me. "Oh no, I'm gonna die."

Chickie gave me a sort of yodeling howl and was on me in seconds. He was so big, part malamute, maybe some husky thrown in there, Caucasian ovcharka for sure, and probably, though no one could say conclusively, some wolf. He was huge. On his back legs, his front paws went easily on my shoulders, and I was five eleven. People saw him coming and ran, except when Sajani held his leash while they walked around together. Then there was only "oohing" and "ahhhing" and "ohmygod, they're freakin' adorable together" from anyone who saw them. Babies and dogs weren't a thing on the internet for nothing.

He whimpered and wiggled and bumped me with his head and licked my hands until I buried them in the long fur Ian and I had to constantly stay on top of. He had to be brushed once a day, and we had just bought a vacuum cleaner we carried like a backpack. Whoever wore it looked like a Ghostbuster.

"Jesus, that dog is a monster," Eli said as Chickie greeted him and then bolted back down the street to Ian. "I see the hair grew back over where he was shot."

"Hair grows everywhere on the dog. That's not an issue."

When we got closer to the Greystone, I saw Ian sitting on the stairs in a pair of old threadbare jeans, one of my ancient University of Chicago T-shirts, and socks. He looked fantastic, like home, like everything I'd ever wanted.

What kind of idiot messed around with their life's happiness? Who did that?

I nearly threw up again.

I finally had Ian; everything else should have been secondary. But that's not what I was doing. I was being selfish, needing my personal and professional lives to be exactly what I wanted. It could be argued that I hadn't picked my new job, that it was chosen for me. But I didn't argue either. I accepted because I could see myself taking care of kids… helping….

But if I lost Ian because of the job… what was the use? It was an impossible choice, and I couldn't move, couldn't take another step, so horrified by the choice I faced. Eli walked by me and then stopped, realizing I wasn't at his side.

He turned to come back, but Ian called to him.

In moments they switched positions, Eli at the top of the stoop and Ian walking quickly down the sidewalk toward me. I had the strangest urge to run, and so I grabbed the streetlight to prop me up and keep me from bolting.

"Don't make me sic the dog on you," Ian warned with a chuckle as he closed in.

I turned slowly, and he was close. Standing my ground, shoving my hands down into the pockets of my dress pants, I waited.

He didn't stop, didn't slow, just walked right up to me, slipped his hand around the back of my neck, and kissed me.

Hard, devouring, claiming, like he meant it, like I belonged to him, like he was trying to get my attention.

I broke the kiss when I couldn't breathe, panting as I leaned my forehead against his. "I'm so sorry."

"Me too."

I snapped my head up and stared into those beautiful blue eyes of his. "You don't have anything to be sorry for. I'm the one who—"

"No," he assured me, massaging the back of my neck, up in my hair. "I was wrong to think that I could stand between you and all the bad shit in your life. I want to protect you, and I missed having you there today, but I forgot that when you're good at your job, people want you to do something more. It happened in the Army. I got good at one thing, and then there was always the next step to take. People expect you to climb up the ladder, not down."

"Yes, they do," I agreed, just soaking in the closeness, not looking away.

"This morning I thought, Kage is out of his fuckin' mind, and then I spent all day being in charge of everyone outside our office, and it was like—"

"Natural."

After a moment he nodded.

"You're a born leader, Ian, just like Becker, just like Kage. People want to do what you tell them because they can see you'll be right behind them."

"And Kage sees that you're good with people, and he knows how great at taking care of kids you are, so that's why he picked you for Custodial."

"I know I'm gonna get hurt, and I know that every day won't be a win."

"No, it won't, but this morning when we left for work, I thought everything but you was the same as it was yesterday. I thought, if I'm going anywhere, it's to SOG."

"Sure."

"But then we get to work and everything's different, and you can't work for me anymore anyway," he said, chuckling. "I can't order around the guy I sleep with."

I grinned.

"You're a pervert, just so you know," Ian assured me.

The tears of relief came fast. The fear had been sitting on my heart all day long, since I'd decided to repress it and focus on the job. I'd been putting it aside, thinking about everything but losing Ian—and there was a whole laundry list of things to concentrate on—but when I saw him, it was like being caught in a landslide, and I was lost in seconds.

"Miro," he rumbled, and the sound sent electric tingles running down my spine, straight to my cock. Nobody else, just with their voice, turned me inside out like Ian. "Nothing with me works without you, so just follow me home, all right? Don't overthink, don't be scared. Everything's okay."

"You promise?"

"I promise."

I heaved in a gulp of air. "We're still gonna fight, and there's still gonna be—"

"We're still us," he said, kissing my eyes, my cheek, and the line of my jaw. When he licked over my lips, I had to take hold of him so I wouldn't fall down.

"Love."

I jolted under his hands, flayed open today between this and the kids and then Kelson. I was needy and vulnerable, and I needed Ian to make my whole world balance out and make sense. "God, I'm sorry, you're gonna be the guy putting me back together every night when I come home."

"Yeah, maybe. And maybe you'll be doing it for me. We work life-and-death jobs, and some days they're gonna totally suck. We just gotta make sure we talk all the time. Nobody gets to go all silent and broody."

I snorted. "But you look so hot when you brood."

"Are you done?" The way he lifted one eyebrow and curled his lips, how his voice got all silvery and soft, nearly stopped my heart. He annihilated me always.

"Yeah, I—"

"Don't leave me," he said quickly, adamantly, kissing my jaw, the side of my neck, inhaling me. "Miro, honey, don't ever leave me."

I was lost, putty in his hands. "I thought—it'd be you."

He stepped into me, hugging me tight, face down in my shoulder. "No, honey, I'm gonna stick right here with you."

I gave him my weight, leaning, letting him shore me up as I soaked up his warmth, his strength, all of him, just Ian and that he belonged to me.

"Stop thinking I could ever leave you, all right, and I'll stop thinking you'll tell me to go."

It was a powerful thing, taking for granted that the person you loved would simply be there through thick and thin, forever. It was faith and trust, neither of which I was any good at before Ian.

"That's what our marriage is gonna be about, sticking it out because we love each other more than anything."

I straightened up, leaned free, and looked at him.

"What?"

"That was very profound."

"Oh yeah?" He grinned. "You like that?"

I nodded.

"Okay, so, we good?"

I needed these simple conversations that put the world under my feet, sky overhead, everything back in its place, and me no longer untethered. Ian made my life solid, and it sounded like I did the same for him. I hadn't been giving myself enough credit. As much as I'd been worried about losing him, he was just as scared over the thought of being without me, and because the marriage was new, I'd been treating it like either one of us could simply walk away.

It was like when you moved into a new apartment but didn't unpack your boxes because you weren't sure how long you were going to be there. That's how I'd felt, like I'd been waiting to see what would happen. My boxes were all still sealed.

"Miro?"

I leaned in, hugged him tight, and heard his low, seductive chuckle. "Yeah, we're good."

"It's my fault. I was scared this morning before we went to work, and I was freaking out and—I'm sorry."

"Me too," I told him.

"Hey!"

We pulled apart slowly and looked down the street to Eli on the stairs.

"I'm starving, the dog's starving. Can we make with the dinner, please?"

Ian grabbed my hand and tugged me after him. "We better go feed him. He gets whiney when he's hungry."

"He does, you're right."

"We should feed Chickie too," Ian said, chuckling. "By the way, what'd you eat today?"

I was not about to tell him I was empty on the inside.

"I mean," he said, turning to look at me, "that you kept down."

"How did you know I was sick?"

"Oh, I dunno, maybe 'cause I know you and know that dealing with anything Hartley-related makes you barf."

"You're not wrong," I agreed, letting go of his hand to move in closer, jostle up next to him so he could put his arm around my shoulders. I had to be closer to him, I'd missed him all day, worried all day, and so the contact was as necessary as breathing.

"Well, I'll fix you up," he promised. "I can't wait to hear about your day."

It was nice to know that although we didn't work together anymore, the talks would be endless, and that was really something to look forward to.

CHAPTER 9

IAN MADE spaghetti with meat sauce, and as Eli looked at it, he realized the same thing I did the first time I ate it: "sauce" was a loose term, and it had a kick to it.

"Isn't this supposed to pour?" Eli asked as he stood next to the soup pot with a ladle of sauce in his hand that would not come out of the spoon onto his plate.

"You have to really kinda fling it," Ian suggested, taking a gulp of his beer from one of the frosted glasses I'd started keeping in the freezer.

"It's more like a stew than a sauce," I acknowledged. "But it's really good. You just tasted it. You know it's great."

"Yeah, but sauce can be ladled."

He had a point. It was probably the sausage, mushrooms, green peppers, onions, and capers Ian put into sauce already thick with ground beef that rendered it unpourable.

"You shouldn't need a knife with spaghetti."

Ian glowered at us. "You guys need to get off my ass on the whole cooking thing because I didn't hear either of you volunteering."

"You're right, I'm sorry," I said sincerely because, really, it was very thoughtful and a gorgeous meal, complete with a tossed salad with the grape tomatoes I liked, crusty garlic bread, and wine for me and Eli. "Thank you, baby."

I leaned sideways, bumping him with my shoulder, and kissed him. I meant it to be a quick peck, but he bit down on my bottom lip, holding me there. When he let go, he slid his tongue over the bite and then went back to eating. My whole body thrummed as I stared at him, unable to look away as arousal buzzed through me.

"You know, Mrs. Svoboda says that your name is wrong," Ian said, making conversation even as he slipped his hand around my thigh under the table.

"My what now?" I asked, squirming a bit, feeling my cock thicken in my dress pants.

"Your name," he said with a grin that should have been illegal. It was seductive, like a cool pond on a hot summer day. "She's originally from the Czech Republic. She used to live just outside of Prague, and she says that the shortened version of Miroslav is not Miro, but Mirek."

"Oh, that's cool," Eli said, clearly enjoying his food by the way he was shoveling it in. "I should start calling him that."

"Or not," I said, willing him to eat even faster, shifting in my seat at the table, needing to relieve the pressure.

"I think Mirek sounds badass."

"I need more wine," I said, getting up and walking to the pantry and the rack full of bottles inside it.

"You want a whole other bottle?" Ian called.

I stood in the pantry, hands flat on the wall, trying to calm down. It was the day, I knew it was. I'd been scared of losing him, and having everything as it should be, plus his closeness, was doing insane things to my libido. I needed Eli gone because I wanted Ian all over me.

"Wait, what?" Ian said suddenly from the doorway to the pantry, clearly talking to Eli and not me.

"I'll be right back. I'm just looking for the bottle I want," I lied, trying to will my erection back down. There was no way Eli would miss it, and then he'd feel like he had to leave, and that wasn't what I wanted.

Well. I *did* want that, but not because he'd be embarrassed or feel like he was a third wheel or something. That wasn't my intent. It was all Ian's fault.

"What're you doing?" Ian asked, leaning into the pantry and looking at me.

I put my cheek on the cold plaster wall, staring at him, at his broad shoulders and wide chest, noting his long muscular legs and the veins in his arms. He was simply mouthwatering, and I was aching for him. "Go away. Talk to Eli."

He scowled but then saw me adjust myself, and the wicked grin made his eyes gleam with the same dangerous intent.

"Get out," I ordered.

"You hard?"

I ignored him, pressing my forehead to the chilled surface. I felt like I had a fever.

His chuckle was simply decadent.

Turning my head, I growled at him. "I hate you right now." He took a step toward me. "Okay, I'm outta here."

"No," Ian ordered, turning to walk back out to the table.

Moving slowly, I made it to the doorway and then bent over the counter so my cock—trying to escape through my zipper—was hidden. Ian stood beside the refrigerator, arms crossed, leaning against it as he talked to Eli.

"You don't have sex with strangers anymore. You're thirty-two years old, man, that's ridiculous. You need to be dating, not fuckin' around."

"You sound like my mother," Eli griped.

"For fuck's sake, Eli, you don't even know this girl."

"That's the point. I will *get* to know her in the biblical sense."

Ian shook his head.

"Listen, just because you can get laid at home doesn't mean the rest of us can," Eli protested, then gulped his wine.

"Having sex with women you meet on an app on your phone is not safe."

"Everybody uses it," he explained, standing up, cupping his hand over his face and doing the breath test. "Awww man, how much garlic is on that bread?"

"It's called garlic bread, you ass, and there's some in the spaghetti too."

"Tell me you have toothbrushes for overnight guests."

"In that bathroom right there," Ian said, shaking his head.

"Don't judge me. Did you actually look at the girl?" Eli asked, walking toward the bathroom, pausing to pet Chickie, who was passed out on the couch. "I know you can appreciate a beautiful woman."

"Yeah, she's hot, but c'mon, Eli, you're not gonna date her."

As I listened to them, I could feel my body start to cool down. It was the banter, the normalcy of them that did it.

"No, man, I'm gonna fuck her," Eli clarified. "I need to get laid."

"You should start being more serious about who you're dating."

"Have you lost your— Where are the tooth—"

"On the left-hand side," Ian directed, levering off the refrigerator and walking over to me.

I really needed him to stay on the other side of the room. He was too much of a temptation, and I was like dry brush at the moment. The tiniest spark and I would combust. "Ian, I—"

He grabbed me roughly, twisted my right arm behind my back, took firm hold of my left shoulder, and shoved me back inside the pantry.

He pinned me face-first to the wall and held my head there, my cheek ground into the smooth, cool plaster as he used his left hand to get into my pants.

"What're you—doing?" I gasped, jolting against him, pressing my ass back into him. "Eli's still in the… the… the place where we are now."

He rumbled in my ear, biting the lobe, breathing down the side of my neck as he worked my belt open, the button of my dress pants and then the zipper. His hand brushed over my hip before he wrapped it around my length and tugged.

I moaned his name.

His chuckle was sinister as he let go of my head, only to wrap that hand around my throat and tip my head so it fell back on his shoulder.

"Ian, I will have a debate about fucking versus dating with you tomorrow," Eli cackled as he moved through the house, away from the kitchen. "In the meantime, I'll call you later and let you know I'm not dead."

"Good," Ian yelled back.

"See ya later, Mirek," Eli continued, and then I heard the door open and slam shut. Clearly he was in a hurry.

"The hell are you thinking?" I shuddered, reaching for him behind me.

"Stop moving," he ordered, passing me a bottle of lube. "Hold this."

"Where was *this*?"

"Under the sink," he told me, shoving my pants to my knees.

"You're always prepared," I teased.

"I was an Army Ranger, and I'm a deputy US marshal," he reminded me, bumping me as he got into his jeans, pushing them to his thighs before snatching the lube out of my hand and opening it with a click. "I'm ready for anything."

"Ian," I mewled, "please."

He slid his slick fingers between my cheeks and then inside of me, ruthlessly, relentlessly, without pause, nothing slow or tentative about him at all.

"Ian!"

He was withdrawing, leaving me shivering and empty, but then I felt the head of his cock at my entrance. With the same inexorable push forward, he pressed inside me.

"Jesus Christ, Miro—every fuckin' time, this feels amazing."

The stretch, the way he opened me up, it hurt because there had been no prep, but he was stroking my cock, tugging, touching me roughly, fast and dirty like we were in a back alley, not our home, my skin catching on the hard calluses, making me buck into his fist, wanting more even as I ground back on his cock, driving him deeper.

"Fuck," he growled, thrusting fast, the angle off because he had to pump up into me. He pulled out only to haul me to the floor, to my hands and knees.

One hand on the small of my back, he guided his cock back into my hole with the other and picked up his rhythm quickly, in and out, the brutal pace bringing me close to orgasm even without his hand on my dick.

"This is the second-best part of bein' married," he groaned loudly, decadently, pounding into me with abandon, holding on to my hips, using me just the way I wanted.

"And the best?" I managed to get out before my back bowed and I yelled his name, my orgasm rushing over me, drenching me in heat as my muscles clamped down around the length of him, holding tight.

He stayed still for only a moment.

"God, your ass," he roared, hands on my shoulders, jerking me back into him as he rammed forward, shoving in deep and hard, leaving me no time to breathe between strokes.

It was an endless loop of pleasure so sharp, radiating through me, that I was left shuddering with the feel of him lodged inside.

I choked on his name, letting my head drop as he found his release, filling my ass with his thick, hot spill, collapsing on top of me, looping his arms under mine and around my shoulders so we were plastered together, his body molded to mine, chest to back.

We panted together, slick with sweat, and I closed my eyes, letting myself feel his skin on mine, bask in the moment, loving his weight draped over me.

Neither of us moved.

"You have my cum dripping out of your ass, even though my dick is there too."

I grunted, smugly happy that my body pleased him.

"And just so you're clear, your ass is amazing, tight and round and just fuckin' edible, but the best part of bein' married is that you love me, so you don't do this with anybody else, and I trust that like I never thought I would or could."

I took a breath so I wouldn't do something stupid to ruin the moment. Like cry.

"You're my husband, and I didn't think that would ever be something I would want, and now it's the only thing I do."

I nodded, and he laughed softly against my back.

"All that goes ditto for you, huh, tough guy?"

"Hold me tighter, 'kay?"

And so he did.

WE FINALLY got up, wiped ourselves down, nuked the spaghetti because it had gotten cold, ate some more, showered, took Chickie for his nightly walk, and then came home and lay on the couch, tangled together.

"I wanna hear," I yawned, "all about your day."

"And I wanna hear about yours."

"You go first," I insisted because I could imagine him being all bossy, and it sounded pretty hot.

"Why don't you just put your head down while I watch a little TV and let my brain rest."

"But I'm really interested in you."

"I know, and I'm happy you are, but right this second, I kinda just want to… be."

"Oh," I sighed. "Well, that sounds pretty good too."

"I thought it would," he said, brushing my hair back and kissing my forehead as I snuggled up against his shoulder.

The knock on the door was a surprise.

"Who're you expecting?" Ian asked as Chickie got up from where he was curled at Ian's feet and padded over to the front door.

We both watched as he stood there, head cocked, listening, tail wagging slowly like an afterthought. Whoever was out there, he knew.

"Shit," Ian grumbled because that was worse. A stranger he could turn away. Extracting himself from me, he got up and walked to the front door and looked out the peephole. "Oh for fuck's sake."

Hurling the door open, he stepped sideways so Cabot and Drake, Josue and another kid could walk through the door.

I scrambled to my feet the second I saw that Cabot had a bloody nose and lip. Drake looked worse and Josue only a bit better. I was pretty sure I knew who the fourth kid was, but I'd wait a second to see.

"The hell happened to you guys?" I yelled as they all bolted across the floor to reach me.

It was a wall of sound, all of them talking at once, over each other, and of course I couldn't understand a word beyond "party" and "drugs" and "the DEA."

Of course it was the fuckin' DEA.

"Who're you," Ian asked to the new kid, "and why're you in my house?"

He too had gotten hit in the face. The pale skin was marred by red splotches that would become very colorful bruises, I knew from experience. He was pretty with his black hair and dark blue eyes, and I understood why Josue, who was stunning himself, had looked twice at him.

"I'm Marcello McKenna."

"Who?" Ian was confused.

"Josue's boyfriend," I explained.

"Okay," Ian said, squinting at Josue. "So what happened?"

"They tried to grab him," Josue wailed, face crumpling, eyes overflowing with tears he'd barely held in check, shivering with cold, I was sure, and fright.

Marcello put his arm around Josue and drew him close before wrapping him up tight and notching his head under his chin. They were very cute together, and when I looked at Ian, I found him glaring.

"What?"

"Don't go all warm and gooey over there. This kid could be a criminal that your kid is mixed up with."

"No, we vetted him when he and Josue first started dating, don't you remember?"

"Clearly not," Ian said, sounding very bored.

"You checked him out?" Josue asked.

"Of course. We had to."

"I told you they would," Drake chimed in. "The only reason Cabot and I didn't have to be checked out was that we came in together."

"That's right," I informed Josue. "Anyone personally involved with you gets run through our system."

"And nothing bad came back on me, right?" Marcello asked.

"Nothing that sent up any red flags, but there must be something or the DEA wouldn't have you in their system."

"It was a long time ago," Marcello confessed with a sigh. "I used to run packages for Tadgh Murphy back in the day, but seriously, it's been years. I don't know how this guy even knew about me. And old man Murphy knows I've been out since his son died."

"You were only a runner, not a dealer?" Ian barked.

"No, never, I swear to God."

Ian nodded and looked over at Drake. "Tell me what happened."

"Well, we were at a party Marcello was having, and then this guy came in to buy drugs, and Marcello says he was never a dealer and basically said everything he just told you, but then Cabot looked at the guy and says he knows him, and I was all 'Where do you know him from?' and then," Drake said as he looked at Ian, "Cabot says that he's your brother."

Both Ian and I turned to Cabot, who was standing there, bleeding from his lip.

"It's your turn," Ian prodded.

"Well, last Thanksgiving when we were here, your stepmother, she showed me a picture of your stepbrother on her phone, and I was surprised because he kinda looks like you."

I myself had never seen any similarity between Ian and Lorcan Doyle. Ian was all chiseled perfection with his sharp-angled bone structure, while Lorcan was softer, blunt-featured, without any of Ian's innate beauty.

"So when I saw him tonight, I said to Josue, I think that's Ian's brother," Cabot said.

"And was it?" I asked.

Cabot nodded. "When I interrupted and said that I knew him, he kinda freaked out."

"No, no, no, that was not *kinda*," Drake assured him. "He attacked you."

Cabot nodded, leaning into Drake, clunking his head on his chest. "Thank you for saving me, as usual."

"Always." Drake smiled, even with his own split lip.

Ian groaned. "So then what happened?"

"Then all hell broke loose, and suddenly there were DEA agents everywhere and… it was a mess," Cabot said shakily.

"How did you guys get outta there?"

"I dunno," Drake answered, looking at me like maybe he needed a hug too.

"Okay, everybody into the kitchen so we can wash faces and make sure nothing's broken."

It was a ridiculous thing to say—they were all over twenty-one, men, not boys—but they still moved fast, even Marcello.

When I tried to go after them, Ian grabbed hold of my bicep and turned me to face him, hands on my sides, possessive but gentle in a way that spoke volumes. No one had ever held me the way Ian did, like I was precious and his at the same time. It was a rush that he did it instinctively because I belonged to him. "You clean 'em up. I'm calling the office to make sure we already know everything we need to know about McKenna," Ian grumbled, clearly not pleased at having his relaxing evening broken up.

"I know that we totally vetted him when they started dating. We just never see him, which is why neither of us can remember what the hell he looks like."

"Well, I'll remember now that he's in trouble," Ian finished, still holding on to me.

"Ian?"

He was thinking, and his gaze met mine.

"I gotta check on the boys."

His grunt was cute as I leaned in to kiss him, and took a nibble of his bottom lip. His soft moan made me smile against his mouth.

"I just wanted you to fall asleep next to me."

The simple things that made him happy were a revelation to me. "Still doable," I promised. "Lemme check on the boys."

They were all banged up—apparently the DEA guys got rough in the thick of things when more people than just the four guys in my kitchen tried to get away—but nothing was broken. Once I had cuts closed with the wide array of bandages under our bathroom sink, Drake was just standing there, and I eased him close and hugged him. He had been big when he was just eighteen and had added muscle over the years. Now when he hugged me, we were close to the same size, and to have his weight, to feel him lean, was nice. It showed trust, and as I glanced over at Ian and saw him shake his head and roll his eyes, I understood that he got it. Whether he wanted to call it what it was or not, we were foster parents, and we had three boys—maybe four now—who looked to us for guidance, safety, and love.

Ian nuked the spaghetti again, and even though Josue and Marcello were concerned about the sauce—"Is it supposed to stick to the spoon like that?" Josue asked—they all started scarfing it down along with more garlic bread, faster than I had ever seen people eat in my life. No one was interested in salad.

Chickie let out a loud booming bark while the boys were having chocolate mousse I had bought a few days before and forgotten about. The pounding on the door a second later was not a surprise.

Ian went to the door, ID in hand, opened it, and yelled in that thunderous way he had. I looked out the front window. Interesting. A SWAT team was parked on our street, and regular CPD officers and DEA agents lined our sidewalk. The best part, though, was the guy standing on my tiny postage stamp of a porch at the top of the stoop, and I moved up behind Ian so I could smile at him.

"Agent Stafford," I greeted cheerfully. "How long's it been?"

His head did a slow tip sideways as he lowered his gun, straightened up, and holstered it.

Ian's grin was downright evil. "You know you never do well when you cross the marshals' office, Agent Stafford. Look what happened the last time."

Two years ago we had taken a witness right out from under him because protocol was not the DEA's best friend. We had a system we followed each and every time. And maybe other districts didn't work like ours, but because we worked for Sam Kage, by the book was the way we did things.

"We want Marcello McKenna," he announced, but there was not a lot of bite to his words. SWAT was already loading back up, and the uniformed CPD officers were walking back to the street. "Where the hell are you going?" he yelled at the retreating lawmen.

"Federal marshals, Corb," one of Stafford's team members said, gesturing at Ian. "The fuck are we gonna do?"

"Why do you want McKenna?" Ian asked, standing casually in the doorway like it hadn't been a big deal moments ago.

"We have a CI that says that McKenna is a dealer for the Murphy crime family, and of course we're looking for him to make a deal."

"Marcello McKenna is involved with a witness of ours, and as such has been fully vetted," Ian told him. I knew that was the truth because he'd been on the phone with whoever was riding the desk at the moment, and they confirmed everything we thought we knew. A stint as a runner for Tadgh Murphy when he was still a juvenile would not, and could not, be held against Marcello now. "He is not a drug dealer. Your intel is faulty."

He stared holes through Ian. "Your own brother gave him up, Doyle."

"Stepbrother," Ian made clear, crossing his arms, in his battle stance. "And did it ever occur to you that Lorcan is probably working from bad information himself?"

"The hell you say."

"Oh, c'mon, Stafford," Ian said, patronizing and judgmental, "you know he's not a dealer. This offense was his one and only, and then you come dangling a get-out-of-jail free card, and so he remembers some shit he heard or someone told him, and you guys mobilize like you're taking down El Chapo without checking anybody out? The fuck are you doing over there?" He took a breath, glancing around at the rest of Stafford's team. "Or maybe it's just you, huh? Maybe the rest of these guys are okay. I have a friend who's worked with the DEA out in San Francisco, and he says they're pretty great."

"I—"

"Maybe you're the only fucktard over there at the moment."

"Shut the fuck up, Doyle," he roared, moving up so he was right in Ian's face. "You don't want to give us McKenna, fine. We'll just grab him when he leaves here or tomorrow or the next day or—"

"No," Ian insisted, moving so he and Stafford were basically nose to nose. "He's in our system as attached to a high-profile witness. You try and do anything with him, I mean fuckin' *anything*, and the system will kick him back out. And if you try and do anything to him off the record and I find out, your boss is talking to mine, and I'll give you one guess how that turns out since my boss is the fuckin' chief deputy," Ian said with a smugness in his tone that had gotten him hit on a number of occasions. "Think about what happened the last time you went in there and demanded something from him."

Stafford took a step back. "I have your brother, and he's the one who's gonna answer for all this shit."

Ian would have said something back, and things would have escalated, I was sure, but the guy behind Stafford gave a quick shake of his head with his brows furrowed, and we knew right then that Stafford was talking out of his ass.

"You do what you think is right," Ian told him with a shrug. "But a malicious prosecution charge is gonna look like ass in your jacket, I'm just sayin'."

"Doyle—"

"Stay clear of our boys, and that includes McKenna, or I will personally fuck you up."

"You don't have the—"

"I'm the new deputy director of the Northern District of Illinois," Ian advised him in that hard, biting, high-handed way he had when he was really pissed off. "And if you screw with anyone who has any connection to me—you're fucked."

It wasn't a threat; Ian never made those. He was a promises kind of guy. But I knew Stafford could not slink off the porch either. It wasn't in him.

"It's not worth your time anyway," I advised Stafford, which turned his attention to me. "This is all small shit, man. What're you doing even running this down?"

He was glaring at me, but I saw him breathe through his nose, take in some air, and maybe calm just a fraction. "We were on Vaughn, you know the commander out at the fourth, but when he was busted for those murders, we got pulled off."

"That's bullshit," Ian growled. "But I can get you in touch with Vaughn now, and with his intel, you could go after O'Brien."

It was working, Stafford was deflating, and no, Ian didn't have to, but he was the deputy director now, and he was supposed to be about building bridges, not slamming doors.

"Chris O'Brien had a lot of friends too, I bet," Ian continued. "You got young guys who can go undercover?"

And of course he did.

"Call me tomorrow," Ian offered, arms uncrossed, hand on the doorjamb as Stafford pulled his phone to put in the direct line he was given. "And I'll get you to Vaughn."

When Stafford met Ian's gaze, he nodded and then turned, his men behind him all glancing at Ian before they thumped down the steps of our stoop.

"Lookit you being all professional and shit," I teased Ian.

"Yeah, well," he sighed, closing the door, rounding on me. "I guess I actually need to be a diplomat now, right?"

"Yes."

"And I get you and Custodial."

"How's that?" I asked, feigning confusion.

"You're an idiot."

"Yeah, you knew that before you married me, so—who's the idiot now?"

"Kage was right."

"Oh?"

"You're a caretaker, and you're the best fit for Custodial," he said, gesturing at the boys crossing the room to us. "You already do it."

"I know."

"And if you get hurt—which you will."

"Which I will, agreed."

"Then I'll be here to take care of you," he finished, stepping into me, my space, and wrapping his arms around my neck to kiss me and throttle me all at once.

Just as Drake cared for Cabot, and Marcello protected Josue, Ian would shelter me. It was how it went when you loved someone.

"You signed on for this," I reminded Ian as I closed my eyes and leaned on him.

"Yes, I did," he agreed. "I most certainly did."

CHAPTER 10

THE BOYS slept over, which made for interesting sleeping arrangements on the couch and floor, but they all wanted to stay to watch a movie with Ian, especially Marcello, who must have thanked him a million times for sticking up for him.

"Just don't be a stranger anymore, and come with Josue when we all do stuff."

"I will," he said, beaming at Ian. "I so will."

The hero worship was cute.

When our alarm went off at six the following morning, I was surprised to find Cabot up already, having made coffee and smiling at me blearily.

"Why're you up?"

"I just wanted to say that I appreciate all you and Ian have done for me and Drake since you got stuck watching over us."

"Never been stuck with anything or anyone in my life, kid," I told him, tousling his hair. "I kinda like you."

His smile got even brighter before he took a sip of his coffee. "What's Custodial?"

I enjoyed talking to him. He was the introspective one, the artist, and when I was done explaining, he was certain I'd do great there. "You take such good care of all of us."

"Stop sucking up, kid," Ian grumbled as he walked into the kitchen, yawning, leaning in to kiss me before staggering toward the coffee maker.

At work an hour later, having rousted the boys and dropped Chickie off with Aruna, I was really not surprised to find Bodhi Callahan, Redeker's partner from Vegas, standing in the hall that led to the locker and breakroom.

"Callahan," I called.

He moved quickly, gracefully, smiling as he came, hand out for me to take.

I grasped tight, grinning at him. "I knew you'd be right behind him."

Instant frown. "Did he tell you this was my idea?"

"No, he didn't."

"Of course not."

"Where are you staying?"

"I have a friend who just moved back to California a couple weeks ago, so he's letting me sublet his place," he told me. "It's a loft over on Michigan Avenue."

"Whereabouts?"

"In the Prairie District?" he said, grimacing. "I dunno what that even means yet."

"It means it's nice," I assured him. "They made a lot of those old industrial buildings into lofts. I looked at those, but I wanted a private gated area and the whole sanctuary when I got home, you know? No neighbors right on top of me."

"Gotcha."

"But you're happy with it?"

"Only been there a day, but yeah."

I had to ask. "And Redeker?"

"What about him?"

"Come on."

He shook his head, and the sun-streaked dirty-blond mop that fell to his shoulders caught the light, the wheat and copper, chestnut and gold. Between the hair and golden tan that was now, I realized, his natural coloring, he was stunning. He was twenty-seven when we met a year ago—with Redeker eleven years his senior—but I could tell he was one of those guys who would never age. I was betting people stopped and stared at him wherever he went, which was not great for a federal marshal, as we preferred to go unnoticed until the

very last second before a bust went down. He and Redeker together,
as striking as they both were, had to be a challenge.

"So?"

He squinted at me. "So what?"

"You transferred here too."

"Obviously."

"Are you supposed to see Kage?"

"Yeah, and then Doyle?"

I nodded. "Ian Doyle's the new deputy director."

"And your guy, right?"

"Yes," I said, feeling it in the pit of my stomach, the warmth of
saying that yes, Ian Doyle was with me.

"I wanted to ask—"

"I thought you were fucking with me on the phone last night."

We both turned to find Redeker there, glowering a few feet away.

Callahan snarled back. "If I fuck with you, you'll damn well
know it."

"Okay, that's my cue," I said, coughing into my closed fist before
taking a step back and retreating around the corner to the entrance
of the breakroom before popping my head back out to eavesdrop on
them. No way was I bailing to be left in the dark. If I was going to
help them work their shit out, I had to know how deep the crap was.

"Well, that was fuckin' great," Redeker groused.

"Like Miro cares, he's not like that."

"It was still rude."

"The only one who's rude and an asshole is you."

Redeker shook his head, and I saw the glower and the clenching
of his jaw. "I told you not to—you can't be here."

"It was my idea to come. I reminded you of that last night on the
phone, so why wouldn't I be here?" he asked indignantly. "I told you
I'd be here this morning. I spent all day yesterday moving into my
new place because, unlike you, I built in time for that."

"This is a mistake."

"Yeah, yours, for not just waiting and coming up here with me,"
Callahan said imperiously, somewhere between condescending and
furious.

"I thought—" Redeker swallowed hard and took a shaky breath. "—you'd be good there if I left."

"If you ran, you mean."

Redeker tugged on his hair again—obviously a nervous habit, self-soothing that I did myself. Light glinted off the ring, and I watched Callahan's attention catch on it. He ghosted his fingers across the silver before he took a step forward and put his hands on Redeker's sides, holding him still exactly as Ian had held me the night before. It looked as possessive and claiming as it felt.

"Don't—I'm trying not to fuck up your life," Redeker whispered, shifting on his feet, ready to ease free.

Callahan moved closer, very clearly not about to let him go, and slipped his hands under the parka Redeker had on. I watched Redeker close his eyes as though it took every drop of concentration to remain standing. He lifted his own hands to Callahan's face but then dropped them back to his sides.

"Where are you staying?" Callahan asked, his tone changing to gentle, coaxing, even as his lips hovered over the side of Redeker's neck, debating, I suspected, whether to press his mouth to the freckled skin, or his teeth. The desire was rolling off him, the need to stake his claim, and I *so* understood. Back when Ian and I were just friends, not touching him whenever I wanted, not making him mine, had been almost physically painful. "You should stay with me."

It was a good offer. I really hoped Redeker would take him up on it.

Redeker's eyes drifted open slowly, languorously, like he was drugged. "I can't—I shouldn't—I don't want it to be just like—"

"Oh, don't worry," Callahan said, easing back, letting him go but remaining in Redeker's space. "It won't be like Vegas at all, I can promise you that."

"And what the hell does that mean?" Redeker muttered, back to scowling but still not pulling away, allowing the touching.

"Everything will be exactly how you want it."

"Why does that not sound good?"

"I have no earthly idea," Callahan said innocently.

"Explain to me what you mean by—"

"What're you doing?"

Redeker's words faded out as I turned to see Ian behind me. "Where did you come from?"

"Over there," he said, grinning, pointing at the ever-present enormous fruit basket in the breakroom. "Sometimes your body just craves citrus," he explained, showing me the Valencia orange in his hand.

I grunted.

He tried to look around me, but I stepped sideways into the hall so he couldn't. "I wanna see who you're spying on."

"No one," I insisted as I turned and saw Redeker and Callahan walking toward us.

"Oh, I see," Ian teased, waggling his eyebrows.

"Just be nice to them. They're working things out."

"I'm always nice," Ian claimed, smirking before tipping his head at the two approaching men. "Are you Callahan?"

"I am," he said, offering Ian his hand. "Are you Doyle?"

"Yeah," Ian replied, shaking hands before tipping his head at Redeker. "You guys were partners in Vegas, right?"

"We were."

"And you both transferred up, so—you good to keep being partners?"

"We are," Callahan answered before Redeker could say a word.

"Great," Ian sighed. "That makes things much easier. Come with me, and we'll get your paperwork done. And you should go down and get a car before all the good ones are gone. There's a Gremlin down there, so you might wanna hurry."

Redeker looked at me, horrified, releasing his breath in a rush. "I thought you were kidding about that."

"Nope."

"Did you say a Gremlin," Callahan asked, the concern flooding his face, looking a bit stunned. "Is that even safe?"

Ian shrugged. "I dunno, but I wouldn't wanna test it."

Redeker bolted for the elevator as Callahan followed Ian like he was in a fog. The horror of the truly frightening automobile—been there.

I SPENT some time that morning doing follow-up calls and checking on the placements made the day before. Eli called right about noon and asked if I wanted to get lunch, and when I asked where Ian was, he said he was stuck in his office with DEA agent Corbin Stafford. Apparently they were working out things to do with Lorcan and a joint task force, so maybe a better working relationship was on the horizon. Maybe. I wasn't going to hold my breath. Perhaps, though, with Ian at the helm, there could be new inroads made with the DEA. But it wasn't anything I would ever be working with him on, and acknowledging that was bittersweet because, yes, Ian and I were still together, still both marshals, but we were separated. I'd decided I was content to be in Custodial—it was the better fit for me—but not having Ian at work was new, and I felt the pang of being without him. It wasn't logical; it simply was. It would take some time to get used to.

I was about to make the turn from the bullpen to head to my office when Becker stopped me. When I turned to him, he pointed at the elevators, which dinged almost as if on cue.

"Oh, what the hell," I said under my breath as I saw a woman getting off the car with six other men in trench coats.

The woman stopped in front of me as Eli sidled up on my right. She opened her credentials so I could see the FBI badge, and her expression was grim and resigned at the same time.

"What happened?" I groaned, terrified of what the answer would be and knowing instinctively her being there had something to do with Hartley.

The agents with her came in close, circling us so it was only me and Eli and Becker together, no one else allowed.

"I'm Christina Stigler from the Office of Partner Engagement, and I flew out here from Langley to speak to you, Marshal Doyle, on Monday, as I'll be working with you going forward to coordinate— and I have no idea why I'm giving you this background, because none of that matters right now." She sighed, and I saw how tired she looked. "What's important at the moment is that Kol Kelson just explained two hours ago that he has a bomb inside of him that could go off at any time."

I shook my head. "So they called the bomb squad and had him checked for radiation, and let me guess: he beeped."

"He did."

"So they transported him where?"

"They were on their way to—"

"And they were forced off the road."

"Yes," she said, sounding like she was a hundred instead of in her midforties like she looked.

"You realize that by now you guys should have Hartley's MO down, right?"

"Agreed." The pained tone did not recede.

"How many times has he done this?"

"It's easy to see in hindsight, not when he's doing it."

I nodded. "And there's more."

"Yes."

Eli's hand on my shoulder was more than comforting. It kept me grounded in the here and now instead of letting me go tripping into scary, dark places where nightmares lived.

"My boss, Director Ryerson, was informed today that though his wife was saved and taken into protective custody yesterday, his son, going to school here at Northwestern, was not."

I took a breath, willing myself to stay calm.

"No," Becker said sharply.

Her eyes scrunched up, and I saw the pain etched on her face. "It's not your call, Marshal. That belongs to Marshal Jones."

"The hell it does," he assured her. "Marshal Jones is—"

"Stop," I ordered. "Where is Hartley?"

"We have no idea," she said, and I heard the tremble in her voice. People got that way where Hartley was concerned. Everyone had to stay constantly vigilant, and being on guard all the time was hard to maintain. "You're just supposed to go out the front door of this building and run as fast as you can straight down the sidewalk, and apparently it will become clear."

"But you don't know if this is Hartley or Kelson."

"What?"

"None of this is how Hartley normally operates. I could be running to Kelson and not Hartley," I clarified.

"Well, yes, I—yes."

"And someone, either Hartley or Kelson, has Ryerson's son?"

"Someone does," she agreed. "We have proof of life."

"None of this sounds like Hartley," I told her. "He doesn't do this."

"Or hasn't before," she cautioned. "Perhaps you don't know him as well as you think you do, Marshal."

"Or I'm absolutely correct, and Kelson's gonna try and kill me."

"Yes."

"Okay," I said and started taking off my blazer.

"No," Eli croaked, his voice rough and brittle. "And definitely not before Ian gets to come out here and talk to you."

"Agreed," Becker said gruffly. "You stay here, I'll get him."

"We don't have time for this," Stigler rasped, worn thin.

"We're making time," Becker insisted before pushing through the press of men.

It took only moments for Ian to join us, and when he did, the stricken look on his face told me exactly how terrified he was.

"It'll be all right," I assured him, wanting to touch him but afraid if I did, I wouldn't go. Leaving him to go to Hartley went against everything in me.

"No," he protested. "I refuse to let you risk your life for—"

"Stop," I whispered, handing him my jacket so I could be unarmed when I met Hartley.

"Miro," he husked, taking the Glock from me, and the new holster he'd bought me for Christmas that was just like his, handmade leather with brass buckles.

"You'd do the same," I ground out. "Just—I'll be right back. He probably wants to have a chat, and it's not like he can call."

He took a quivering breath. "I don't—I can't—"

"I know," I whispered as Kage joined us.

"The hell do you have my guy doing?" Kage thundered at Stigler.

She took a breath and retold the story quickly as I put back on my jacket.

"Everyone goes downstairs right now," Kage demanded, turning on Becker. "I want SOG on standby now."

He said "now" about eight more times before I was allowed on the elevator. Ian came with me, standing directly behind me, hands on my shoulders.

On the way down in the elevator, Stigler passed me a dime.

"What is—"

"You feel the weight?" I nodded as she took a deep breath. "It's a tracker. He won't be able to tell unless he holds it in his hand."

"Okay."

"He will not take you out of this area. We won't let him. We have all the streets in a two-mile radius sealed off. Just get the boy and get out any way you can," she stressed, grabbing hold of my shoulder. "We don't want Hartley. We just want you and Max both in one piece."

"Yes."

"Good," she barely got out, forcing a smile.

I stepped away from Ian and watched him clench his jaw. "I'll be right back."

His eyes filled, but he did not shed a tear. "Hurry."

The sidewalk was full of federal agents and CPD, and into that crowd came Kage and everyone from upstairs. When I saw Ching arrive, I turned to Kage, who gave me a nod. Turning fast, I bolted down the sidewalk.

It was a long, busy street—all the driveways that opened out onto the road, with the endless purge of cars, thick crowds, homeless people, stragglers from groups—a continual tide I had to dodge or, in a few cases, leap, even veer into the street to avoid, only to almost get hit before careening back onto the sidewalk and running on. I was in good shape—I ran with Ian every other day, did my cardio, lifted weights—but still, after twenty minutes of running all-out, I was tiring. Ian was the distance runner, his muscles compact, tight, lean, and sleek like a big cat. I was more bull, with what Ian called my massive shoulders and hard, heavy muscle. When I saw the van out of the corner of my eye, I was thankful. When it stopped ahead, double-parking beside another car so two others couldn't pull out, I ran to catch up, certain that was where I was going.

It rolled forward half a car length into the crosswalk, and upon reaching it, I dived inside the open door as a young man with his hands tied behind his back and duct tape over his mouth was shoved out onto the hood of a parked Honda Civic.

I scrambled to sit up as the van lurched forward and saw—

Craig Hartley.

Immaculately put together as always. As usual he looked like he was styled for a magazine shoot, from the three-hundred-dollar haircut to the Carlos Santos brown wingtip boots. The Soho-fit herringbone navy wool suit was stunning on him, setting off his thick blond hair, styled in a side part that looked particularly good. Funny, his boots were the exact ones I'd been shopping for just weeks before. We had always shared a similar taste in footwear.

Even after how many times our paths had crossed over the years, it was still a surprise to see him. I always expected each time to be the last.

"Nice gun," I commented, swallowing hard, tipping my head at the automatic rifle.

"Oh, thank you," he said, smiling fondly. "I found that I needed more bullets than the Desert Eagle afforded me, and I'm not a terribly good shot, but with this," he said, lifting the Heckler & Koch MP7A1 I'd taken off more than one would-be gangster, "I don't have to be."

"It probably scares people too."

"Yes," he agreed. "And you know how much I hate raising my voice."

"I do."

"Speaking of 'I do,' I understand you got married."

A chill ran down my back, almost jolting as sharp and sudden as it was. It was strange. I wasn't scared of him in regards to me, but I didn't want him knowing anything personal about Ian. That made no sense because Ian and I were entwined—we were one entity—but having Hartley "see" Ian in relation to me was unsettling. "Yes."

"Well, congratulations."

"Thank you." I sighed, leaning back against the wall of the van and staring at him. "Nice shoes," I said, as was our usual.

"Thank you. You're the only one in law enforcement who appreciates these things."

I doubted that. But no one else got the opportunity to give him compliments before he killed them.

A topcoat, scarf, and hat lay on the seat beside him, and it occurred to me I was looking at traveling clothes.

"Are you going somewhere?"

He smiled, and the laugh lines around his eyes crinkled. I wouldn't have thought serial killers would have those, but Hartley did. "I am, and I wanted to say goodbye."

I glanced around and saw Kelson in the passenger seat and another man driving. "You could just call next time."

He nodded. "I would have, but I wanted to see you before I left."

I jumped at a kernel of hope. "Not planning to come back?"

"Perhaps not," he sighed, yawning but never taking the gun off me. "I haven't decided yet. I'm planning to travel through Europe for the foreseeable future."

I nodded.

"You wouldn't want to come along, would you?"

"No," I said gently. "Just got married, as you said, but I do appreciate the offer."

"I know you do." He sighed and leaned forward, surveying, taking my measure. "I could insist you accompany me."

"Yeah, but you won't," I said with certainty.

He grunted as he sat back. "You're right, I won't."

It hit me then, how much the two of us had changed.

Over the years I'd been told by several reporters, members of law enforcement, and even prison staff that intensity simmered between Hartley and me. We had a thing, a way of talking, communicating, that people found riveting, even flirty, probably because they didn't understand that to have a personal relationship with Craig Hartley meant giving up a piece of yourself—in my case, literally—to him. A brilliant man, he could peel layers away so expertly even as he answered benign questions about himself that before you knew it, you were naked in front of him, turned inside out.

I'd seen so many people—from followers, worshippers really, to badass FBI agents—crumble under his scrutiny. I'd always stood apart, even from the beginning, because we started out in a place where he owed me. I'd saved his life. I'd put my body between him and death, and as I'd sprawled there on top of him, bleeding to death, he pressed his hand to the wound he himself had made and whispered soft words of comfort into my ear. We were connected from then on.

But now, after our last collision… confrontation… communion… it was different. We were different. We no longer circled each other, trying to pick apart the other's weaknesses, looking for a chinks in the armor. We simply sat there, not quite like friends—we could never be that—but something close.

"Miro."

"Sorry," I said absently, again astounded that I let my mind wander in his presence. Not many others could, and live.

"No, it's fine, nice, actually," he said with a trace of a smile. "But I have something to ask."

"What's that?" I exhaled sharply. I really *was* calm, sitting there comfortably with my wrists resting on my knees as I rode in a van with him holding a gun on me. When had this become... normal?

"Did Kelson try to shoot you yesterday?"

"No," I lied. "Why would he?"

"Because like everyone else I know, he's jealous of you."

All of them just as insane as he was, because no one in their right mind wanted to be Hartley's favorite. "It's how I knew he was a fake."

"Oh?"

I realized I'd said too much and almost choked. I spoke without thought because somewhere in all the time spent in his presence, I'd lost my natural fear of him. It was how a fly forgot about the spiderweb, or the mongoose got a bit too cocky, or a pigeon thought the hawk wouldn't even see it from way over there.

I watched a documentary once about orcas and how they would play with young seals for weeks close to the shore to get them all good and lulled into a false sense of security before one day they just ate them. It was diabolical. The whales never saw the seals as friends, and I thought that, beyond surprise, the seals must have had their feelings hurt as they were being eaten alive.

It felt like that.

As Hartley sat there like a circling orca waiting to eat me, I thought, how stupid am I? Letting my guard down was idiotic. How had I ever been soothed into trusting Hartley?

It all went back to the last time I'd seen him and had everything to do with my dog.

All of my fear had been expelled because of Chickie.

He'd saved my dog.

How were you supposed to be scared of someone who saved your dog?

"Miro?" he prodded gently.

"I— When his boss said he knew you best... I was suspicious."

"Suspicious or jealous?"

"Jealous?" Had I heard him right?

"That someone was claiming to be closer to me than you."

"But there are lots of people, I'm sure."

"I've outgrown so many."

"Well, he was talkin' out of his ass," I said, looking past him at Kelson when I said it.

"I was not!" he roared, which got a slow pan from Hartley.

Instant silence as Kelson swung around to look out the front window.

"How he was trying to blame that mess on you was ridiculous," I continued.

"He told me you'd believe it, but I knew better."

I shrugged. "You know I pay attention."

"Yes, I do," he practically purred.

I took a breath. "So what's the plan now?"

"I have no idea," he answered, his smile serene, almost bored. No, *really* bored.

"Holy shit," I blurted. What I thought I was hearing, seeing, was actually God's honest truth. He all but sighed like an angsty teen with nothing to do on a Saturday night. I had seen hundreds of emotions cross the man's face over the years, but this was brand-new, and I was stunned. How in the world did a serial killer wake up in the morning and find themselves filled with ennui? How was that even possible?

He startled. "What?"

"You're bored," I announced, matter-of-fact. "Jesus Christ."

He gave me a dismissive wave.

"You are. That's why you're leaving. That's why you haven't killed anybody in—how long's it been?"

He had to think. "Since whatshisname in your house, the one who was passed out."

"When you killed him, that was more to prove a point than anything else."

"It was." He yawned. "True."

"You know, for fun, you might let the FBI catch you. Then you can fuck with the profilers, play mind games with them."

He sighed. "I actually thought about that, but when you're captured, there's always so much manhandling, and people are so rough. I just want to be spoken to nicely, treated like a gentleman, not like a common criminal."

He really was ten kinds of crazy.

"And the supermax was so boring, you really have no idea."

"You realize they're made like that on purpose."

He made a noise of agreement.

"What if I stayed with you the whole time until you were incarcerated, and what if the supermax was off the table?"

"Well, for one, you would have to go home eventually, and for two, you can't say for certain where I'll go, and now this Ryerson thinks I've done something to him personally, and that's going to be—"

"I can fix that," I asserted, studying him. "I told him that wasn't you, and I can let him know that it was Kelson who took his son."

He grimaced, unconvinced.

"Your track record speaks for itself. It's not like you to target anyone in law enforcement."

"Except you."

"Not because I was a cop and now a marshal, but because I saved your life."

"That's true."

"Believe me, I can explain what happened."

"And you'd do that for me?"

"It's the truth," I said, avoiding that trap.

He pointed over his shoulder at Kelson. "Well, all I ever wanted was access to the FBI, which I had first with Wojno and then with Kelson."

"Right."

"But my interests have changed," he said deliberately, flicking his pale blue eyes to mine, holding for a moment, and then dropping them. The action told me all I needed to know about Kelson's life expectancy. He was one step from the grave.

But Hartley would never kill him in the van. He wouldn't want any splatter.

"So you're flying to Europe?" I asked for clarification.

"Yes," he said with an indulgent smile, and we both heard my question as I intended it, that he, no one else, was traveling. I couldn't see the driver's face, but he was good, whoever he was, because the van had not slowed once since I got in. Of course Stigler was wrong; they had taken me rather quickly past the safe zone she'd set up.

"You know," he said after only moments, "I do believe you're the only person I've ever truly cared for."

"Such as that is," I teased, but gently. Poking a viper was never a wise decision.

"True," he said, smiling fondly before turning to look over his shoulder out the front window.

I could have rushed him, done something, but we'd developed a strange trust between us that I didn't want to mess with. The idea of returning to a time when I feared what he would do to me was exhausting even to consider. In my life now, he was not one of my day-to-day concerns. I didn't want to change that. I didn't need the arrow back on me. I did need to check something, though.

"I don't want us to be on bad terms, but I also can't have you hurting people, because then that's on my head too."

"How?" he asked, turning back to me.

"I'm responsible for what you do."

"Why? Because you won't trade your life to stop me?"

"You won't kill me."

"If it's me or you, you know I would. I only do not because you allow the charade of power."

"The whole 'you holding a gun on me that I know you won't fire' thing."

"Unless, of course, you come at me with some kind of murderous intent."

"I have confinement intent," I admitted and couldn't help chuckling.

"Yes," he agreed, unable to keep from smiling in return. "But you know the rules, and we both play by them."

We did, it was true. I didn't push; he offered me no real peril.

"But see, I can't have you out there killing people again."

He thought about that before saying, "I have no intention of killing anyone at the moment. I think it was a phase that ran its course, but I'll make you a deal."

"G'head."

"If I get any new homicidal urges, I'll call first and tell you where I am, and you can hop on a plane and try to stop me."

"From halfway around the world?"

"This is your issue, not mine; don't make it an annoyance simply because you don't have a valid passport."

"I'm a federal marshal. Of course I have a passport."

"Well, then," he contended like it was a done deal. "I'll alert you, and you can come try to stop me. It will be just like old times."

"I'm going to put out a red notice on you, you know."

"Do what you feel you must."

"You don't sweat Interpol, huh?"

"Not ever, no."

"All right, so I have your word? No one dies unless you call me?"

"Absolutely."

"Okay."

He held out his hand. "Let's shake on it."

I rolled forward to my knees and stretched for his hand, not about to crawl over to him.

His hand was warm and dry, and he wrapped his long, elegant fingers around my hand as he stared into my eyes. Unlike Kelson, Hartley's eyes were clear, intent, and showed his happiness at having made a pact with me.

I squeezed tight and would have let go, but he held on.

"Whyever did you squeeze my hand?" he asked, lashes fluttering as he smiled, bemused.

"I have no idea," I sighed, shaking my head.

"You know, I suspect this will be the last time we'll talk, maybe ever."

"I would agree," I said softly.

The van stopped then, and he rose to slide open the door.

I moved quickly, hopping out, and when I was standing on the side of the road, I looked up at him.

He breathed in deeply. "Leaving Chicago is so odd. I never thought I would."

I nodded.

"I'm glad I was able to see you."

"So am I," I whispered, and I realized a part of me *was* happy because this, right here, was finally closure.

"That's it?" Kelson gasped, scrambling out of the van, charging up on me, his Glock 20 leveled at the center of my chest. "You're just going to let him go?"

"Of course," Hartley replied smoothly but snidely, the disgust on his tongue and all over his face as he stared down Kelson. "I'm not a barbarian."

"But he's an idiot, and he thinks he—"

"He doesn't *think* anything…. He knows," Hartley corrected, turning to smile at me. "He's my oldest friend."

"Friend." Kelson heaved out the breath, and I saw in that instant, with those last four words, that Hartley had broken him.

Completely, utterly, annihilated him.

Kelson had been so clever. He'd planned, done everything to impress the man he so desperately wanted to be. The problem was, though, I'd gotten there first.

It was simply a matter of timing.

I was the one who saved him.

I was the one who visited him when he was locked up in Elgin.

I was the one who sat and listened for hours on end to his thoughts, to the why of what he'd done and became his witness—the voice in his head, he'd told me once—and eventually, after he saved my werewolf, a man I didn't break out in cold sweats over anymore.

We weren't friends, it wasn't that, but we were… something. I'd have to figure out what at some point.

But Kelson didn't have the benefit of knowing our history and was instead hampered by his own jealousy and hatred and bitterness. What he thought would never matter more than what I did, and it was killing him. His face said everything. Where I couldn't read him at all the day before, now I saw his intent clear as day as he squinted at me and pulled the trigger.

I didn't have time to yell. I didn't think about Ian and how much he'd miss me. I didn't see Aruna or Catherine, Janet or Min. I didn't regret all the kids I wouldn't be around to help, or even think if Redeker would pull his head out of his ass and tell Callahan that, fuck yeah, he wanted him too.

Nothing went through my head except for the fact I was going to die with Hartley looking down at me after all. And somehow that wasn't as bad as it once was.

Something hit me hard and hurled me into the grass and mud on the side of the road. It had snowed the day before, and because it hadn't been warm enough to melt, when I went down under what I abruptly recognized as a hundred and eighty pounds of Craig Hartley, my back hit the ice over snow, and it took every puff of air from my lungs.

Stunned, shaken, I saw the pale sky, heard a high-pitched shrieking wail before the weight on my chest lifted and the sound of machine-gun fire filled the air in quick staccato bursts.

Kelson screamed, and when I lifted only my head, I saw him lying on the same cold, hard, ice-covered ground I was splayed out on.

Already my back was damp. The chill was seeping into my skin, sending a quick tremor through my frame as I gulped air and sat up. When I turned my head to the left… only then did I see Hartley.

His mouth was open, and he was breathing, but it was labored, and in the next second I saw the reason. Blood staining his jacket over his heart.

Scrambling sideways, I pressed both hands to his chest, pushing hard, which made him wince in pain.

"Useless," he husked as a tear rolled from his left eye down toward his ear.

"The hell were you thinking?" I rasped, my voice, fractured, stilted, sounding odd, frightened and hollow.

"Well," he huffed, each syllable a labor. "I was thinking that no one is allowed to kill Miro Jones… but me."

"Smooth talker," I murmured, hearing my heart pound in my ears. He tried to smile.

Lifting one hand, I struggled to get my jacket off. I needed to slow the bleeding and warm him up so he didn't go into shock.

"Do not ruin a perfectly good Tom Ford jacket," he scolded. "It's no use. Just sit here for a moment and take the gun."

I looked at the automatic rifle and then back at his rapidly graying face. "What?"

"Honestly," he sighed, "how you've stayed alive this long… the driver is still—"

The sound of an engine revving caught our attention before the van drove off with a squeal of tires.

"Well, that's heartening," he deadpanned before he coughed up some blood.

"Shit," I choked out, rummaging through his jacket for his phone, having left mine with Ian. "Where the hell is your—"

"In the van," he whispered, letting go of the gun and lifting his left hand toward me.

I grabbed it fast with my right, felt how cold it was, and held tighter even as blood pooled between the fingers of my left. "Goddammit, where the fuck is everyone?!"

"Oh," he said so softly I had to lean down, my ear close to his mouth. "You're really scared, aren't you?"

It was so useless now. He wasn't a threat anymore, and yes, he was a horror, but somehow… not. It made no sense and revolved as much around the life of a mixed-breed dog as it did me and him and how he'd been in my life longer than even Ian. A very big part of me was defined by my interactions with him. I could feel it in my heart, in my stomach, the rising ache.

"I don't—this isn't how I wanted—we're supposed to be even," I said, turning to look at him, into his eyes, so close, our noses almost bumping. "I saved you, you saved me—how am I gonna pay you back?" I asked, my eyes filling.

"Next time," he whispered, lifting his chin. "Come here."

Without thought, I turned my head so his lips pressed to my cheek as he squeezed my hand, so tight for just a moment.

"Always knew you were mine," he said, exhaling.

I stayed there, frozen for a second, and then turned to meet his gaze as his grip slowly lessened, and his hand would have slipped from mine if I wasn't the one holding on.

The last tear slipped down the side of his face, and I brushed it away before closing his eyes.

It made no sense to cry. He was not a good man. He was, in fact, a monster. But somewhere between him shoving a kitchen knife into my side and taking a rib from me, and telling me that, no, my dog was not dead… he had become *my* monster. We were not what we once were, and in the end, he took a pair of bullets meant for me and saved my life. People would be writing about him for years.

I had no idea how to feel, what to think, but sitting there, holding his hand, seemed like the only right thing to do.

IT WAS quiet and still, like the whole world had stopped, but in another few minutes, I caught the faint sound of sirens.

I slowly let Hartley's hand go and placed both, together, on his chest. He looked like he was resting, peaceful, and when he blurred, I realized my eyes were filling, and I put my face in my hands and let myself cry, in private, and mourn a man no one, even Ian, would understand the why of.

He'd done horrific things to me, but they were mine to forgive, and so I would. Not because he'd saved me. Nothing so cut-and-dry. If he'd left me on the side of the road like he wanted with a "Have a nice life, Miro," my feelings would be the same. God help me, but he was my friend in some freaky way that made no logical sense.

So I sat there, bawling, chest tight, tears running down my face because Craig Hartley was the first person I'd ever lost who meant something to me, who was close to me and who had altered the course of my life. I had no parents, no birth family, no one besides Ian and the girls and a few other friends who loved me, and none of them had ever died. This serial killer was the first, and so I broke down there beside him in the mud and felt what it was to lose one of the people who'd helped shape the man I'd become.

I was glad the cavalry wasn't there yet because it was allowing me time to grieve, to pour my tears into the ground and come completely apart. It was fortunate no one was there to see me purge the vault of my heart.

Then a wall of police cars raced by.

"Miro!"

Wiping at my eyes roughly, I took a breath, lifted my head, and saw the row of SUVs stopping beside me and Hartley and Kelson.

"Holy shit," Ian gasped as he climbed out of the passenger-side door and charged over to me, dropping to his knees and wrapping his arms around me.

I couldn't breathe, and I was pretty sure he crushed my ribs. But that was okay because he was there, solid and warm, and as long as I was in his arms at the end of things, I called that a win.

"Oh, baby, what happened?"

But I couldn't, not quite yet. All of it too much to vocalize at the moment.

He held me to his heart, kissed my eyes, my cheeks, the line of my jaw, and then brushed his mouth over mine. I wanted more, and he murmured a promise of showing me how much I was loved when we got home.

When the Feds arrived along with CPD, Ian helped me to my feet because no way could I walk alone. I couldn't watch them touch Hartley, didn't want to see whatever they were going to do with him, so I didn't look back when Ian put me in the back behind the passenger seat. Eli was driving, and even as Stigler walked toward the SUV, he pulled out and whipped the SUV around, doing a U-turn in the middle of the road leading to the Chicago Executive Airport in Wheeling where Hartley had been headed.

"He saved me," I said to Ian and Eli—and Ryan and Dorsey, who were also in the SUV—new tears coming fast. "I—Kelson tried to kill me, and Hartley.... He saved me."

No one said a word.

"He took the bullets that Kelson fired at me."

"Jesus Christ," Ian croaked, turning in his seat to give me his hand.

"Only you, Jones," Ryan sighed, and when I glanced over at him, he was smiling ruefully. "I don't know anyone but you who gets saved by a serial killer."

We rode the rest of the way back to the office in silence.

Once there, Ian went with me to one of the smaller meeting rooms, where a forensic team met us.

He left to get me a set of sweats while the supervisor and two others stripped me down to my underwear, combed mud from my hair, scraped blood from under my nails, and shot an endless amount of pictures of me from every imaginable angle. It didn't take long, but I was shivering by the time they were done. Ian came in once they finished, pulled the sweatshirt down over my head, and helped me into the pants before he lunged and wrapped me up tight.

I hugged him back so hard I pulled a groan from deep in his chest.

"You're alive and you're here with me," he whispered into my hair. "As soon as you're done talking to the Feds, I'm gonna take you home, and we're gonna wreck the bed, all right?"

I nodded into his shoulder. Not that I didn't always want him, but now I needed him. I needed his warmth over me, around me, in me.... I was cold to my core, and only Ian could make me *me* again.

Outside in the hall, Eli was there waiting to lead Ian and me to the large meeting room. Kage was there, along with Stigler and Ryerson and Adair and many others, all of them taking up one side of the enormous table and fanned out around the room.

Once I was sitting between Ian and Eli, I looked up at Ryerson, who was leaning forward, hands clasped in front of him on the table.

"How is your son, sir?"

"Scared but fine, thanks to you, Marshal."

I nodded. "I hope that you checked on Kelson before your men got close."

"I'm sorry?"

"He did maybe have a bomb in him after all."

All eyes lifted to Kage, who was standing somewhere behind me. I couldn't see him, but I could feel him there.

"I told you when I got there to call the bomb squad first, as you will recall."

Ryerson turned first to Stigler and then swiveled in his seat to Adair. "Did someone do as the chief deputy suggested and call them?"

Stigler leaped from her chair and bolted from the room.

"You people run the biggest clusterfuck I've ever seen," Kage informed Ryerson. "From how many times Hartley got away to this latest debacle. I swear to God, if I ran my office like this, there would be bodies stacked up to the sky."

"Chief Deputy, we—"

"Oh dear God," Stigler yelled as she rushed back into the room. "No one was hurt, but because the bomb squad wasn't on-site to check and defuse the device inside Kelson, his body exploded and destroyed two of the SUVs parked on-site."

"Holy fuckin' shit," Eli snorted, and I did a slow pan to him.

"What?" he said, gesturing with both hands at Ryerson. "Are you *kidding*?"

"And Hartley's body?" Ryerson asked.

"Destroyed," she whispered.

And suddenly everyone was talking at once.

I couldn't even deal. It was too ridiculous. Who didn't listen to the goddamn chief deputy of Northern Illinois? What kind of idiots just blew him off? How did they not call the bomb squad first fucking thing? It was… insane.

Leaning my head in my hand, the tears came again even as I started laughing.

"Marshal?" Ryerson asked.

How much would Hartley have loved this? His legend was growing already.

"He's done," Ian informed him.

"But we have questions."

"Put it in a memo," Kage said flatly, patting my shoulder at the same time. "You get up, go home. I don't want to see you until Monday."

"Yessir," I said, getting to my feet.

"You too, Doyle. You're relieved."

"Thank you, sir."

We were out in the hall, where I could breathe, when Eli joined us. Even through walls that were supposed to be pretty damn well-insulated, I could hear Kage yelling.

"He's going to eat them," I told Ian.

"I certainly fuckin' hope so."

As we walked by the break room on the way out of the office, Eli ducked in and grabbed a couple of kiwis from the enormous basket Mrs. Guzman still sent monthly for Ian and me.

"I sent her an email again," I told Ian as Eli caught back up with us. "But I don't think she's ever gonna stop sending us fruit."

"No," he agreed, slipping his hand into mine, "I don't think so either, but that's okay, right? She can send the fruit if she wants to."

"Yeah," I agreed.

"We think we were just doing our jobs, but that's not what she thinks. She's allowed to feel how she wants. We all are."

And I got, then, that when I thought before Ian wouldn't understand how I felt, I was wrong about him. He could read me like a book.

In the elevator I leaned into him, kissing the side of his neck, inhaling citrus and leather, gun oil, a trace of cedarwood, and just Ian. He smelled like home, and that fast my eyes were swimming again.

"I really need to take a shower," I said gruffly, my voice breaking as I rubbed my eyes hard, trying to grind the tears away.

"Don't do that," he cautioned, turning so I could put my cheek down on his shoulder, wiping my whole face on his wool peacoat. "Just hold on, we'll be home soon."

But I was about to dissolve all over again. Everything felt unsteady, like there was nothing underneath me and I wasn't tethered to anything. I could float away so easily.

"Can you drive us?" I heard Ian ask Eli.

"You bet."

It was a fog I was walking through, and only Ian's hands on me, guiding me, steering me forward, kept me moving.

He got on the phone with someone, but I couldn't tell who, and honestly, I hardly cared. He was there with me, and that was all that mattered.

There was snow falling outside my window as I sat in the back seat, my face against the cold glass, wondering what would happen to all of Hartley's shoes. He had so many.

And his suits.

And his art collection, and everything else. If a life came down to what was accumulated, where was it all?

"Do you think they'll cremate what's left of Hartley?" I asked Ian.

"I dunno," he murmured gently, taking hold of my hand. "Jesus, you're like ice," he grumbled. "C'mon already, Eli."

"This is Chicago in rush hour, are you kidding?"

I closed my eyes for a second, and then Ian was telling me to watch my head as he helped me out of the car.

Eli hugged me, for whatever reason, and I felt bad for not giving him my regular full-body one back—he was one of my best friends now too—but I just couldn't summon the energy. And then I was at the front door, having somehow climbed the stoop with Ian.

"I fell asleep in the car, huh?"

"Yes, love," he said, his voice deep and gravelly. "C'mon."

Inside, he dropped the keys, locked the door, got me out of my parka, and led me upstairs. He got the shower going, stripped me down, and then had me step in under the warm spray.

"I'm gonna hang everything up, stow the guns, make you some soup—"

"But I'm not—"

"You're gonna eat," he promised. "But just for now, shower. You'll feel better after you do."

I nodded, and he closed the door.

"I'll be right back to check on you, all right?"

"Okay," I said, putting my head under the water.

It was weird, but it was like I couldn't feel the water, like it wasn't touching me. I couldn't feel the warmth, like I hadn't felt anything when Eli hugged me. It was strange, off, and I wasn't sure what would turn it back on.

I went through the motions of washing my hair and body and stood there until the water was turned off and Ian was there, easing me out, putting a towel over my head.

He was gentle, towel-drying my hair, kissing my cheek when he was done, then drying my face and smiling at me.

"You're gorgeous," I told him, sighing deeply. My beautiful man with his chiseled features and sculpted body was a work of art. "Holy fuck, did I win the lottery or what?"

"Man, if I didn't know better, I'd think you were stoned," he teased, drying the rest of me, but not slow like he did when he wanted to fool around, but fast, deliberate, like he wanted it done. "Come on. Aruna's downstairs, and she brought Chickie and food so you have something better than just chicken noodle."

"I like chicken noodle soup," I said as he passed me my deodorant.

"Yeah, but Aruna's food is always a step up, right?"

There was no argument to be made.

"Just come on," he prodded, piloting me out of the bathroom to our bedroom. I got a kiss on the cheek, and then he was gone.

I could hear them downstairs, and a minute later, Chickie came up the stairs and padded over to the bed where I was sitting with only sweats on.

Seeing him made me think again of Hartley, and it was stupid, but there were fresh tears as I wrapped my arms around the dog and hugged him.

Chickie, who outweighed some people I knew, namely Aruna, always considered himself to be a lap dog, so he maneuvered his way up and into my lap, and that was where Ian found us, sitting on the bed together, Chickie rumbling happily as I sobbed into his fur.

"Oh, baby, you're gonna hafta take another shower if you smell like wet dog," he grumbled. "Chickie, get down—go see Aru—don't you growl at me, you piece of crap, he doesn't belong to you!" He sounded very affronted, and that, finally, made me smile.

"Oh, there he is," Ian murmured before he took my face in his hands, leaned in, and laid a kiss on me that curled my toes. His mouth on mine was mauling, firm, parting my lips as I moaned deeply, needing more, wanting more, craving the heat of him because I was absolutely freezing inside.

He broke the kiss, and I gasped, clutching at him, wanting him back, my body more than ready for him, willing, able, shivering with something utterly primal. The connection was utterly necessary, and I had to have it.

Climbing off the bed, he leaned over the railing and yelled down to Aruna. "I need you to walk the dog for me, three times around the block'll do it, all right?"

"Going now," she called back up.

He was back on the bed in seconds, climbing over me, and I reached up as he bent and took my mouth again, tenderly but possessively, opening me up, rubbing his tongue over mine.

I wanted his clothes off, but he swatted my hands away, rolling me to my side and holding me there as I sank down into the bed.

I was a block of ice until Ian was there at my back, his sleek, warm skin sliding over mine as he spooned me, shucking down my sweats at the same time as I felt the head of his cock notch against my crease.

"Oh please," I moaned as I heard the cap of the lube flicked open.

He nuzzled his face into my hair and kissed the back of my neck, taking hold of my shaft and stroking from balls to head as I arched back into him. His hard, muscular thighs were against mine, his ridged stomach and broad chest on my back as he fumbled for a moment, slicking his cock, and I could hear it and smell the mint flavoring of the lubricant he'd purchased by accident last time and ended up liking.

He used the tee he'd been wearing under his dress shirt and wiped his hand on it, throwing it off the bed as he positioned himself against my hole and pressed slowly inside.

I cried out his name.

"I'll take care of you," he growled into my hair before he kissed the side of my neck and my cheek. "Turn your head."

I twisted for him, and he lifted to kiss me at the same time he pulled me back, pushing deeper, the long, hard, hot length of him so very welcome as he seated himself fully.

"Miro," he gasped, releasing my mouth, stroking in and easing out over and over, rolling his hips in a seamless, searing rhythm I ached for. "You're alive, love, and I've got you, I'll always be here… I'll always have you. I'm your safety net. You can count on me."

I could, I knew that. He was mine, my husband, my partner in all things, and the job didn't matter, only life did, and for my life, there was Ian.

"Jesus, Miro, you feel so fuckin' good."

So did he.

I wanted more, craved more, and so tried to close the distance between us so he could piston inside, faster, harder, the burn of his entry, the stretch and fill, forcing out the cold, only his heat remaining.

"Miro, honey—you're killing me. I'm trying to be—fuck—gentle."

"Don't need gentle," I mewled, the ache in my voice making it crack and strain. "Need you all over me."

Without hesitation he rolled me to my stomach and then lifted me roughly to my knees, rutting inside, hands on my shoulders so I couldn't move.

"Ian," I moaned, the domination, his power, making my whole body shudder as I clutched at the sheets and held on.

"You don't belong to Craig Hartley, you understand?"

"Yes."

"I know you're hurt, but I won't allow you to be lost, you understand?"

"Ian," I whined as he bent over me, one arm around my chest, and lifted me up, back, back until I was impaled on his cock and he was pushing up into me.

"You belong to me. You're mine, and no one and nothing comes between us, not ever."

"Yes."

Ian stroking my shaft with his rough, callused hand, his cock finding the spot inside of me, driving me wild, pumping mercilessly up into me, had me chanting his name in an endless litany.

"Look at you coming apart," he said, the low, seductive chuckle sending new ripples of electricity dancing over my skin. "I think I see my boy coming back to life."

And I was. I was there in my head, in my body, feeling everything, wanting desperately to be able to have as much of him as I wanted.

"What do you need?" Ian rumbled.

"You under me."

Carefully he lifted me off the end of his dick and then toppled over beside me, down onto the bed, rolling to his back. I pounced on him, straddling his thighs, and he took hold of his cock as I sank down over him, slowly but steadily until all of him was buried inside of me.

"Ride me."

I wasn't gentle, and he bowed up off the bed as I ground down onto him, over and over, taking what I needed until I pushed Ian to his limit and he manhandled me to my back, curled over me, lifted my legs over his shoulders, and stuffed me full, thrusting as hard as he could.

My muscles clenched around him as I came, and he was seconds behind, my name crawling out of his throat in a husky roar.

We were slick with sweat, panting, and Ian was still above me, still pushing in, still coming until he collapsed down into my arms, utterly spent.

I rubbed his damp hair, turned and kissed his cheek, and then lifted his head so I could see his face. Always, how dark his eyes got made me smile.

"I want you here with me."

"I am," I sighed.

"You have to talk to me all the time."

I grinned. "You telling me that I hafta talk is kinda funny."

"Just—do what you're told, all right? Don't be such a smartass."

"Yes, dear," I said playfully, easing him down for a kiss.

"You two better be done gettin' your freak on up there because some people around here have husbands and daughters to feed!"

Ian ended the kiss and yelled down at her to keep her panties on.

"Chickie, your daddy wants you," Aruna cooed. "Where's Daddy?"

We both heard the dog galloping up the stairs.

"Goddamn, Chick, don't—oh God, he broke my back!"

"Serves you right, asshat!" Aruna yelled.

I couldn't stop laughing.

ONCE WE got up and dressed, Ian went down first, and then I followed, falling into Aruna's arms when I reached her.

"Oh, baby," she crooned, stroking my hair, petting me. "I'm not sorry the man's dead, but I know that it had to be messy for you, not just one thing, so for that, you have my sympathy."

I hugged her tight, and she squeezed me back.

"Let's get some food in you, all right?"

Nodding, I sat down on a barstool, one of three that went on one side of our new kitchen island. The entire Greystone had improved quite a bit since Ian moved in.

I was eating, not really paying attention as Ian and Aruna talked, but when Aruna hauled off and smacked him, I was surprised.

"Why're you hitting him?"

"Because he told Min about his promotion before me," she snapped, scowling at him. "I'm right here, for heaven's sake!"

I turned to look at Ian. "You talked to Min yesterday?"

"I talk to Min every week. You know that."

I did, and it never ceased to amaze me because it was the weirdest thing. Of all my girlfriends, he'd bonded with Min. He really liked Aruna, but it was more sisterly, like he couldn't say anything bad to her. He tolerated Catherine, and I got that. She could be a bit high-handed, conceited, and snooty, but I adored her. Janet, Ian wasn't sure about. He liked her well enough, but she was definitely more my friend than anything else.

Min, however, he gelled with. She was low-key, blunt, prickly, did not suffer fools, and she had an affinity for all the same video games Ian did, from *Call of Duty* to *Horizon* to *Borderlands*. They played online with others, and it was uber-nerdy. They took it very seriously, and I'd been banned from playing or talking to either of them when they were on a "mission." They even had headsets. Ian bought them at Christmas, and Min cried over FaceTime when she opened her present. Her new boyfriend, Jensen Drake, who owned a very well-respected custom car shop there in Burbank, had given her a ring—*the* ring—and she'd seriously been more excited about the headset. I apologized to Jensen, who just grinned and said that was why he loved her.

They made an interesting pair, the thousand-dollar-an-hour criminal attorney and the tatted-up car guy. They met at a fundraiser, and Min took one look and moved toward him, he said, like a shark in the water. He was entranced. She was beautiful and scary, and he told me he never knew what hit him. He wanted to marry her on their second date; she was worried he was too clingy. She finally agreed to move in with him because his house in Topanga Canyon was apparently just lovely. She could breathe there. That was a very good thing.

Jensen had impressed Ian, as he'd been a Navy SEAL who got out when he realized he wanted more for his life, and that included art and a family. With Min agreeing to marry him—even if the Harry Winston ring on her finger played second fiddle to a gaming headset—he had everything he wanted. Ian told me he knew the feeling.

"So you told Min all about your promotion?" I asked.

"Yeah."

I smiled.

"What? She gets me."

I knew that. "Did she have any advice? I mean, she always does, right?"

"She did."

"What was it?"

"To be my best self."

I squinted at him. "The fuck does that mean?"

"I have no clue, but she was really pleased about my promotion—and yours—so that's—"

"You got a promotion too?" Aruna yelled.

"God," I groaned.

She swatted me, hard, and I rubbed my bicep as I told her all about Custodial, and then Ian explained what he was doing as well.

"Ohmygod, that's perfect for you guys," she sighed, beaming. "You were a ward of the state too; you'll know exactly how to talk to those kids to make them feel cared for. My goodness, but your boss is a smart man. Moving Ian into a position where he can use his natural bossiness to cut through the red tape—"

"Hey!"

"—and you being a caretaker of kids since you suck at being a grown-up sometimes, especially in terms of your personal safety."

"I… what?" I griped.

"That chief deputy, what a clever, clever man."

I really couldn't disagree.

CHAPTER 11

MY PHONE woke me early the following morning, much too early for a Saturday, and when I moved, still tangled with Ian, he tightened his grip on me, as was his instinct.

"Phone," I muttered, and he reached over me to grab it and hand it over at the same time his went off.

"Oh, what the hell," he grumbled, rolling toward his nightstand to grab it as Chickie laid his head on the end of the bed to look at us. A voice blasted at me as soon as I answered it.

"Miro!"

It took me a second. "Min?" It was her, but I'd never heard that exact tremor in her voice before in my life. It was almost scary.

"I need help."

My head cleared instantly. "What's wrong?"

"Ned has lost his fuckin' mind."

"Ned?" I wasn't sure I was understanding her. "Janet's Ned?"

"Yes, Janet's Ned."

"What happened?"

"He checked Janet into the hospital yesterday and is trying to have her committed."

I sat up straight. "But she just had a baby."

"What does that have to do with what I'm telling you?"

I had no earthly idea, but it had made sense in my head.

A month ago Janet had delivered her first child. She was still out on maternity leave. Ian and I were supposed to go on our honeymoon, but we agreed we'd skip that and use our vacation for the birth of the baby instead. But I had wanted to wait until Cody, Janet's son, was at least three months old so he wasn't so boneless. I had held Sajani when she was a month old, and it freaked me out.

"Honey, I need you to wake up because I need you to save Janet."

"Okay, go back," I demanded, throwing off the covers, getting out of bed.

"It sounds like Ned's mother got him going because Janet didn't want to leave the baby with her. She convinced him that Janet is suffering from postpartum depression and suggested she go with Ned to a spa and rest."

"There's more, tell me more."

"As I understand it, Janet and Ned were in the bedroom fighting about going out. Ned wanted to; Janet wanted to stay home with the baby, but when he tried to take Cody out of Janet's arms to put him back into the crib, she tightened her hold, and Ned pulled at the same time," she sighed. "In the process of this teeny tug-of-war, Cody fell, and as Janet was crying, Ned's mother, who was also there, called the police."

"The police?" I rasped, not believing how quickly something so innocent had escalated.

"Yeah. So when the police got there, Ned's mother said that Janet was endangering her child. When they asked Ned for confirmation, he said that yes, she was, and had purposely dropped the baby. He blamed postpartum depression, and the cops took Janet to the hospital, but Ned had her transferred immediately to The Meadows Treatment Facility, which is where I need you to go spring her from this morning."

"Wait."

"Yes?" she said, and I could hear the tension and exasperation in her voice, like she didn't want to explain things to me, she just wanted me to listen.

"Janet's not some dying calf in a thunderstorm, right? I mean she's strong and gutsy and—there's no way she doesn't stick up for herself in that situation and get the cops to listen to her," I contended, knowing Janet, certain she would have argued, had a rebuttal for Ned's allegation to defend her actions. "She would have told them that it was his fault, that he was the one trying to grab the baby away from her."

"Normally, yes, I agree. I know she would have been able to handle this and stop it from blowing up, but this time she lost it."

"Why?"

Sharp exhale of breath. "I don't know. I think maybe she must have gotten scared, because it said on the police report that she started screaming and threatening Ned and his mother, and then she threw her cell phone at him while the police were right there."

Hurling the phone at Ned was bad enough, but the fact there was an infant in the house compounded it. The big-picture concern would be that Janet was a danger to herself and others. Once the police made that determination, that would have been all they needed to take her into custody and remove her from her home.

I could feel my heart starting to pound. "And?"

"And that's it."

I couldn't breathe. "When Cody fell—how—"

"He fell probably three feet onto the bed."

It took me a moment. "I'm sorry?"

"No, you heard me right."

"He fell onto the bed?" I could barely believe what I was hearing, and I was getting angrier by the second.

"Yeah."

"Onto the bed?" I was flabbergasted. "Are you kidding?"

"I wish I was."

"But—"

"I know. Believe me, I know."

"So Cody's fine."

"Totally fine, yes."

"Then all this is because of Ned's mother."

"And Ned," Min snapped, the anger seeping through her words. "Don't forget him. But yes, his mother was there, and—well—it escalated from bad to worse."

"No shit. So what now?"

"Now you go get her skinny ass out."

"How?"

"Well, as you know, I don't practice law in DC, but I have a colleague there, and he filed a restraining order for me on Janet's behalf against Ned and his mother."

"Just tell me what I need to do."

"I need you to go there, get her out of the hospital, and go with her so she can take custody of Cody."

"Where's Cody now?"

"He's with Ned and his mother," she explained and then continued on, talking to me using so much legalese that I couldn't even follow her. Clearly she was speaking to me like I was a colleague and not her friend.

"Min, tell me again and use small words."

In the midst of her freaking out about Janet, she took a breath. "Okay, sorry, honey, I'm just—you know."

"I know."

"Okay, so, I filed for a court order to stop what Ned was doing with Janet at the hospital, and the restraining order had to be approved and served to make the baby legally Janet's until this gets straightened out. I did that all yesterday, and it was in fact approved, but it was too late to be served by the court, you understand?"

"Yes."

"So it's all good, there's just no one there to serve it on a Saturday."

"Right. So did you send me a copy?"

"Yes. I emailed it to you, so print it out and get on a plane. I don't want her in there any longer than she needs to be. She's probably losing her fucking mind."

"Course."

"I'll be in Chicago tomorrow morning. That's the quickest I can get there because I'm in goddamn Puerto Vallarta instead of where I should be at home with Jensen!"

There was no time to ask. She was probably doing something for work, meeting a client or something else, but whatever it was, I suspected she wouldn't ever do it again.

"It's fine. Try not to worry. I'll take care of it."

"I know you will, I know," she said frantically. "It's just when Janet called me yesterday, I—she was hysterical, and I—I know she called me because I'm the lawyer, right, and I couldn't fix it right away, and if she'd called you or Ian, I just—"

"It wouldn't have been any better," I assured her. "And there was no way she could have gotten hold of me yesterday. I was dealing with my own shit."

"Yeah, no, sure—I—"

"Min, sweetie, you're doin' awesome."

She took a quick breath. "Okay, so, listen, Catherine will meet you there at the hospital. She left Manhattan about ten minutes ago."

"Leaving now."

"Listen to me," she said solemnly, and I heard the tears in her voice. "You do not let them keep her or that baby, do you understand me?"

"Yes."

"Aruna should be there to get you and Ian in twenty minutes. Shower, shave, wear your suits, take your badges, get it done."

In the middle of something this scary, I was struck by her absolute faith in not only me, but Ian too.

"Min—"

"Put Ian on the phone, please."

Turning, I found him growling, obviously annoyed at whatever his call had been about.

"So that was my father on the phone, and he doesn't think that the deal Stafford and I worked out for Lorcan is good enough, and he—Miro? What's wrong?"

"Min wants to talk to you," I said, holding my phone out for him.

"What's wrong?" he repeated gruffly.

I jiggled the phone, and he grabbed it from me.

"Hello?"

He listened while I ran around and got into the shower. Even under the water, I heard him yelling.

"Are you fucking *kidding* me?"

I left the water on so Ian could get in right after, and as soon as I stepped out, he went in, slamming the shower door behind him.

"I'll fuckin' kill him."

Meaning Ned, of course.

The doorbell rang, and I raced downstairs in only a towel to meet Aruna, who was there with Liam, holding Sajani's hand.

"Minnow!" Sajani greeted me cheerfully, holding up her arms. Miro was not in her vocabulary, but the name of a small fish was.

Frickin' kid.

Scooping her up, I carried her inside as Chickie barreled around the couch and up to me because I had his prize.

"Chickie!" she squealed, contorting in my arms to get down to be with him.

As soon as I set the tiny bird-boned toddler down, she opened her arms and wrapped them around Chickie's muzzle. It should have been scary—he could have eaten her in one bite, maybe two—but instead it was sweet because her trust was complete and his protection unlimited. He'd stand between her and anything.

"Why are you not ready?" Aruna asked me irritably. "We've got a plane to catch."

I was surprised. "She bought plane tickets?"

"This is Min," she reminded me as Ian pounded down the stairs. "Of course she bought plane tickets."

"Ian!" Sajani announced loudly, almost shrill.

"How come she can say Ian?" I questioned Aruna.

"I'm sure I have no idea," she answered, clearly bored with the topic.

"Here's what I think—"

"Hey. You take care of my girl," Liam said seriously, patting my bare shoulder before hooking the nylon leash, made out of the same stuff people used when they went mountain climbing, to Chickie's collar. "I've got your dog."

Ian leaned in, hugged Liam, kissed Sajani, and then bolted for the kitchen to grab keys and probably see if he could get one cup of coffee in before we had to go.

Aruna turned, kissed her husband, then her daughter, and shooed them away before following Ian.

"Don't screw up," the mass of muscle that was Liam Duffy warned me.

"I won't. Get out."

He pointed at his wife—in my kitchen with Ian as they decided if tea would be better; we had Assam, and that was good in the morning—"I want her back just like that."

"I promise."

He left then, holding his daughter and leading my dog.

"I hate it when I'm not around when he goes for walks with those two," Aruna yelled from the kitchen.

"Why?"

She gestured at the door he left through. "Are you kidding? Beautiful man with a cute kid and a gorgeous dog—he's a chick magnet."

I rolled my eyes and headed back for the stairs.

"Ovaries exploding all over the place!"

Dressing quickly, I was back downstairs in minutes as Ian and Aruna both gulped down some apple juice—no time for tea—and the three of us headed for the front door.

"You both strapped?" Aruna asked.

"Ohmygod!" I yelled.

"What?"

"Yes," Ian answered as he grabbed his wool topcoat and headed outside.

I shoved her out after him.

"Watch it," she groused.

"Are we strapped…? Who talks like that?"

She was cackling as the Lyft driver pulled up alongside our truck on the street.

"Seriously," I said as I got into the back beside Aruna. "Min is fuckin' scary."

"She's thorough," Ian corrected. "I like it."

Aruna gagged.

"He's her favorite, you know."

"That's because he's a bootlicker," Aruna taunted.

He reached between the seats and swatted her leg.

"Owww, you ass!"

"Not a bootlicker. Ask Miro."

I leered. "He licks other things."

"I'm gonna throw up."

The driver couldn't keep from chuckling.

WE GOT serious once we were at the airport. After we checked in, the TSA had to determine that our clearances were good. Even law enforcement didn't get to just carry a gun on a plane. But as federal officers, we were required to carry at all times, so even on vacation, even going on a fishing trip or something inconsequential, we had to be armed.

Badges, credentials, tickets, routine check with our office and Homeland to make sure we were who we said we were, and once we were approved and wanded and patted down—watches, gun holsters, belts, shoes, and our guns looked at again—we joined Aruna, who was waiting for us.

"It's amazing that I made it through before you guys," she grumbled. "Now I need coffee before we get on that plane."

Once we were in the boarding area, Aruna's face crumpled.

"It's gonna be all right," I promised, wrapping an arm around her and tucking her up against my chest even as I watched Ian talk on the phone. He was pacing as he explained where we were going and what we were doing. I wasn't sure if he'd called Kage or Becker, but whoever it was, he was doing a lot of nodding.

She took a halting breath. "Of course it will."

Several women and a few men turned as they passed Ian, taking another look at the gorgeous man they walked by.

"Yeah, if I wasn't married, I'd take another look at him too."

"I can't stop looking at him," I told her.

"I like the sweater and sport coat and scarf you've got him in. All those layers of earth tones are very handsome," she said, turning to look at me. "Well done."

"It helps when you're built like that," I agreed, gesturing at him. "I mean, what can't he wear?"

"Are you guys talking about me?" Ian asked as he sat down beside me and put a hand on my thigh.

"Yes, of course we are."

"The clothes?" he surmised because he knew us.

"Mmmmm," Aruna murmured, smiling at him.

He bumped me with his shoulder. "You know how he is. I just have to put it on."

She nodded. "Well, you look fantastic. What is that pattern, windowpane?"

"Very good," I praised. "You'll notice that the stripes go with the sweater."

"I do," she said brightly, looking better now, more her, more upbeat.

"Windowpane?" Ian said like the word burned his mouth coming out. "Who cares?"

"Well, clearly your husband wants to make sure that you don't look like a shmuck, even before coffee on a Saturday morning," Aruna defended me.

He left to go to the bathroom, and we watched him walk away.

"Yep, very handsome man," she sighed before turning back to me. "And it's cliché, but really, what's on the inside is better."

"I know."

"May I just say that this blazer, jeans, and cashmere sweater combo you've got going on is very handsome as well?"

"And the gray lace-ups?" I teased, lifting my feet.

"A very nice touch," she said, giggling. "But Ian's Chelsea boots are better."

"They're mine."

She laughed, but then she took a shaky breath, remembering, I was sure, that we were in the airport for a reason and not a vacation. I stood quickly and yanked her into my arms, hugging her tight as she pressed her face into my chest and sobbed.

"It'll be all right," I promised hoarsely. "We'll fix it."

"The fuck happened?" Ian grumbled as he walked up beside me. "I left you with a perfectly happy woman, and now look at her. What'd you do?"

"I didn't do anything. She's a crybaby," I told him, and she laughed and hiccupped before ordering me to find the Kleenex in her purse.

As soon as I had it, Ian snatched it from me and then held a tissue over her nose so she could blow. It was adorable. We got on the plane fifteen minutes later.

THE PLANE ride was an hour and fifty minutes, and as predicted, Catherine was there when we walked out of the terminal. She ran to Aruna and grabbed her, and as they hugged, I got ready to be next. But she lunged for Ian as soon as she was released, and what started out awkward changed to him holding her like she would break in seconds.

"I knew Miro would come," she said, sobbing into his sweater. "But I wasn't sure you would. Thank you, Ian, I'll never forget this."

She and Ian would be different going forward, closer, and I was so much more than pleased.

In the line at the car rental, Ian explained his plan.

"Miro, you and Catherine go get Janet out. Me and Aruna will get the baby."

"So we need two cars," I told him.

"We have two cars," he assured me.

"She really is just terrifying," Aruna said with a whistle, referring to Min again.

After stopping quickly at a copy shop on the way to the facility to print out the paperwork Min sent, we reached the very-high-end rehabilitation center just after ten in the morning.

"I wonder why us," I said absently to Catherine.

"What?" she asked, getting out of the Cadillac Escalade we'd paid for the upgrade on, since Catherine refused to ride in the Dodge Dart the guy at the Enterprise counter tried to give us. She looked stunning, I noticed, hair swept up, diamond studs in, Dolce&Gabbana black power suit and sunglasses on, black clutch tucked under her arm.

"You look kinda scary."

"You look like you're ready for a day of antiquing."

I scowled.

"But to your question," she said as we began toward the front door, her black Louboutin heels sliding over the gravel as she walked. "I'm a doctor, so me at the mental health facility makes sense, and Janet will want to see you first. I just hope when Ian kicks down the door of Janet and Ned's place that he doesn't scare the crap out of everyone. He can be a bit—intense."

"He can be, yes."

"But perhaps, in this instance, that's what's needed."

At the front desk—it was more like a five-star hotel inside than what I was expecting—a woman smiled at us.

"Hello," Catherine greeted. "We need to speak to the doctor in charge, as well as to one of your patients who we have an order of release for."

"I'm sorry, but—"

"Ma'am," I said, stepping forward, holding up my credentials, "deputy US marshal. I'm afraid I'm going to need to insist."

And with that little, she went from combative to helpful. This was the nation's capital, after all; they knew how to obey people with badges.

Catherine went to the office with the doctor on duty, Dr. Abbott, who seemed more than a little blown away by one of the top neurosurgeons in the country striding through the corridors of his facility. Did it make sense? No. But Catherine was using her big words, her smile, the feeling of money that oozed off her, and the hard click of her heels on the floor as she walked to intimidate the man but good.

I followed a nurse and two orderlies. "It must be hard, coming here every day."

"The hard part is when you meet people who have no support systems," the nurse told me. "People who've had their families turn their backs on them for whatever reason—that's what breaks my heart."

I cleared my throat. "I have a new job with the marshals service working with kids."

She reached out and patted my arm. "Oh, then you understand how I feel. When there's no one for your kids, you're going to have a heck of a time, but just remember, never stop trying and never stop caring, that's my motto."

"It's a good motto."

Her smile was bright. "You don't get into this line of work, or yours, I suspect, unless you're a fighter—am I right?"

"You are."

At Janet's door, the bigger orderly gestured for me to go ahead and open the door.

"It's not locked?"

"No, of course not," he said. "That's not the kind of facility we're running here. She can leave her room, just not the building."

I opened the door and found Janet sitting up on a made bed she clearly had not slept in, legs crossed, breathing deeply in and out.

She was dressed as she'd probably been at home, in yoga pants, socks, a Lululemon short-sleeved shirt, and a large sweater coat with pockets. Her bright red hair was tied back in a messy ponytail, and when she saw me, her face went from slack and ashen to infused with light.

"Oh," the nurse almost cried as Janet leaped off the bed and rushed across the room to me, leaping at the last second so I had to catch her in my arms. "I'm glad you're taking her. She didn't strike me like some of the other postpartum moms we got in here."

While hugging Janet tight, I heard her start to cry, face resting against my shoulder, trembling hard, breathing rapidly. "If she seemed all right, why did you let her husband check her in?"

"Because he said she was a danger to herself and their baby, and we can do a seventy-two-hour hold without question if the husband signs off on it."

"Which he did."

"Yes," the nurse answered, looking like she might cry as she watched Janet shuddering in my arms. "Poor dear."

"Well, I appreciate your help, and—"

"I need to see my baby," Janet whispered, lifting her head to look into my eyes. "Miro, where is he, do you know if he's safe and—"

"He's okay," I promised, putting her on her feet, hands on her face, wiping away her tears. "Ian and Aruna are getting him, all right?"

She was having trouble talking and catching her breath. "Ian and Aruna?"

"Yes, honey, we're all here."

Leaning into me again, arms back around my neck, she clung as I rubbed circles on her back and told her that everything was going to be all right.

"I knew you'd get here, I knew you'd come," she chanted. "I knew it, I knew it."

"Min mobilized us."

"I knew that too," she said, her voice breaking as the tears started again.

"Come on, let's get outta here."

Once we were out in the hall, Janet clung to my arm with a death grip as we walked toward the front exit.

"It was so surreal."

"Ned, you mean?"

"Yeah."

"What do you think happened?"

"I don't know. Maybe he got scared that his life was going to change—and it is, I mean, of course it is, because, you know, baby."

"Sure."

"I thought about it all last night, and the only thing I came up with is that he had an idea in his mind of how I was supposed to be, and what he thought and the reality didn't mesh."

She was so logical; of course she'd thought about it and come up with an explanation for his behavior. "And his mother didn't help."

"Oh hell no," she said flatly, "and I tell you what, if I see her—oh," her voice dropped suddenly as she saw Catherine. "I knew she'd be here too, just like you. All of you guys, my friends, I swear to God, you're the blessing of my life."

I patted her hand as we closed in on Catherine.

"When I lost my mother, she said, 'Baby, you're gonna be all right. You have the girls, your sisters, and you have Miro. All of them will stand in for me until I see you again.'"

"Don't make me cry," I grumbled. "I haven't had enough coffee."

When we reached Catherine, they enfolded each other, hugging so tight, neither of them breathing. After a moment Catherine let Janet go, and she returned to my side, plastered there as Catherine rounded on the doctor.

"Thank you for taking such good care of her," she said graciously to Dr. Abbott, who nodded and smiled before shaking her hand.

And just like that, the three of us strolled outside and into the sun.

WE DROVE to Janet's house in Georgetown, and as she showered and changed, Catherine found luggage and packed her up, and I packed for Cody.

Janet did not want to stay. The perfect crib, the perfect room she'd painted herself, all the details she lovingly put in place, she could barely stomach to look at. The bouncer, some kind of contraption that jiggled the baby, was necessary, as were a few other things that folded down easily as I packed them into more suitcases.

"Aruna has baby stuff at home," I told her as she dried her hair.

"Yes," she agreed, nodding, looking nervous.

I took her hands in mine. "This is Ian and Aruna, honey. Do you think they're not coming back here without Cody?"

Tears filled her eyes, and I drew her in close and hugged her.

Catherine put Janet's many, many face and eye and lip products into bags.

"Don't ever tell me again that I have a lot of crap," I warned, and for the first time since we sprang her, she smiled.

"Why did I think that Ned's mother lived in Maryland?" Catherine asked after she pronounced the bathroom done.

"She did live there," Janet explained as the three of us went downstairs, me toting the four massive suitcases stuffed to the gills. "But she moved to be close to us right after Cody was born, to help, she said."

"Yeah, but doesn't she have, like, a million grandchildren already?"

"But Ned's her baby," Janet sighed, looking wrung-out and…. "Ohmygod, this hurts so bad."

"What?" I asked anxiously.

"Where's your breast pump?" Catherine inquired, knowing exactly what the issue was without having to be told.

"How'd you know?" I asked her.

"Because she was holding her breast, Miroslav."

"I love it when you use my whole name."

"Oh, I know," she scoffed, getting the pump for Janet while I turned on the TV as they messed with the electric contraption that would also make the trip.

"Miro, honey," Janet said, chuckling, which was nice to hear, "instead of trying to drown out the pump, why don't you go put the suitcases in the car."

I did as I was told.

Once they were done, I packed the breast pump in the trunk as well, and then I asked Janet if there were things of her mother's she wanted to take from the house.

"You're gonna laugh," she said softly.

Both Catherine and I turned to look at her.

"All the stuff my mom left me is still in storage in Chicago."

"In that place we all shared?" I asked.

She nodded.

"No shit?" Catherine exhaled sharply, smiling brightly. "How fortuitous."

I snorted as we all heard a car pull up beside the row house. After walking out the front door, the three of us stood on the stoop and looked at the car. I saw Aruna first, smiling like a crazy woman, waving from the front seat, and then Ian emerged from the driver's side before opening the back door and getting out a car seat. He came around the trunk of the car and up onto the stoop as Aruna stepped out on the sidewalk.

Janet burst into tears as Ian passed Cody to her. He was very pink, with wisps of red hair, and he had Janet's cute little button nose. There was a moment of yawning, then squirming before he settled again and made bubbles on his lips.

"Oh, he's beautiful," Catherine gushed.

"He's pink," I said.

"He's perfect," Aruna sighed as she joined us.

"He's got some serious lungs," Ian remarked, eyes big for a second.

Aruna chuckled, patting his face for a moment before moving around me to reach Janet.

"You guys," she whimpered, back to crying.

"What took you so long?" I asked Ian. "You go there, you kick down the door, you grab the kid—what the hell?"

"Oh no," Aruna corrected me. "We went to the police station first."

I looked at Ian.

"What?"

I crossed my arms, waiting.

"New job had me thinking," he said, reaching up to brush my hair out of my eyes. "That going in by the book, doing things with a handshake instead of a fist—I mean, that's the way to do it, right?"

"It is."

"Oh, you should have seen him," Aruna sighed like she was smitten with him, sliding one arm around Ian's back, one hand on his abdomen. "He was so calm."

"Were you calm?" Catherine asked as Janet rocked the baby.

"No," Aruna admitted, "but I kept my mouth shut while Ian talked to the desk sergeant and then the police captain, and showed them the approved restraining order and explained the situation. Then when we got to the house, he knocked, and when Ned came to the door, he showed him the order and asked him to give Cody to him."

"And?" Catherine prodded.

"And when he said they couldn't come in, one of the policemen stepped in front of Ned, served him the restraining order, and told him that they were there to take the child into protective custody, and to step aside or they would make him."

"But Ned has as much right to the baby as Janet does, then," I said, glancing at her.

"Yes," Aruna answered. "Except that he had Janet placed on a seventy-two-hour psych hold that was bullshit, and he's going to have to explain that to try to reverse the restraining order, as well as during the divorce."

"Divorce?" I asked.

"Oh hell yeah," Janet said, starting to cry again.

"So we all packed up?" Ian wanted to know, trying to change the subject, crying having always been hard on him. He'd watched his mother cry herself a river after his father left, and then go silent and dead inside. He had an aversion to it that, somehow, did not include me. When I did it, it brought out every protective instinct he had. Fortunate for me it worked like that.

Janet nodded quickly before passing me Cody and launching herself at Ian. He rocked her with as much gentleness as she had her child.

We caravanned back to the airport, and after we checked the bags, paying a mint because they were *way* overweight, we got out the stroller and car seat for inspection, let them wand the baby and Janet, and then Janet and Cody together checked Catherine over because she kept beeping, finally figuring out it was probably her diamond tennis bracelet—even with all that, the girls made it through before Ian and me with our guns.

"Holy crap." Janet was amazed, finally smiling, feeling truly safe and untouchable on the other side of the security checkpoint. "I thought they were going to strip-search you guys."

"I've had that done. It's not enjoyable," Ian told her.

"I could have lived my whole life without knowing that," Aruna told him.

As we sat in the boarding area and Janet prepared to breastfeed Cody while Catherine draped his baby blanket over the top of baby and boob, Janet started to shake.

"What?" I asked, seeing the fear flood her features.

"I just—what if cops come and surround us, and Ned gets them to take Cody, and—"

"That's why I took the cops with me when I picked him up," Ian explained. "That way if any new paperwork comes across their desk, they know that the restraining order trumps it, and they have my contact information for questions. They've also got the number for Min's lawyer friend who filed the papers for you."

She inhaled quickly. "Okay. Okay."

"So a divorce?" I asked Janet. "You're sure?"

"It feels like the only answer right this second," she said, taking a breath. "But I guess thinking about it from his perspective, he might truly think that me not wanting to leave the baby for even a dinner out is me being depressed."

I was quiet, just listening.

"I mean, he might actually be worried about me, and all of this was him showing his love," she conceded. "But if you guys could have seen him yesterday, looking at his mother instead of me, taking his prompts from her…. I can't… I can't have that. I've always known I was second to her, but when I saw her nodding, and then the way she smiled at me as they were dragging me away from my baby—there's no way."

"Don't worry anymore," Ian murmured, and we all looked at him because his voice had gone cold in a way that was a little scary. Every now and then, I was reminded Ian was trained to kill because… every now and then… it slithered to the surface, and it was there in the slow blink of his eyes, the sneer on his lips, and the languid sprawl of his body that could come, instantly, to deadly movement.

"Okay," Janet agreed, eyes big as she stared at him.

On the plane, Janet passed Cody to Aruna, took a shuddering breath, lifted the armrest between us, leaned into me, and was out seconds later. Aruna gave Cody some water during takeoff because we needed his ears to pop.

"I think we should go into business doing this," Aruna said brightly. We sat three and three, Aruna and Catherine next to a stranger who appeared pleased to see Catherine until he saw the ice rink on her ring finger. "Rescuing people, saving kids."

"Miro already does that," Ian said hoarsely, sliding a hand up my thigh.

"Oh? What are you doing?" Catherine wanted to know.

So I explained about Custodial WITSEC on the ride home, and I noted Catherine's huge smile along with Aruna's.

"What?" I rumbled.

"Oh, honey," Catherine almost squeaked, all choked up, "that's like the perfect job for you. You'll be so good with the kids because you'll totally get where they're coming from."

"I know," Aruna whimpered. "He's gonna save all the babies."

"It's not gonna be all sunshine and roses," I protested.

"Wow, that boss of yours," Catherine went on, completely ignoring me. "Can he spot talent or what?"

"I know," Aruna agreed. "And he's yummy too. Remember how great he looked at their wedding in that suit that fit like a glove?"

"Ohmygod, that's right," Catherine agreed, nodding, eyes wide. "So hot. If I wasn't married, I'd tap that."

It was horrifying to think of Kage in any kind of sexual anything. "That's disgusting," I assured them, and when I glanced over at Ian, he looked just as revolted.

"Oh, Ian got a new job too," Aruna announced. "He's in charge now, aren't you, bunny?"

"Bunny?" Ian repeated, looking pale.

"Tell me all about it," Catherine purred, elbow on the armrest, looking at him like he was the second coming.

And Ian, who always found Catherine overbearing, found that being the center of her attention really wasn't all that bad.

WHEN WE got to O'Hare and exited the terminal, Aruna pushing Cody in his stroller—the way it all hooked together was beyond me, but apparently Ian had it down after having only done it once before—we found Min waiting. She was looking for us, and when we got closer, she put her hand over her mouth and started crying. Janet was a go with the waterworks then too.

They ran to each other, arms out, and collapsed to the floor together, sobbing, laughing, hugging the daylights out of each other, and generally making a spectacle of themselves in public as people had to walk around them.

I saw Jensen standing off to the side, and when I waved, he returned the gesture but moved for Ian, hand out, ready to shake. I was surprised Ian hugged him instead, though briefly, before they turned to watch the wailing women.

We clustered around them, and then Jensen lifted Min while I lifted Janet. There was more hugging then; Min hugged us all one by one and then went into Ian's arms and stayed there, shivering, content not to move as he bent and whispered to her as she nodded furiously.

"She really likes him," Jensen said, shoulder-checking me.

"The feeling's mutual," I told him and then turned to really look at him. "I thought she wasn't getting here until later tonight."

He nodded. "I have a plane."

"Huh."

"I flew to Mexico and then here."

"That's handy."

"Yeah," he said, shoving his hands into his pockets.

He was a handsome man. I wasn't sure about the beanie inside, but I liked the Crossroads Gin T-shirt, the vintage jeans, brogue boots, leather jacket, and the chunky Pierre DeRoche watch. The fact that he paired the timepiece with beaded bracelets and a silver cuff on the opposite wrist was a bit too hipster for me.

"So," I said, "you rich?"

He turned his head. "Yeah."

"I thought you restored cars."

"I do, but, yanno, for celebrities and on TV and stuff."

I nodded. "Min wouldn't care about that. The rich part, I mean."

"I am aware," he agreed.

I cleared my throat. "Not that I'm not glad you're here, but... why are you here?"

"Because," he said, his eyes on Min as he answered, "there's going to be a moment when she's gonna come undone, and when… that… hap… pens…."

She turned from Ian, took two steps, saw Jensen, and reached.

He was there fast, sweeping her up off her feet, into his arms, hugging her tight, and she cried into his shoulder, howled. She'd been a rock and put her faith in us because it had to be Catherine going, and me, had to be Aruna and Ian, not her. She was the general. We did what she asked; we were her minions. But now in her moment of need, of total breakdown, Jensen was there to pick up the pieces, and I had to give it to him—it was damn smart.

I stepped close and swatted his back as he crooned to his girl. "Did you meet her mother?"

"Nailed that," he said, lifting his head and giving me a superior smirk.

Ass.

I would have to grill Min later about how much her mother, who hated me and Catherine, liked the man who looked like a bad boy but was, in reality, the complete opposite.

When I glanced over at Aruna, I realized she wasn't paying any attention, and I quickly understood why. She was smiling at Liam and Sajani, who had come to the airport to see her.

Liam, who realized when Aruna was graduating from college that letting her go back to her family in Dallas would be a huge mistake, was still smitten with his wife. And Aruna felt the same about the six-foot-five lieutenant in the Chicago Fire Department. They had always been my idea of what a good relationship was, the trust, the communication, and the humor. I'd been so glad to share them with Ian.

"Let's go eat," Liam suggested, and everyone agreed that was a fantastic idea.

Jensen had rented a car, and between that and the Honda Odyssey Liam brought, we were ready to caravan for the second time that day. I was just happy we were all together.

CHAPTER 12

JANET WAS going to stay with Aruna and Liam for the foreseeable future; she could do her job from there just as well as she could from Georgetown, and now she would have lots more people to help her. She was also considering moving to LA to be close to Min, and since Min still owned her condo in Santa Monica, she could move Janet in there easy with, she said… her mother.

"Your mother?" I asked Min, horrified.

"What?" Min was defensive. "My mother would love it, and so would Janet."

"Ohmygod, I love your mother," Janet almost cried, "and she would love to take care of Cody."

"Yes, she would," Min agreed, smirking at me.

I looked to Catherine for help.

"Oh, I'm with you," she said, hands up. "I'd rather be lobotomized."

Jensen stuck up for Min's mom, but she patted him and told him he didn't have to work so hard. "They all know her, honey. Don't worry about it."

He was certain Catherine and I just needed to be more open-minded.

"Uh-huh," I said, only to find Ian scowling at me. "What?"

"Min's mother is lovely," he asserted. "Jensen's right. You need to give her a break."

I glanced over at Min.

She coughed. "The last time Ian and I were on Skype, she was over, and they got to talking," she explained. "Did you know Ian is, like, a Korean food savant?"

I turned back to Ian.

"What? I like Korean food. What do you think I ate when I was stationed in Seoul?"

"I'm outta here," I announced, getting up from Aruna's huge dining room table. "I'm leaving my husband here to do dishes."

And suddenly I was being smothered with hugs and kisses, and there was no way I was getting out of the house anytime soon.

Eventually Min and Jensen took Catherine downtown with them to the Four Seasons for the night. We all agreed to reconvene for breakfast the following morning before the three of them flew out.

Ian and I cabbed it home with Chickie and had the driver drop us a couple blocks away so we could get our werewolf's walk in.

"So who were you talking to before we left this morning?" I asked as I walked beside Ian, his arm around my shoulder.

"Kage. I needed to let him know we were flying."

"And he must've let you tell people that you were there on official business."

"He did."

I grunted.

"What?"

"It's not like him to break the rules."

"It wasn't rule-breaking, though, right? It was just being able to say, 'I'm here as a federal marshal, not just as Ian Doyle.'"

"Still, that was nice of him."

"I'm in his direct chain of command now. He has to do stuff for me; it's part of picking me in the first place."

I chuckled.

"What? It is."

"I guess you—Ian?"

He had stopped walking and didn't let me take another step forward. As I looked down the street toward our house, four other houses between us and it, I saw a man sitting on our front stoop.

"Who is that?" I asked.

"I don't—"

"Oh no, wait," I said as the man stood up and waved to me. "I know him. That's Efrem Lahm from Homeland."

"Who?"

"Efrem Lahm," I repeated, waving back. "I met him in Phoenix at the hospital when I went in the ambulance with the Guzman kids."

"And what is he doing here?"

"I don't know, baby. Let's go ask."

Ian wasn't thrilled, but the closer we got, and when Efrem came down the steps and stood on the sidewalk, looking crisp and polished in a cashmere trench coat, dress pants, and Prada wingtips, but not in any way threatening, Ian calmed. Seeing also, up close, that Ian had easily fifty pounds of muscle on the smaller, more delicate man, helped put him even more at ease.

"Efrem," I greeted when we got close, hand out, reaching.

He took my hand, shook warmly, and then repeated the motion when I introduced him to Ian.

"It's nice to see you," I said as he pet Chickie. "To what do I owe the pleasure?"

"This is going to sound odd, but I need you to bear with me."

"Course."

With that he reached into his coat pocket and withdrew a beautiful antique gold pocket watch and passed it to me.

I turned it over in my hands, opened the case, and saw the inscription. It was simple, just the words *For Miro* with the initials CH underneath. I took a breath before I lifted my head to meet his green gaze.

"The fuck is this?" Ian asked coldly, on edge, there to protect me, glancing around the street, scanning for a threat.

"Efrem?" I questioned, squeezing the watch in my hand, not about to let it go and wanting to at the exact same time. "Tell me what's going on."

"What you have there is an eighteen-karat-gold Phillippe Patek chronograph pocket watch that has a matching eighteen-karat-gold watch chain with the key to Doctor Craig Hartley's safe on the other end."

"His safe?"

"Yes."

"Explain."

He cleared his throat, pivoted, and waved to someone on the other side of the street.

A moment ago Ian and I had just scanned the street for other people, and there was no one else there. But evidently there had been, and that that someone managed to evade our notice until now, obviously put Ian on edge. Briefly he looked scared, almost panicked, but just as quickly, he squinted and his expression grew irritated. "Harris?" he said after a second.

"Doyle," whoever Harris was called back from the shadows. I couldn't see anybody at all, but apparently Ian could.

"What's the deal?"

"I wasn't sure what you'd heard. I didn't want to spook you, plus your husband knows Ef, so I figured that was the best way to make contact."

"We were in Afghanistan together," Ian said, hand on my shoulder, squeezing gently. "We're good."

And with that, a stunning man stepped out of the darkness he'd blended so well into, looked both ways, and then jogged across the street to us.

He had warm eyes of the most unusual color, like a spring green with gold all swirled together. When he got close, he held out his hand for Ian, who took it quickly.

"I apologize for the subterfuge," Harris said, addressing me. "I just didn't know if your husband would shoot me on sight."

I glanced at Ian. "Why would you do that?"

"Because this man used to be a CIA operative, and the last I heard, he was a contract killer, so I would have assumed that Hartley's last request was to put you in the ground."

"Which couldn't be further from the truth," Harris informed us both. "He left that in my care with orders that it be delivered to you the moment he died."

"You knew him?" I asked.

"Only by reputation. We never actually spoke. I'm now the curator of a service that clients use to deposit things for safekeeping, and that's what this watch was. There were instructions for it to be delivered as soon as possible after his death was announced. I wasn't notified until this morning, but I came as quickly as possible."

I nodded. "May I ask the name of your business?"

"There's not a name, per se. It's just a service where people—"

"Criminals," I suggested.

"Some, yes," he allowed, his voice deep and resonant, "but not all."

"I'm sorry, that was rude. Please go on."

"People entrust me with all manner of treasures, and I hold on to them until they remove them or I'm asked to do something else."

"Huh."

I turned back to Ian. "What?"

He moved closer to Harris, studying his face. "You know what you sound like."

"No, what?" he asked, but he smiled, which was weird.

"That's a real thing? The Vault is real?"

"You didn't think it was?"

Ian shrugged. "It's a fairy tale. Stuff like that doesn't actually exist."

"There are more things in heaven and earth, as it were," Harris said, grinning at Ian, passing him a card I hadn't even seen him holding. But maybe ex–CIA operatives were good with the whole sleight-of-hand thing. "If you ever want a job... or if you need help outside of what you can do... feel free."

Ian took the card and met Harris's remarkable eyes. "Thank you."

Harris turned back to me. "The key opens an actual vault in Switzerland, so you'll have to travel if you want to look through Dr. Hartley's possessions."

"Okay."

"He didn't want the bank's information coming with the key in case you were pressured into surrendering both to the authorities. So if you decide you want to go through it, use the card I gave your husband, call me, and I'll have someone meet you in Zürich and take you to the bank."

"And that's all part of the process?"

"It's the process that Dr. Hartley set up specifically for you. My understanding is that even with the key, if it's not *you* with the key, there's no entry."

"And if I never go?"

"Then I suspect that the contents of his vault will simply remain there until the bank itself is torn down, though I think the oldest bank in Switzerland was built back in the 1800s, so it may outlive you."

"And if that happens?"

"Then that's not your worry anymore, now is it?"

I nodded. "True."

"Anyway, you let me know," he said kindly, reaching out to squeeze my shoulder before looking at Ian. "And you as well."

Ian gave him a nod.

"I don't know if I should thank you for bringing me the watch or not."

"I'm glad it was given into my keeping so I could meet you. It's been my pleasure."

"And mine," I said, offering him my hand. "Any friend of Ian's."

"Friend might be a stretch." Harris smiled one more time, and wow, it struck me again that he was a really handsome man.

"Good to see you, Miro," Efrem said quickly, patting my shoulder, "and to meet you, Ian."

"You as well," Ian said as he shook Harris's hand and then Efrem's before they turned and headed back across the street, then down the sidewalk. They must have parked on another street, because they turned at the next corner and disappeared from view.

"It's cold for them to not have parked closer," I said, draping my arm around Ian's neck.

"Fuckin' Harris," he growled.

"What?"

"If he wanted us dead, you know how easy that would be for him?"

"Why would he want us dead? He seemed like a good guy."

"Jesus, Miro, your life is filled with scary-ass men."

"No," I corrected him. "My life is full of one good man with a scary skill set."

He grunted.

I tightened my arm, curling him close so I could kiss his cheek and then his lips, playfully biting his lower lip, sucking on it before letting go.

"What're you gonna do with the watch?"

"Go put it in our safety deposit box on Monday. I don't want it in the house, but I don't want to lose it either."

"Good plan. I'll go with you."

Inside our Greystone, I carefully put Hartley's watch in the pocket of my topcoat to be ready for Monday, then started stripping.

"Hey," I said, a thought hitting me, walking over to the railing to look down into the living room. "You never got to finish about Lorcan. What's going on with that?"

Ian walked over by the couch so I could see him. "My father was pissed because Lorcan has to do a thousand hours of community service, volunteer at one of those free legal help places for the next six months, and submit to biweekly drug testing for the next two years."

I leaned over on the railing. "That's the deal Stafford gave you?"

"Yep."

"That's really fuckin' great."

"Yeah, no shit, but my father says that he didn't pay for him to go to the University of Chicago Law School to use his degree to help drug addicts and prostitutes."

"What?"

"I know. He's living in a bad seventies police drama—who does he think does drugs, just poor people in the ghetto?"

"Lorcan should be kissing Stafford's ass."

"Yeah, I know."

"And so, what, you and Stafford are buddies now?"

"'Buddies' is pushing it, but I think we're gonna work together, yeah."

"Huh. The marshals and the DEA," I said, grinning. "Lookit you already building bridges and shit."

"That's what Kage hired me to do, jackass. Build fuckin' bridges."

"Oh, you diplomat, you."

He flipped me off and went back to the kitchen, and I heard him talk to Chickie. "Oh, you do not need to go out, it's like twenty degrees out there, you stupid dog."

And it was nice, after the craziness my life had been over the past two days, to hear the normalcy of Ian arguing with our werewolf.

"I love my life," I yelled down to him.

"That's lucky 'cause you're stuck with it."

"And I love you."

"Same principle applies."

Lucky.

IT HAD to be early in the morning when I woke because it was still dark outside. The sheet and heavy quilt were tucked around me, and I realized the temperature had dropped and my skin was icy. Ian had gotten up to turn off the lights at some point, and it was nice, serene in the quiet and dark. I heard the toilet flush, and then he was back in bed, diving under the covers, snuggled to my back, his face in my hair as it started to rain outside. I could hear the drops pelting the skylight, and my sigh was long.

"What?"

"I'm having a perfect moment."

"Jesus, you're easy to please."

"Shuddup and go back to sleep."

He made a contented noise and fell silent.

I had almost drifted off.

"Hey."

I grunted.

"I love you too. Marrying you was smartest thing I ever fuckin' did."

"Oh, you romantic, you," I said, turning my head to kiss him over my shoulder.

He made sure to find my lips in the dark.

MARY CALMES believes in romance, happily ever afters, and the faith it takes for her characters to get there. She bleeds coffee, thinks chocolate should be its own food group, and currently lives in Kentucky with a five-pound furry ninja that protects her from baby birds, spiders, and the neighbor's dogs.

To stay up to date on her ponderings and pandemonium (as well as the adventures of the ninja), follow her on Twitter @MaryCalmes, connect with her on Facebook, and subscribe to her Mary's Mob newsletter.

ALL KINDS OF TIED DOWN

Mary Calmes

Marshals: Book One

Deputy US Marshal Miro Jones has a reputation for being calm and collected under fire. These traits serve him well with his hotshot partner, Ian Doyle, the kind of guy who can start a fight in an empty room. In the past three years of their life-and-death job, they've gone from strangers to professional coworkers to devoted teammates and best friends. Miro's cultivated blind faith in the man who has his back… faith and something more.

As a marshal and a soldier, Ian's expected to lead. But the power and control that brings Ian success and fulfillment in the field isn't working anywhere else. Ian's always resisted all kinds of tied down, but having no home—and no one to come home to—is slowly eating him up inside. Over time, Ian has grudgingly accepted that going anywhere without his partner simply doesn't work. Now Miro just has to convince him that getting tangled up in heartstrings isn't being tied down at all.

www.dreamspinnerpress.com

FIT TO BE TIED

Mary Calmes

Marshals: Book Two

Deputy US Marshals Miro Jones and Ian Doyle are now partners on *and* off the job: Miro's calm professionalism provides an ideal balance to Ian's passion and quick temper. In a job where one misstep can be the difference between life and death, trust means everything. But every relationship has growing pains, and sometimes Miro stews about where he stands with his fiery lover. Could the heartstrings that so recently tied them together be in danger of unraveling?

Those new bonds are constantly challenged by family intrusions, well-intentioned friends, their personal insecurities, and their dangerous careers—including a trial by fire when an old case of Miro's comes back to haunt them. It might just be enough to make Ian rethink his decision to let himself be tied down, and Miro can only hope the links they've forged will be strong enough to hold.

www.dreamspinnerpress.com

TIED UP IN KNOTS

Mary Calmes

Marshals: Book Three

Miro Jones is living the life: he's got his exciting, fulfilling job as a US deputy marshal, his gorgeous Greystone in suburban Chicago, his beloved adopted family, and most importantly, the man who captured his heart, Ian Doyle. Problem is, Ian isn't just his partner at work—Ian's a soldier through and through. That commitment takes him away from Miro, unexpectedly and often, and it's casting a shadow over what could be everything Miro could ever dream of.

Work isn't the same without Ian. Home isn't the same, either, and Miro's having to face his fears alone… how to keep it together at the office, how to survive looming threats from the past, and worst of all, how to keep living without Ian's rock-solid presence at his side. His life is tied up in knots, but what if unknotting them requires something more permanent? What would that mean for him and Ian? Miro's stuck between two bad choices, and sometimes the only way to get out of the knot is to hold tight to your lifeline and pull.

www.dreamspinnerpress.com

A DAY MAKES

Mary Calmes

First from The Vault

Mob enforcer Ceaton Mercer has killed a lot of people in a lot of different ways—he stashed the last two bodies in a toolshed belonging to a sweetheart marine researcher in an idyllic island community—but he's really not such a bad guy. Over time he's found a home of sorts, and he even learns he's found a place in the hearts of the people he works with… at least enough so that they won't put a bullet in his head because he's outlived his usefulness to the boss.

But he never thought he'd find one day could change his life, and he's about to discover how wrong he is.

Because in a single day, he meets the man who looks to be *the one*, the love of his life. It's an improbable idea—a man who deals in death finding love—but it's like it's meant to be. That single day gets weirder and troubles pile up, forcing Ceaton to take a hard look at his dreary life and accept that one day *can* change everything, especially himself. His future might be brighter than he expects—if he can stay alive long enough to find out.

www.dreamspinnerpress.com

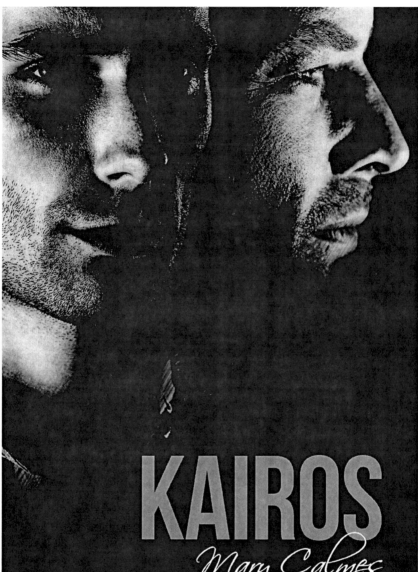

KAIROS

Mary Calmes

Sometimes the best day of your life is the one you never saw coming.

Joe Cohen has devoted the past two years of his life to one thing: the care and feeding of Kade Bosa. His partner in their PI business, roommate, and best friend, Kade is everything to Joe, even if their relationship falls short of what Joe desires most. But he won't push. Kade has suffered a rough road, and Joe's pretty sure he's the only thing holding Kade together.

Estranged from his own family, Joe knows the value of desperately holding on to someone dear, but he never expected his present and past to collide just as Kade's is doing the same. Now they've stumbled across evidence that could change their lives: the impact of Kade's tragic past, their job partnership, and any future Joe might allow himself to wish for....

www.dreamspinnerpress.com

Mary Calmes

YOU NEVER KNOW

Hagen Wylie has it all figured out. He's going to live in his hometown, be everybody's friend, explore new relationships, and rebuild his life after the horrors of war. No muss, no fuss is the plan. He's well on his way—until he finds out his first love has come home too. Hagen says it's no big deal, but a chance encounter with Mitch Thayer's two cute sons puts him directly in the path of the only guy he's never gotten out of his head.

Mitch returned for three reasons: to raise his sons where he grew up, to move his furniture business and encourage it to thrive, and to win Hagen back. Years away made it perfectly clear the young man he loved in high school is the only one for him. The problem? He left town and they have not talked since.

If Hagen's going to trust him again, Mitch needs to show him how he's grown up and isn't going to let go. They could have a new chance at love… but Hagen is insistent he's not reviving a relationship with Mitch. Then again, you never know.

www.dreamspinnerpress.com

CPSIA information can be obtained
at www.ICGtesting.com
Printed in the USA
FFOW03n2322230318
45819003-46704FF